Praise for *Fire Conditions*

A captivating depiction of young Mike's coming-of-age in the naïveté of 1950s rural Wisconsin. You can almost hear the jukebox blaring in the local tavern and smell the Friday night fish fry as you help Mike, and the local citizens of Friendship, search for his missing brother. *Fire Conditions* is a must-read, paired with a brandy old fashioned.

~ KD Allbaugh, *Face Down in the Rising Sun*

Thomas Malin does an excellent job of showing us what happens when a marriage begins to fall apart, and two little boys seem to be in the way. Mike is 13 and Jimmy is 7. Their mother puts them on a train in Evanston, Illinois—destination: their Grandmother Flowers's home in Friendship, Wisconsin. Arriving in Friendship, they quickly learn that their grandmother is a quirky character, with a house full of dogs. She also owns a tavern and their bedroom is on the second floor of the place. The book is a page turner.

~ Jerry Apps, Author of *In a Pickle*
and several other novels and nonfiction books.

Set in the late 1950s, *Fire Conditions* is a captivating account of brothers sent to spend the summer in central Wisconsin with their maternal grandmother. With an authentic voice, this gripping story offers a wide range of human emotions. Malin combines nostalgia, heartbreak, dread, and heroism masterfully. A page turner you won't want to end.

~ Pete Sheild, author of *Bad Medicine* and *Remnants*

Fire Conditions is a bittersweet tale of family strife set in a simpler time and told through the lens of a thirteen-year-old boy.

Tom Malin tells a story of separation, abduction, and arson that is both thrilling and tender. Set in 1950s rural Wisconsin, the author thoroughly immerses his readers in time and place. But Malin's unique talent is to capture the voice of an exquisitely sensitive older brother with tenderness and grace.

~ Jennifer Trethewey,
author of the Highlanders of Balforss series

Malin captures the essence of a small town in the late 1950s where the tavern, not the barbershop, is where promises are made, dreams are realized, and secrets are learned. While reading this book I saw a piece of myself in every character—I applauded their antics and accomplishments and bit my fingernails during the struggles. *Fire Conditions* left me contemplating the smoldering embers long after the layers of smoke had cleared.

~ Chris Marcotte, author of the Reminisce column,
Grand Rapids Herald-Review,
articles, short stories, and poems

Fire Conditions

Books by WWA Press

Red Road Redemption:
Country Tales from the Heart of Wisconsin
PJA Fullerton

Red Road Redemption is an unforgettable collection of short stories filled with haunting characters both human and animal, overflowing with thought-provoking drama, humor, and nostalgia. Take an unquiet walk in the woods, peer through a poignant lens at disappearing family farms, and cheer for the dog pack struggling to bring home the best gifts ever.

My Homecoming Dance: Reflections on Teaching in Wisconsin
Sue Leamy Kies

In her memoir *My Homecoming Dance: Reflections on Teaching in Wisconsin*, Sue Leamy Kies returns to her alma mater to teach high school English. What's changed in the twenty years since graduation? What hasn't? Compassion and empathy present powerful lessons as Sue experiences the deaths of students, her beloved mentor, and her own son. Sue's story will inform and entertain anyone who has entered the doors of an American high school. You are cordially invited to *My Homecoming Dance*. Unlike in the author's day, no date is required.

Coming Spring 2025
Milking for Barn Cats
Memoir
PJA Fullerton

This is the truth of my tribe...
Once there was a tight-knit band of Wisconsin preacher's kids who grew up in rural poverty during the 1950s and 60s to become doctors, lawyers, teachers, writers, one noble felon, and an honest-to-goodness All-American Hero. These short narratives from the middle child of sixteen siblings sparkle with laugh-out-loud humor, real life drama, and more than a touch of poignant tragedy and loss.

Fire Conditions

Thomas C. Malin

Fire Conditions

Copyright ©2024 by Thomas C. Malin
All Rights Reserved
First Edition, October 20, 2024
Fiction

Cover design by Paul Ruane

Except for legitimate use in critical reviews, the reproduction or utilization of this work in whole or in part in any form by any electronic, mechanical, or other means, now known or hereafter invented, including xerography, photocopying and recording, or in any information storage or retrieval system, is forbidden without the written permission of the author and publisher. With the exception of certain names of public record, names used throughout this work are fictional and not meant to represent any individuals, living or deceased.

Library of Congress Cataloging-in-Publication Data
Names: Malin, Thomas C., Fire Conditions
Library of Congress Control Number: 2024941667
ISBN 979-8-3304-2844-1 (pbk. book) | ISBN 979-8-9863365-8-9 (hardback) | ISBN 979-8-9863365-7-2 (epub)
Subjects: Fiction /coming-of-age/ Wisconsin/ mid-twentieth-century family / arson
More info available at https://lccn.loc.gov

Published by
Wisconsin Writers Association Press
www.WiWrite.org
10490 Fox Ridge Drive
Hillsboro, Wisconsin 54634

For Shelly Malin, the love of my life.

PART ONE: FRIENDSHIP

Chapter 1

My mother put my little brother and me on a train from Chicago north to Friendship, Wisconsin, the first week of June 1958. We were going to stay with our grandma, my mother's mother. As we boarded, I held our tickets in one hand and Jimmy's hand tight with the other. I hid my tears as my father would have expected of me. I had turned thirteen in March, too old to cry. Jimmy was seven, going on eight in November, but he still acted six, sometimes five. I was angry and afraid at the same time. The weight of my responsibility for my brother fell on my shoulders.

I arranged our small plastic kid suitcases and my large bag of books for a comfortable ride despite my feelings. When I was settled, I looked up and caught sight of Mom in her tight red dress through the window, already dashing off and disappearing into the mass of people who scurried about Northwestern Station. I handed Jimmy one of my Superman comics and told him the villain was Lex Luther, his favorite.

"Thank you, Mikey," he said, though his eyes were blank, as if he had been dealt a blow. "Why isn't Mom coming?"

I didn't want to fib, so I gave him a shrug. His eyes told me that he expected more from me.

"She wants us to see where she grew up. She's coming later," I said, which I hoped was true.

He considered this, then, in a pout, angrily flipped open the comic as the train lurched and screeched to announce its journey north.

Three days before, Mom had caught Jimmy in the garage playing with matches near a gasoline can without a cap. I was not there to witness the capture, except for its end, when Mom dragged him into the living room, of all places; not into his bedroom, or to the bad-boy closet, but to where I was reading *Tom Sawyer*.

"I'm having lunch with friends," she announced. "Can you keep an eye on him? He could've burned down the garage."

I felt way too pissed-off to say anything. I had just finished chapter three, where Becky Thatcher is first mentioned. Tom and she sounded as if they were destined to be sweethearts, and I wanted to keep reading.

"Well, answer me!"

I nodded.

She didn't see my answer. "You'll watch him?"

I nodded again.

Satisfied, or pretending to be, she left to meet her friends.

I asked Jimmy what had happened in the garage. His story was sketchy. For an almost eight-year-old, he was good, given his innocent eyes and darling expression, at making excuses grown-ups would believe. He tried to soft-sell me when I asked him where he found the matches, since he'd left out that little detail. He told me "A friend." Which friend? He wouldn't say. I might've reminded him he didn't have friends that I was aware of, but that would have been mean. I said, instead, "You know you could've burned down the garage."

"Mom already told me that."

"What if you burned off your face?"

He paused to think what it might be like.

"No one would kiss you. Or want to touch you." I poked him with my finger for emphasis. "How would you like that?"

"I didn't know about gasoline," he said, not as miserable as he should've been.

I set down *Tom Sawyer* and walked to Jimmy's toy chest. I decided on the can of Pick-Up Sticks. We'd always liked to play that with Dad. We would sit on the carpet, the three of us. Now we sat down alone. I reminded him of the rules (always a good idea), and of how many points each color of a stick was worth. We played long enough to put what had happened in the garage out of our minds. Sprawled on the floor, we played Tiddlywinks, dominoes, and Chinese checkers until Mom returned from lunch. I glanced at the Timex I got for my birthday. She had been gone for two hours.

"Nice to see you two having fun," she said as she passed through the room. She had fixed a drink for herself in the kitchen and returned without shoes. She settled on our new fancy chair, an unwanted, showy gift from my father's rich parents, Grandpa George Calloway and Grandma Phoebe, who we referred to as just BeBe because Jimmy couldn't pronounce her real name.

Mom watched us play dominoes. A red toothpick speared two olives inside her glass. It looked like a baby Pick-up stick. Her eyes dulled as she continued to sip her drink.

I let Jimmy win. Dominoes weren't fun anymore. I opened a

box of checkers. Jimmy cheated right from the start. His pieces were red. He jumped his own checkers to get an advantage on me, the black, but never took his own piece off the board. Mom didn't notice. We could have been playing Bloody Murder, for all she knew.

"How was lunch?" I asked. We hadn't eaten yet.

Her gaze wandered to the ceiling then back at me. "What did you say?"

"How was lunch."

"Your father's not coming home tonight."

He had not been home in days, though this was the first time she had mentioned what I already knew. I looked at her as if to say, "So what?"

She retreated to the kitchen and returned with a "refresher," her fancy name for another drink at their parties. I never heard what they called a third refresher because I was in bed by then. Mom crossed her legs as though she was still at lunch with her girlfriends. "But don't be worried," she told us. "We'll figure it all out when your father gets sick of the slut. He'll come back. He always does."

I wanted Dad to come home but didn't understand why she believed he would. I had heard rumors from friends about a father who had walked out on his family. Was this happening to Jimmy and me? Would we be a rumor?

Jimmy begged me with his blue eyes—a jumble of sadness, anger, and fear—that I would promise him Dad would come home again. As much as I wanted to comfort him, I doubted he would believe what I said. I took him by the arm and led him down the hall to my bedroom. I waited for Mom to come and tell us everything would be all right, but she didn't. Not that I had expected her to.

I handed Jimmy two of my model cars to play with, the blue Corvette and my green army jeep. Normally, I wouldn't have let him touch them. I had carefully glued them together, painted them, and set their wheels on axles that spun. Today I didn't care if he broke them. I looked at my pennants hanging on the walls, then the pile of books I piled on the dresser. My things, especially my books, calmed me and helped put Mom out of my mind. Jimmy sat beside me on my bed. I put my arm around his shoulders and found myself wishing he had burned down the garage. That would have caught our parents' attention.

After the train pulled out of the station, a conductor entered our car to collect tickets. Old white people avoided his eyes like their tickets were handouts.

"You boys alone?" he asked.

I nodded. I had seen people of color in the Loop and Southside, neither of which I had been often. We lived in Evanston. Neighborhoods were changing. Grandpa Calloway sounded bitter whenever he spoke about decreases in North Shore property value, whatever that meant.

"If you boys need anything, you let me know, okay?"

"Thank you," I said.

Suddenly he winced and grabbed a knee. With the seat open on the aisle across from us, he asked whether he might sit a spell. His question had been addressed to me, as if I were my brother's "adult."

"My bursitis's acting up," he explained.

I caught sight of a woman two rows ahead of us, saw her raise her head like a periscope and glance, scowling, at the conductor. When my eyes met hers, she dove behind her seat.

"Can I ask something?" said Jimmy.

"You sure can," the conductor said.

"Do you have kids?"

"I do."

"How old?"

"A daughter. A lot older than you."

"I don't have a sister," Jimmy said.

"You have a brother. He's right there beside you."

"I would've had a sister," Jimmy persisted, "but her heart was broken, and she died."

"Oh my."

"Before I was born."

The periscope's eyes were now accompanied by ears. "Quit bothering those boys. Don't you have work to do?"

The conductor lowered his head. It wasn't about my sister, I knew. It was because the woman was mean.

I had never heard Jimmy speak of our sister, nor had I imagined he even knew she had existed. Maybe I had never said anything about her to him because she wasn't all that real to me, either, having seen her only once, in her casket. What I knew was she had died in the hospital the day she was born, but I had not heard about her bad heart until after Jimmy was born.

Fire Conditions

I looked at the countryside as the train gathered speed. Jimmy returned to his comic book. The conductor sat across from us either in prayer or in torment from a suffering knee. As I watched red barns, large white farmhouses, and rotted-out sheds pass by, I remembered our sister's name had been Elizabeth.

I was five years old, younger than Jimmy was now, when I heard my parents cry night after night. It had to do with the funeral. The baby in the tiniest white box, covered with a blanket of pink flowers, was my sister. I had felt like I was supposed to be sad but was confused and afraid. I remembered—or knew from talk since—Grandpa and Grandma Flowers were at the funeral but left before they ate at my other grandparents' house in Lake Forest.

I punched Jimmy in the arm because he reminded me of a bad memory I didn't like to think about. He shot me a "why did you do that" look as he rubbed his upper arm. I told him to switch seats with me. Stubborn, he kept his butt where it was. I reached into my bag and pulled out a comic book he'd never seen, a bribe, of sorts. One Dad told me never to show him. He'd bought it a week ago along with three others. He promised to take Jimmy and me to a Cubs game when he was less busy with work, sometime in July. He told me to keep it a surprise, between me and him. I shouldn't tell Jimmy and ruin the surprise, or Mom, for that matter.

The comic books Dad bought for me were Classic Comic Books, illustrated literary classics that were published by a company Dad viewed better for children than Marvel. I offered Jimmy Frankenstein. The cover portrayed the monster strangling someone. He quickly switched seats with me.

Mike looked up at the conductor, feeling relieved and safe. "We're happy you're here."

"You might say so," the conductor said, his eyes wide, surprised by my comment. "Do you know why they call this train the 400?"

I shook my head.

"It's a piece of work, this train. A steam engine. Better than any train out East, even the new diesel engines these days. Imagine that! It's the '400' 'cuz it goes four hundred miles in four hundred minutes. You'll feel how fast that is when we hit the flats."

Minutes later the clatter of iron-on-iron wheel on rail reached a crescendo, then leveled off. We were flying along without clattering and were able to hear each other.

"Folks don't know what to think seeing me not in my place," he grumbled.

"Maybe they just need to get to know you," I said.

He looked kindly at me. "How'd you come to be here without you' mama?" he asked.

I told him we were going to stay with our grandma for a while. I didn't know when we'd go home. Or for how long. I'd said enough. It was none of his business. I'd never tell a stranger that my parents might get divorced. I wanted to pretend that we had a happy family like Ozzie and Harriet.

"I gotta keep an eye on him. They don't have time right now."

I glanced at Jimmy and was pleased to see he had not been listening. He was engrossed in Frankenstein; most likely looking for pictures of the monster strangling people.

Fire Conditions

"Where are you getting off?" he asked.

"Friendship," I said.

He scratched his head. "There's no Friendship on this line. I wish there was, but the next stop's Adams." He laughed lightly. "There's a stop in Adams. Friendship and Adams are like St. Paul and Minneapolis. Twin places but these are small."

I checked my ticket, on the edge of panic. It read "Adams." Mom had said Friendship would be our destination.

"Don't worry," he said. "I'll make sure you get where you're supposed to be."

At the stop, before he headed down the aisle, smiling despite the stares, he helped us take our suitcases and my bag of books down to the platform, and slipped each of us a caramel.

"Remember," he said, "Mamas love their babies. Yours loves you. You know how I know?"

I shook my head. Jimmy was unwrapping his caramel.

"Your bow ties say so," he said and smiled. Mine was navy blue, Jimmy's fire engine red. Mom had wanted us to look presentable to Grandma, I figured. She wouldn't want her mother to know how our family was falling apart.

When we said goodbye, he said, "Godspeed," and I knew I'd likely never see him again.

A large woman in a dress with daffodils spotted us. She charged at us like she was an ox, but quick on her feet. "Oh, Jimmy Jammer! I can't believe it's you!" she said. Jimmy squealed as she lifted him off the ground and swung him like a rag doll, his spindly legs flying. After she put him down, he staggered like he did when he got off a merry-go-round. She shook his scrawny shoulders and smothered him with kisses. Her expression told me she could hardly believe he was real and was standing in front of her.

Other people waited along the tracks, watching us. I didn't know then that the daily arrival of the passenger train was a big deal in town. People watched who came on or off the train. Today Jimmy and I had their full attention. Jimmy's dizzy walk gave them a laugh.

I set my book bag on the platform. Grandma looked right at me. I didn't expect she would be much different from how I remembered her years ago. Her love was on display with my brother. I braced myself. She sized me up. Was there something wrong with me? I was a gangly weed of a boy. I had not sprouted or filled out enough to satisfy her. That was how I interpreted her look.

"Hi, Grandma," I said. I smiled to see the caramel smear on her cheek where Jimmy kissed her. Or licked her.

Her strong arms buried me between her breasts and I gasped to breathe. Her dresses were remarkable, I vaguely remembered my mother telling me. Grandma's dresses were like gardens, spread to cover her body from shoulders to midway between her shins and ankles, all roses and tulips in late spring, mums and geraniums in early fall. The fabric, in the crevice where my nose was pressed, smelled like sweat, not flowers.

Finally, she released me, saying, "You're still my little Mikey. My little man now."

I felt happy and proud to still be special to her. It was that easy,

Fire Conditions

like a magic wand had been waved over my head.

So, Jimmy and I had arrived. Not necessarily safe and sound here, but better off than where we'd been. Not quite there, yet; not at her house, where we would stay. Our Friendship family was a mystery, rarely mentioned by Mom, and disdained by Dad's family. For Jimmy, though, I thought it was a safe place, free of adult complications.

Our audience cleared the platform when a blast of steam announced the end of their day's entertainment.

"What do you have in there?" Grandma asked.

"My books," I said.

"You read?"

"I do."

She gave me a curious look. "The car's over there," she said, and bobbed her head toward the last car left on the strip of gravel alongside the depot. It was a bright pink, two-door Nash Rambler, not nearly as big as Grandma Bebe's and Grandpa Calloway's black Cadillac, but flashier.

Jimmy leaned toward me and asked in a hush voice, "Is that a clown car?"

"Shhh," I said.

"Is Grandma a clown?"

"Shhh!"

She slammed the trunk shut on our suitcases and my bag of books. When she turned back to us, I saw there was something she didn't like. Apparently, our bow ties. She reached down to Jimmy's first, then mine, and unsnapped our ties off our shirts.

"For Christ's sake," she said, "we can't have you looking like Little Lord Fauntleroys."

I was afraid momentarily that she would throw our ties in the dirt. Instead, she opened the door to the car, stuffed them under the driver's seat, and told us to climb in. I sat beside Jimmy in the backseat.

Grandma passed a ham and cheese sandwich to each of us. She must've heard our stomachs growl.

Grandma parked the car on a patch of gravel alongside a small house. Its paint hung in flakes. If this was her house it would have been a smidgeon of our house in Evanston. Her yard was sandy with clumps of grass and weeds. A sparse number of lilacs and peonies lined the concrete foundation. For a woman who wore flowery dresses, and whose last name was Flowers, I suspected she was lazy or busy.

"Why don't we go in for a minute," Grandma said, which confused us. We looked at each other. A minute? Wasn't she going to unpack the car's trunk and bring in our suitcases?

"You're in for a big surprise!" she announced. "I have a few little friends I want you to meet."

Inside, she hurried to a door and swung it open, unleashing a pack of little tan tigers saying, "Don't you just love my Pom Poms?"

The dogs looked older than pups and were too big to be cute anymore and came with the stink of a kennel. They didn't greet Grandma as good dogs would. They rushed Jimmy. Their nails clattered across the wood floor. They surrounded him, nipping and

Fire Conditions

growling at each other for a turn at the cuffs of his pants.

He froze.

Grandma laughed. "Don't ya' just love 'em?"

Jimmy did not love them. I found the looks on their faces funny when they shook his cuffs with vigor. But they were also incredibly nasty.

"Penny! Ginger!" Grandma yelled. Did she even know which was which? "Get away from him! Scoot!" She brushed one of them aside with a foot. Jimmy did the same with the other, but gently, like her. She reached into her handbag and scattered what sounded like pebbles through the doorway, shouting, "Treats, treats, get the treats!"

The dogs spun around, slipped, and slid across the floor, little butts striving to beat each other for a treat. Once they were all back from where they had come from, Grandma slammed the door behind them.

I knew my brother better than anyone, and knew he wasn't afraid of dogs, and that Grandma didn't need to feel sorry for him. The look on his face told me that being terrorized could be exciting, a brief thrill.

The living room smelled like dogs. And not nice dogs. Where did she expect us to sleep? The next thing I knew she was leading us through a swinging door to the kitchen. "Now let's meet Pookah!"

I saw nothing anywhere that could be a Pookah. Jimmy stared at the ceiling, expecting a thrilling new creature, a giant spider or monkey, to jump down on him. Grandma looked amused and mischievous.

"Hey there!" came a response, not from Grandma but from something not human. A large black bird sat rocking on a small trapeze in a gilt cage that stood in a nook near the back door. The cage could have held a half-dozen parakeets. Pookah's head twitched, short and snappy in sync with each tic of its head and blink of its eyes. On the sides of its neck were purplish-black feathers, and a few yellow feathers covered the back of its neck. With its sharp, bright orange beak and calculating eyes, it appeared to be on the lookout for something to kill. Maybe a parakeet or canary or two.

Jimmy rushed to the cage and, tall enough, pressed his nose between two of its bars. Pookah snapped its beady eyes on him and swung on its trapeze faster. Its bowl of food sat underneath Jimmy's nose. I didn't learn until later that myna birds weren't seed eaters, like regular birds, but ate what looked like gray lumps of matter resembling dead baby birds, directly below my brother's nose. As Grandma pulled him away from the cage, she laughed nervously and said, "Pookah, say hi to my boys."

"Hello Joe," said the bird.

"I'm Jimmy."

"Nice to meet you, Joe."

"I'm not Joe, dummy."

"I'm a chicken."

"Chickens don't talk."

"I'm a chicken."

"Polly wanna cracker?" Jimmy asked.

"That's what parrots say," I cut in. "Pookah's a myna bird."

Jimmy frowned.

"Hi Pookah," I said.

Jimmy looked like he wanted to slug me for butting in but smirked when the bird didn't say hi to me, either.

Grandma laughed in delight. "You can teach her words," she said.

My eyes widened at the thought of improving a bird's vocabulary, even if she—not he—appeared to be instinctively angry.

"Just don't turn her into an Einstein," Grandma warned.

"How about swears?" Jimmy asked.

Grandma's grin told me that he would be continually amusing her. He didn't know he could be so cute. Never did I think he was cute. Funny, maybe. Adults trusted him. I didn't get it.

The bird provided an opportunity. The ritual assignment on the topic "how I spent my summer vacation" would amaze my classmates. I would title mine "How I taught a bird to talk." The class would think I was an egghead, or a suck-up to the coming year's teacher. Privately, I would tell my friends that I had taught Pookah to swear and they would laugh.

"Say bye," Grandma told Pookah.

"Bye Joe."

"Bye Pookah," said Jimmy.

"Bye Joe."

Grandma led us out of the house. We climbed into the Rambler, unsure where she would take us next. A spark plug misfired, but quickly jumped into the rhythm of the rest of the engine. We arrived at Aggie's Tap in less than a minute. We could've walked faster. It was close to seven p.m., still daylight. The solstice was less than three weeks away. The sun wouldn't set for hours but inside the Tap it was dark. Grandma held Jimmy's hand and carried his suitcase. I paused and adjusted my eyes so as not to stumble. A couple of shadow figures sat at the bar. Suddenly a blaze of bright neon lit up the room. I had seen the Hamm's bear commercials during Cubs' broadcasts in black and white, but this was like walking into Oz when the movie burst into color.

"Hurry up!" Grandma shouted from the top of the stairs.

I was dazzled by a bear paddling a canoe, trying to catch a fish with its paw. The bear grinned to the beat of tom-toms, unaware of the waterfall ahead. Just when he would drop, he found himself starting over, repeatedly, to a jolly song: "From the land of sky-blue waters...."

"Mike!"

I grabbed my suitcase and book bag and hurried upstairs. I caught up with them on the landing. Grandma was sucking wind. I took a deep breath myself of an all-encompassing smell of must, mold, and smoke. A lightbulb dangled from the ceiling. The wallpaper was a dingy brown. Jimmy wandered in circles, pinching his nose. I wondered who lived in the rooms, who had lived in them forever.

"Here's your bathroom," Grandma said, pleasantly, as she indicated a door to her right. "If there's a line downstairs at the john, people come up to use this one if they can't wait," she

Fire Conditions

informed us. They were our customers. The bathroom was a common convenience, after all. "That happens mostly Fridays and Saturdays," she added. "Mondays and Tuesdays are slow."

She didn't show us the bathroom for reasons strange and unknown. She sounded like she was in a hurry. She turned to the door across the hall, saying, "I keep a lot of stuff in here." She opened the door and told us to peek. She was right about the stuff: mops, pails, brooms, cleaning supplies, large bags of animal food, and a roulette wheel. "If you can't find what you're looking for here," she offered, "you can check the cellar. I store stuff there, too. And you can hide from a tornado if you have to."

Jimmy followed Grandma ahead of me to what I hoped was our room. He glanced back at me once to stick out his tongue and scrunch up his face. He did this to me whenever he found something weird, funny, icky, or scary. When Grandma farted, rather than make another face at me, he squealed like a baby pig to stifle a laugh. She didn't notice.

"Here's your room," she announced, and allowed us time to take in two twin beds covered with blankets, unneeded, considering it was almost officially summer. Beyond that there was a lamp on a nightstand between the beds, a small wooden chair in a corner, and a door that probably hid a closet, but no dresser to store our clothes.

"Dibs!" Jimmy called.

I didn't care which bed he chose. They were the same.

"You have a nice view," said Grandma as she demonstrated how to work the brown paper shade on our window. I stepped to the shade and gave its string a practice pull to prove I could do it. Duh. Main Street's lights were on. Only two cars passed the Tap. A Sinclair gas station with its green dinosaur sign was open. Some nice view.

"I bet your bedroom at home is fancier than this, but we'll make the best of it, right?"

I nodded.

She told us to unpack and sat down to watch us. I set my clothes at the foot of the bed closest to me. Jimmy jumped on his chosen bed. He ordered Grandma to "Do it for me!"

"Do it yourself," I said.

Grandma laughed.

She shouldn't encourage him, I thought.

Despite my sour mood I felt obliged to be grateful to her for taking us in. I didn't complain about sharing a bedroom with Jimmy. Fancy or not, I liked my bedroom in Evanston, bigger and all my own. The light from the lamp flickered dimly. Abraham Lincoln could've gone blind reading here. I considered asking Grandma for a candle but decided it was a bad idea. Jimmy and matches and a candle were a recipe for disaster.

I moved my book bag out of Grandma's way and intentionally dropped it hard on the floor. I didn't know why, other than I wanted to protest something, anything that came to mind, but not because of Grandma. I had my parents to blame.

"Is something wrong?" she asked.

I shook my head.

She walked to the nightstand and reached inside the lamp

shade. After a click the light glowed. "The bulb was loose," she said.

"Thank you," I mumbled, embarrassed.

Jimmy yawned.

Was I supposed to put him to bed? That wasn't my job. That was Mom's and Dad's. I asked Grandma what was inside the room across from us.

"That's Joe's room."

"Who's Joe?"

"My brother," she said, "like Jimmy's yours."

"Can we swap rooms with him?"

"There's only one bed."

So what?

"I moved the TV there for him."

"Why?"

"He acts up if he can't watch his shows."

I wondered what she meant by "act up," but let it go.

I put on my pair of blue plaid pj's. Grandma had finished dressing Jimmy in his favorite red and white candy cane stripes. She untangled his limbs, and loosened his muscles, what there were of them. His eyelids fluttered and he sank into sleep.

When I heard loud voices and mean laughter downstairs, Grandma told me she had to stop what was going on. I retrieved *Tom Sawyer* from his place in my bag and went to bed. I must've read it for a short time but couldn't recall any of it when I awoke. The book was open, lying on my chest, its spine raised like a teepee. Jimmy had not moved.

When Grandma returned I quickly closed my eyes. She gave

each of us a quick glance to be sure we were asleep. Then, apparently satisfied, she left again and returned with three cardboard boxes. She quietly moved the chair to where we had set our suitcases and began to sort through our clothes. One box was for Jimmy's, one was mine, and the third for items to discard, based on her disgusted expression and flicks of her hand. She had already thrown away our bow ties with hardly a thought; what was she discarding now?

She slid two boxes in the closet with her foot and disappeared with the third. When she returned, she dragged my book bag to her. She mumbled softly, not knowing how good my hearing could be, "How many bricks does he have in this thing? A whole library?"

She thumbed methodically through the pile she had made of my comics. One caught her attention. As her fingers lingered over the cover, I realized that two thin inner pages hid the *Playboy* centerfolds I shared with my friends. This month, Miss April, ripped out of Sam's father's magazine. She riffled the pages of my Wonder Woman comic, but, to my relief, she stopped before two glossy, semi-naked breasts slipped out. Poor Sam, I thought. He would have to wait for Miss May.

Grandma gave up on the rest of the comics, stood, came over to me, and sat down. She brushed my arm reaching over me to pick up my hardcovered *Tom Sawyer*. I heard her breathing. She studied the book's cover; a happy-go-lucky boy on his way to go fishing. After she closed the book, she leaned over me and whispered, "You need your sleep, my little man," and kissed my forehead. She then kissed Jimmy, and I knew we'd be okay.

Chapter 2

As I lay in bed, I wanted to tell my mother a thing or two. Dad, too, but I began with her. After all, she was the one who put us on the train and sent us away. Dad had to have been involved, no doubt. My thoughts put into words ran:

Mom, we're in Adams, not Friendship, like you'd told us we'd be. We're staying upstairs of Grandma's tavern, not at her house. She has a bunch of ugly little dogs. I think that's why we're here. The dogs have the room that should be ours at the house. Another thing, she has a bathroom upstairs that we have to share with drunks on busy nights. And they have tornadoes.

I hoped she'd feel guilty if she could read my mind.

When I woke up Jimmy's bed was empty. I found him on a stool at the bar, fishing maraschino cherries out of a jar. We were still in pajamas. An old man sat next to him, Grandma's brother Joe, I figured. He was staring at himself in the mirror, lost in thought, expressionless. He looked like he'd slept in a barn. His chin and jaw bristled with whiskers ear to ear. His complexion was as beige as his pajamas were thin. His hair was combed down over his forehead and would occasionally flutter in the wind of a nearby fan. He might as well have been the Hamm's bear in the beer sign waiting to be plugged in for the day.

"You're Joe," I said to be sociable. He was kin, after all; plus, he had a TV across the hall from us. "I'm Mike."

He turned from his reflection. "I'm Aggie's brother," he said. "Who's he?"

Jimmy was pretending not to listen, but I knew he was. "His name's James, but we call him Jimmy. He's my little booger...oh, I mean brother," I said, knowing I could get a reaction if I sank to his level. And, sure enough, he cracked a smile.

"What day is it?"

I told him Wednesday. He closed his eyes. I couldn't tell whether he was thinking. "Ah," he said, "Aggie takes food to Lena today."

"Who's Lena?"

He closed his eyes, thought another moment, and said, "Old friend. Rattlesnake Mountain. Don't come to town."

When Grandma woke up, she made the three of us plates of piping-hot pancakes with blueberries and maple syrup. I hadn't had such a good breakfast in months. Her dress today was like a field of blue morning glories. She told me that she had to run an errand; one she did every Wednesday morning. Her good friend couldn't get into town, she said. She shopped for groceries for Lena, food that would last her a week. As she headed toward the door I asked if I could go with her. She said, not today, maybe next week. She opened the door, then turned and added, "Keep an eye on your brother."

After she had gone Joe told me to wash the dishes. I'd intended to wash them but didn't appreciate being told to do so by him. Did he think he was my boss?

"I'll do it when I'm ready." I went upstairs to change out of my pajamas. As I passed through the bar, Joe and Jimmy were laughing. Upstairs I found that Grandma had laid out our denim jeans and matching plaid cowboy shirts. The shirts were Christmas presents that Grandma BeBe and Grandpa George had bought for us at a Dude Ranch in Colorado. I especially liked the ivory buttons that snapped together. The sleeves were fringed with what felt like rubbery rawhide. If Grandma Flowers knew who had given us the shirts, considering her relationship with my father's family, she might've burned them.

Duded up, I came downstairs, looking forward to getting the lay of the land. As I passed through the bar again, I heard Jimmy ask Joe whether he knew Pookah.

"I love Pookah," said Joe.

"I do too," Jimmy gushed.

"Where's Grandma sleep?" I asked Joe.

"In the gambler's den."

"Where's that?"

He motioned for me to follow him. We walked through the kitchen to a room where deliveries were made. We kept quiet. I noticed the door was double bolted, with a peep hole like on the Eliot Ness TV show. Everyone in Chicago who had never heard about mobsters had to be dead. Grandpa Frank, it was rumored by my father's family, which I'd overheard, played cards with Grandpa Flowers on the mobsters' way to their hideouts further up north.

He would let them win and would reward them with bottles of brandy.

I left Jimmy with Joe. They were having a good time playing cards at the bar. Before I went out, I heard Jimmy ask Joe about a dusty fishbowl at the end of the bar. This was the first time I'd noticed it. There was a faded picture of a boy taped to its side.

I opened the outside door from the gambler's den and entered the mid-morning glare of the sun and a sweltering heat.

Outside I decided to check on Pookah. I'd noticed that Grandma hadn't locked the door to her house the night we arrived. I intended to go back to the tavern a short time later, long before Grandma returned.

A boy called to me, "Hey you!"

By the sound of the voice, and from what I could see, he was about my age. He approached me from the corner of Main and Pine.

"Are you one of the kids who got off the train?" he called.

Was I so memorable to strangers for getting off of a train?

"I am," I called.

He lowered his voice when he reached me. "What's your name?" he asked.

"Mike."

"I'm Roscoe."

He was an inch or two taller than me, and overall bigger, broader, and undoubtedly stronger. A husky kid, people might say. I envied the short sleeves of his T-shirt. My cowboy shirt was making me itch.

"What grade are you in?"

"Eighth in September."

"Me too. Wanna be friends?"

"Yeah!" I was thrilled.

"Where're you staying?"

Normally I would have been embarrassed to answer but felt different with him. "Upstairs, there." I pointed to where he should look.

He glanced at the tavern and turned back to me. "Your shirt's really fancy," he said.

"Not really." Sweat was building under my arms.

"Do you have a cowboy hat too?"

"I didn't bring it." As soon as the words came out, I didn't know why I had lied.

If I had a hat, Mom would have remembered to pack it; there being no hat to begin with. BeBe had bought only shirts.

"How long are you around for?"

"All summer, maybe." I didn't know if that was true. I would stay as long as it took Mom and Dad to get back together.

"I can show you where I live."

As we walked Roscoe told me that his friends were kids that he had known all his life. He asked who my friends were. Sam and Rashid, I said, though I was immediately concerned he might have notions about them, because of their names. Where my friends and I lived, there were people who would have concluded one was Jewish, the other Muslim, which would have been correct. My father claimed that small towns were notorious for bigots. He mentioned nothing about the fact that big cities had bigots, too.

Had Dad forgotten his own father?

My friends and I were nerds.

Thankfully, Roscoe, in easy stride, showed no concern about anything I had said. Shamelessly, I exaggerated Sam's and Rashid's popularity—that they were invited to all the cool birthday parties, went to movies that most kids weren't allowed to see, and had girlfriends. I identified one flaw to make us more real. We weren't good at sports. Which was true. None of us could catch or dribble a ball if our lives depended on it. At least I could run fast after years of running cross country.

We came to a church across the street and he stopped. "That's St. Joseph's. It's Catholic." He turned and pointed out a brick house with a small sign that read "Hospital."

"That's where we get polio shots," he said. "Those needles, man, they hurt! Mom says it's better to get shots than making her cry." He lowered his eyes. "Getting shots is better than being like Will," he said. "There weren't shots then."

"Who's Will?"

"My friend, he got polio. He's in our club. I visit him. Tell him what we're doing. Do you want to be in our club?"

I accepted immediately.

"We're meeting at my house. Two o'clock today. Can you come?"

"If I can bring my brother."

"That's cool."

"He's seven—almost eight."

"So's Gertrude," he said. "Gertie, for short. They can play

together."

I checked my Timex; it read ten after eleven, which allowed plenty of time for Grandma to return from Lena's and earn her consent to attend the meeting.

A low growl of a siren suddenly rose to a crescendo that caused dogs to howl. I took Roscoe's cue and covered my ears. The siren reached its peak and held steady for nearly a half-minute. When the sound fell the pressure in my ears went away. Roscoe slapped the side of his head. I asked him what had just happened. Were the Russians coming?

He laughed. I was a doofus, of course the Russians would bomb Chicago first. The siren was the noon whistle. It was tested at noon Monday to Friday, but it wasn't just for a fire. If the siren held steady, there could be a tornado on the way.

But noon! I scratched my head. It couldn't be noon. A few minutes ago, it was ten after eleven. I checked my watch. Its hands were where they were fifty minutes ago. I must have forgotten to wind it.

"Where do you live?" I asked.

"I'll take you," Roscoe said. "Meet me here. You couldn't miss it if you just follow Main Street."

Jimmy and Joe were still in their pajamas. Grandma wasn't home yet. Next to Joe two burned butts lay in a tin foil ashtray giving off the odor of a dirty, unwashed sock. A half-glass of beer sat nearby. Cherry-mouthed Jimmy had emptied the jar. He was slouched, his head on the edge of the bar. I wanted to give him a punch to wake him up but did not because he looked sick.

When Grandma returned, I asked her if we could talk in the kitchen, hoping she had noticed that I'd washed the dishes. "Did you have a good morning?"

She pulled up a stool, sat down, and began to stroke her chin with her index finger. "What's up?"

"I made a new friend."

"Where? What's his name?"

"Outside. His name is Roscoe."

"What were you doing outside?"

"Just looking around." I told her that I had been asked to join a club. The meeting started soon. "I can take Jimmy. Can we go?"

She mulled this over. "Must be one of the Larsen boys. Only Roscoe I know. Big family but a good one." She added, "Jimmy looks sick. Make him puke up all those cherries he ate before you go. Or you'll be sorry."

I dragged Jimmy upstairs. He puked on his own. "We're going to meet new kids. It'll be fun. Change your clothes. They're on your bed. You can't go in pajamas."

Outside, despite the muggy heat, Jimmy skipped. I walked fast to keep up with him, not wanting to let him out of my sight. Passersby paused to stare at us, watching two boys, joyfully galloping toward Friendship in fancy cowboy shirts.

A kid on a bike approached us on a slight curve into Friendship. Another new friend, I thought. The kid swerved his bike to greet us, his foot planted on the pavement to create a skid.

Fire Conditions

He stayed on the bike while he looked us over. He had to be older than I was because he had a few whiskers. His T-shirt looked like Marlon Brando's in the movie *A Streetcar Named Desire*, showing off his brawny chest and thick upper arms.

I said, "Hi."

"Who the hell are you? You look like a couple of jokers."

My good feeling toward him dissolved in the heat.

"I'm Mike," I said.

"I'm Jimmy."

The kid laughed. "You can call me Goofy."

Jimmy laughed. I didn't.

"What's your real name?" Like I had a right to know.

Goofy looked me over. Whatever he saw, I was sure it was nothing nice. "The circus ain't comin' till August," he said.

I smirked. "Are you selling the tickets?"

"You a smart aleck?"

"Let's go," I told Jimmy. We stepped away. The meeting would start soon. I took Jimmy's hand, and we skipped up Main Street to where I knew the Courthouse would be.

I heard the kid shout behind us. "I'm Butch!"

To me, he was just a creep.

Chapter 3

Roscoe met us where I had left him after the noon whistle blew. It felt like a reunion despite the fact that we had just met. Jimmy looked at him, and he looked back, smiling. "Gertie's going to play with you," he said. "You'll have fun."

Jimmy crinkled his nose. "It's a girl?"

We walked four blocks due west of the Courthouse on Third Street when Roscoe announced we had reached his home. The house was the first on a dead-end road; a one-story ranch with a large picture window. One end of the house was under construction. Lumber was stacked nearby.

The yard looked like every sad yard I had seen since I had arrived. Nobody landscaped their yards, unlike where I had come from. Hardly any flowers grew here because the area's soil seemed to be mostly sand. Roscoe's yard lived a weedy life, littered with old plastic toys, some broken, like they had been abandoned by Santa Claus on a bad Christmas Eve.

Roscoe led us up the steps to the door. At the top, the entire concrete stoop had disconnected from the foundation, leaving an inch gap between us and the door. The house appeared to be sinking. On entering I found myself in a clean, tidy living room that smelled of warm sugar and spices.

In the kitchen, Roscoe introduced Jimmy and me to his mother.

She was big boned like her son. She stirred dough with a strong hand then delicately dropped dollops on baking sheets. My mother was probably out drinking with friends.

"Gertie's in her room," Mrs. Larsen said.

Jimmy lowered his eyes. I knew he was eager to play with someone, even a girl.

"Goose is in the basement. So's Badger. Is anyone else coming?" she asked.

"I think, Squirrel. Probably not Will."

An egg timer clattered until she silenced its tinny ring. When Mrs. Larsen opened the oven, the kitchen was flooded with delicious heat. One baking sheet smelled like peanut butter, the other like ginger snaps.

Roscoe motioned for Jimmy and me to follow him. He led us down the hall to Gertie's room. "Hey there. Here's Jimmy!" he said.

Gertie looked up and smiled. Jimmy hesitated. I nudged him forward. She was sitting on the floor beside a large plastic dollhouse around which was spread a cluster of dolls. The dolls, most of them partially dressed, one missing a head, towered over the playhouse, reminding me of a billboard outside a theater in Evanston. Sam, Rashid, and I stood on the sidewalk, staring in titillation. The movie playing was *Attack of the Fifty Foot Woman*. The woman was enormous, a beautiful blonde, as if King Kong had turned into Marilyn Monroe. We were too afraid to buy tickets and went home to do what boys sometimes did, which was nothing except watch TV.

"Wanna play Barbies?" She made a naked blond pony-tailed

doll dance in his face. "Aunt Gladys got her at a Toy Fair in New York. She's brand new. Here, you dress her." She handed the Barbie to Jimmy.

"Do you have boy dolls?"

I didn't wait for her answer.

I followed Roscoe down to the basement where the concrete walls smelled like the turtle exhibit at the Shedd Aquarium.

"This is Mike," he announced to the two club members present. They must not have heard of me based on their puzzled stares. Roscoe explained that he had just met me that morning. "He's gonna be in our club," he said. "He's here for the summer. From Chicago."

As soon as they smiled, I knew I was welcome.

"This is Goose," said Roscoe, introducing a kid whose skin was darker than the rest of us, but not as dark as Rashid.

"We'll have lots of fun," Goose assured me as he stepped forward and shook my hand. "I am Joshua Wildgoose." He lifted his chin exhibiting his pride. "I'm a Winnebago, our people will be part of the Ho-Chunk nation."

I knew Ho-Chunk was a Native American people from overhearing my father and Grandpa Calloway argue about Indian treaty rights at the family Compound. I didn't follow the point of the disagreement. Grandpa had bought land and had built a house on Castle Rock Lake, not more than fifteen miles from where we were, and was now worried that his ownership could be disputed. He opposed the Ho-Chunk people's return from wherever they had been sent, now to "re-settle" near their ancestral lakes.

Fire Conditions

It's nice to meet you," I said. Goose nodded, returning respect despite my awkward cowboy shirt.

"I'm Bucky," said the second kid, "but my friends call me Badger. Either way. Mom and Dad named me after the mascot at their college. Your shirt's cool, by the way. It's a cowboy shirt, right?"

It was, I confirmed.

Between sweating and attracting kids like Butch to my "come-hit-me-shirt," I did not feel cool. "If you have a Milwaukee Brave shirt, I'll swap with you."

"Oh, sorry. My dog chewed it up."

I half expected Roscoe to tell me he had an animal name too. "I'm just Roscoe," he said like he knew what I was thinking.

The door at the top of the stairs creaked. Another kid came down the steps. He carried a brown paper bag spotted with grease. He had to be Squirrel, I figured. Squirrel was shorter than the rest of us. He had a slender face and a narrow nose that he could probably twitch. His ears were oddly rounded on top and ended in tiny lobes below.

He handed the grease-stained paper bag to Roscoe. "Your mom told me to bring this to you. They're cookies. Hey, isn't Will here?" And then he noticed me. "Who's that?"

Roscoe introduced me all over again. The squirrely kid who brought down the cookies flicked his eyes at me, up and down, without introducing himself and looked sneaky. "Tell him who you are," Roscoe told the odd kid.

"I'm Franklin. I get called Squirrel at school. I hate that. I'm glad it's summer. These guys call me Squirrel because I don't mind it from them. You can, too. It's okay because here we can have an animal name if we want."

I didn't understand why he would prefer Squirrel to Franklin, though Goose to Wildgoose made sense, as did Bucky to Badger.

"Let's get down to business," Roscoe said, and showed us into the clubhouse. Two-by-four cross-cut lengths of lumber framed an area that wasn't a real clubhouse, but just an area of the basement floor, without drywall. We stepped from one place outside the concrete floor into another, except for Squirrel, who waited for us to sit down. Without walls, the space was an open stage. Anyone coming downstairs could see us.

Roscoe took the place at the head of the beat-up card table with rusty metal folding chairs that I knew would chill my butt. I sat to Roscoe's left, at his invitation. Across from me sat Squirrel. He told us he'd come through the door while "you guys came through the wall." No one laughed. Nor did we quite understand. Goose sat next to me; Badger across from him, next to Squirrel. There wasn't a chair at the opposite end from Roscoe; but a space reserved for Will.

Roscoe opened a manila folder and passed out hand-written copies of an agenda. These guys meant business; or at least Roscoe did. The sack of cookies followed. By the time the sack reached me there was one extra agenda and only one cookie, not two like everyone else had taken, except Badger, who I had noticed had taken three. I admired Roscoe's organizational skill as I scanned the topics:

Fire Conditions

June 4, 1958

Agenda

1. Name Our Club
2. Mascot
3. Fort
4. Will

Roscoe pounded his gavel. "Any questions?"

"Today's the fifth. Not the fourth," said Squirrel.

"Okay," said Roscoe. "I'll make the correction. Anything else?"

Squirrel spoke up again. "Now you're supposed to say 'hereby, hereby,' like the chief munchkin."

Badger snorted. "This ain't Lollipop Land."

Squirrel laughed.

Roscoe shrugged; no offense taken.

Goose raised his hand.

Badger stole Roscoe's attention before Goose could speak. With a wary glance and secretive whispers, Badger asked Roscoe whether he knew what our two rivals were up to. I didn't know what to think, who were they, these rivals?

"I don't know," Roscoe said. "The seventh grade hasn't started. I doubt they'll have a name."

I glanced at Goose and his eyes caught mine. I nodded to him to raise his hand again to catch Roscoe's attention. Although he needn't raise his hand, he looked uneasy to speak without permission.

"We don't wanna use anyone else's name," Squirrel said.

"Don't worry about it. They're the Gophers, like last year,"

Roscoe replied. "We're talking about our name."

"Goose has an idea," I reminded Roscoe.

Goose snapped to attention, pleased to have been seen.

"Well?"

"Something Ho-Chunk," Goose suggested.

"Like what?" Badger asked.

"Big Fish People? Do you like that?"

"It's okay with me," said Roscoe. I nodded because it was cool. Badger abstained. Squirrel said it wasn't snappy enough.

"Nobody else is going to use that name," said Goose, defensively.

"What does it mean?" I asked.

"It's the name of someone important to a small tribe, but no one in any big tribe knows the important person is even alive. Like a big fish in a small lake."

"Wow, that's cool," I said.

He smiled.

"Let's go with Big Fish People," Roscoe said. The vote was unanimous. "Now item two, our mascot!"

Squirrel tittered. "How 'bout a squirrel?"

"Naw," said Badger. "Someone'll shoot it."

"There's lot of 'em out there."

"How do we keep track of which one's ours?"

"We catch it."

"And do what? Eat it?"

"Not funny. I mean, keep it in a cage."

Roscoe asked Badger whether he had a different idea. "A dog

Fire Conditions

would be good," he said. "How 'bout Manfred?"

Squirrel groaned. "He's in Tom Terrific cartoons."

"Manfred's real! He's my dog!"

"Hate to say it, but he's half blind and pees in your house," Squirrel said. "I smell it when I'm there."

Goose pointed out that we were the only club that had mascots. But if we had one, shouldn't it be a walleye? After all, we were the Big Fish People.

"We don't wanna get too fishy," said Squirrel. None of us laughed.

"I have an idea," I said. They looked a little surprised. Was I—the new kid—too bold to speak? I held them in suspense to raise their expectations, then asked, "How 'bout a myna bird?"

My new friends looked at each other, confused, not knowing what to say, as they tried to comprehend what kind of bird was a myna. Squirrel spoke first. "It's like a parakeet, right?"

"It's some kind of a crow," said Badger.

"I've heard of myna birds," Roscoe said, "but there are none around here."

"My grandma has one," I said, then waited a moment before I told them about Pookah. They stared at me, mesmerized. "No one's gonna shoot her or eat her at Grandma's house," I continued. "We can hang out there, meet there if we want, when Grandma's at work. And we can teach Pookah to talk, more words than 'hello, Joe.'" I saw their minds spinning with possibilities, made possible by me.

"Can we teach it our names?" asked Badger.

"Our motto!" said Squirrel.

"We don't have a motto," Goose pointed out.

"How about we get an oath," Badger offered, "like last year's?"

"We didn't have one last year," Roscoe reminded him.

"Oh yeah." Badger lowered his eyes.

"All in favor of the myna bird," said Roscoe, "say 'aye.'" The outcome of the vote was once more unanimous.

"The third item, our fort," Roscoe announced.

The Gophers had a head start on us, Roscoe continued. He had scoped out Palmer's woods. The Gophers were building near an old shed with the big hornets' nest in the wall. The place made it through deer season and winter, but it was pretty much wrecked.

"Let's chop it down. Like they did to ours last year," said Squirrel.

"And get stung?" Goose said.

"Ours was on the ground last year. Forts gotta be in a tree to be safer," Badger said.

"Badger's right. Each of you look for a good tree that'll hold a fort. Report your findings at the next meeting."

"Why not a cave?" Goose asked. "There's one at Roche-A-Cri Rock."

Too far away, said Badger, then reminded those of us who were here last year, that a kid died by falling off the edge of a cliff. "It could happen to any one of us."

"What about the kid that disappeared?" Squirrel asked.

"What about him?" Goose said, irritated.

"My grandma says she heard he was probably dead, too," said

Fire Conditions

Badger. "That he got in someone's car, and that was it."

Although I enjoyed my new friends and looked forward to being with them over the summer, I didn't want to hear about dead kids. But of course I was naturally curious, as were the others, to learn more.

The door at the top of the stairs creaked open. Footsteps followed. We stopped talking. Roscoe's mother's feet came into view, then her hands holding a basket of laundry before the rest of her appeared. "It's time for your friends to go."

"Oh geez, Mom," Roscoe whined.

"Hope you all liked the cookies."

We chimed in, "Thank you, Mrs. Larsen."

"One minute, Mom," Roscoe pleaded. "Okay, guys. See you same time, Wednesday, next week."

"That's the eleventh," said Squirrel.

"No, it's the twelfth," Roscoe corrected him. Squirrel sniffed at him the way Jimmy might sniff at me if I irritated him.

"And Mike," she said, "don't forget your brother."

Why would she say that, did Jimmy misbehave? Or was it that she just didn't know me well enough yet?

"And Roscoe, don't forget I have PTA tonight. I still have to put the agenda together. So, you need to watch the kids."

"Even the baby?"

"Who else would? You're good with her."

"How 'bout Dad?"

"He's a klutz with a diaper and pins."

By then everyone else was gone except for Mrs. Larsen, who

stayed behind to finish washing their clothes.

Roscoe, sulking, led me upstairs. In the hall, we paused to let Jimmy and Gertie finish their play. "I'd like you to meet Will," he said. "He's a cool kid. We've been friends forever. In second grade he got polio. He didn't show up for school one day. The janitor came to our classroom wearing gloves. He carried Will's desk out to be burned. And then, I didn't see him for years but prayed for him. He's home now. He'd like to meet you. But be careful," he warned, "if his sister's around. She can be mean."

Mention of a mean sister led me to ask him whether he knew a kid named Butch.

"Oh man, he's the biggest jerk in the world! Did he pick on you?"

"He tried to."

"He picks on new kids at school. Steer clear of his friends too."

Butch had friends! Little Butches? No, butchers, as I pictured them running around Eli's Deli looking for something to chop. I had to be careful. I couldn't hide in the Tap all day.

We parted with Roscoe promising to arrange a time to introduce me to Will. I felt fortunate to have made such nice friends. I held Jimmy's hand on our way back to the Tap. When he started to skip, I skipped along, aware of how stupid we must look in our shirts, but I didn't care because I was one of the Big Fish People.

Chapter 4

Two days later, Friday morning, I woke, startled by the sound of what I thought was the noon whistle. I rolled over and covered my ears with my pillow, ignoring the fact the room was dark and shadowless, and that it wasn't noon. The siren rose but when it fell, I knew there was a real fire somewhere.

Jimmy pounded me on the back to get me up.

I took a swing at him with my pillow to leave me alone. He promptly swatted me back.

"Get up!" he yelled.

Did he expect me to spring into action? I didn't smell smoke but did what I thought was right. I opened the bedroom door, then remembered that I had done what my father had told me never to do. An open door invited flames and smoke to gobble up all the fresh air and suffocate anyone there.

Before that he'd also told me to crawl to a prearranged place in the backyard where our family could account for each other. There had been a tragedy at a nursing home in Iowa where sixteen people were killed in a fire. The reason: someone had opened a window or door to escape but had let death surge in to take the others. Someday, he predicted, a school would burn down and kill kids if schools didn't start having fire drills.

I told Jimmy the fire was elsewhere.

"Where is it, then?"

I covered my forehead like my head ached. "I have no idea."

"Boys!" Grandma shouted from the bottom of the stairs. "Get up if you wanna see a fire!"

Jimmy rushed past me, shouting, "Let's go, Mikey!"

I grabbed at his arm but missed. He escaped down the stairs. I caught up to him in the bar, both of us still in pajamas. Grandma stood waiting, swinging an arm urgently. Were we running for shelter? Jimmy sneered at me.

Outside by the curb, the engine of her bright-pink Nash Rambler was running and raring to go, with no one inside. "Get in the back!" she shouted. After I climbed in, Grandma tossed Jimmy next to me. He laughed in anticipation of a rollicking good time.

Grandma checked the side and rearview mirrors. With the old car's engine still running, she grabbed the steering wheel until her knuckles turned white. She didn't look like my grandma, but like a hot rod driver in a muumuu, bouncing, eager for a race to start.

A fire truck with hooks and ladders chugged onto Main Street, which doubled as a state highway. As the truck idled, we watched the last of the volunteers arrive and jump aboard. One volunteer worked himself out of an apron. Another hopped as he ran, struggling to zip up his jeans. After all of them were in their fireproof gear, they secured themselves with belts to the sides of the truck. Soon a water tanker rounded the corner like a lumbering pig, taking its position to follow. Lights began to flash, and the fire engine's siren kicked in.

Jimmy's eyes were never wider. He hugged his knees. As the

fire trucks began to move, a black and white police car marked Sheriff stuck its nose into the nose of the Rambler. The police car's red flashing lights washed over us again and again.

Grandma pounded the steering wheel and swore before I could cover Jimmy's ears. I was afraid we were under arrest. A uniformed officer rapped on Grandma's window. She snorted as she cranked it down. The policeman looked to be about her age but less roly-poly than her. He leaned into the car. His thick goofy glasses looked heavy. He blinked each time his car's red lights swept across the windshield.

"Aggie," he said, pleading for reason, "keep your distance."

"Where're we headed?"

"None of your business."

I wished I could have seen Grandma's face when the officer added, "Don't look at me like that."

"Like what?" she asked, as sweet as honey.

"I'll ticket you if you try to pass me." He then noticed Jimmy and me. "Who're they?"

"My grandkids."

"Oh, for crying out loud." He shook his head and returned to his car.

"He means well," Grandma told us. "He's just Acting Sheriff. The real one's outta town with his wife. Won't be back till September."

The police car backed away from our car, its lights still flashing, and pulled in line behind the tanker. Grandma made a quick U-turn to join the parade.

I wondered if she was a secret fireman.

Our parade sped up quickly and rounded a bend out of town, passing Friendship Mound with a tall outcropping Grandma called Chimney Rock on the left, and a large pond called Friendship Lake on the right. She gunned the engine as we hit a straightaway. With a hard punch of the gas pedal, the old Rambler surprised me. It responded like a horse, rearing its head, lifting the hood against the wind before breaking into a full gallop. Yet she was keeping her distance, as the policeman had warned.

"Giddyap!" Jimmy yelled.

"Hi-Yo Silver! Away!" I yelled back, getting into the spirit.

Grandma cracked up with laughter. There was no other traffic except our parade for as far as I could see. Surprisingly, Grandma turned chatty.

"We had a forest fire outside of town a while back," Grandma said. "Burnt the new 4-H building and acres of trees. Worse, ten years ago, a few counties east, a forest got wiped out by a fire. Acres 'n acres turned black in a flash. Summer was dry, like this year, unless we get some rain." She paused to adjust the rearview mirror, her eyes off the road, and kept talking. "Another bad one was down by the Dells. Coupl'a folk burned to a crisp, asleep in their trailer. The Dells police didn't let me get close. You'd think a jailbird got loose."

"It would've been something to see," I said to be agreeable.

"Even worse," she continued, spurred by my interest, "a resort on the Wisconsin River burned. That was before the dam went in. Your grandpa was alive then. But I always drove. And all that burned was a tavern, a few cottages, and a couple of cars. Not the whole resort, for sure. We sat on a trestle over the river and watched the fire. We drank brandy straight from the bottle till your grandpa couldn't walk." She laughed and shook her head.

I felt older when Grandma gave away adult secrets. Surely, she had more. "I guess those were the good old days," I said.

An unexpected rise and fall in the highway tickled our bellies. Jimmy giggled. The ride dizzied me. "How'd you like that?" she called, laughing. Jimmy said, "Do it again!"

A sign for Roche-A-Cri State Park came into view. I remembered Badger's mention of a kid who fell off a cliff here and was killed. Curious to see where it might've happened, I riveted my eyes to the landscape, though it was difficult to see anything between the fast-passing trees. The bluff itself seemed to flirt with me between glimpses, leaving the impression of a ruined castle in hiding. I imagined its bare face, with its outcroppings and ledges, must have tempted the dead boy to climb up for a view. The place was dangerous if you had no sense. If we built a fort there, we would need to stay near the base of the bluff. A place like that would be perfect.

I saw Grandma looking in the rearview mirror with a worried expression. "Oh hell, and hockey sticks," she said. I looked out the back window. Two cars were gaining on us, racing each other for Grandma's position.

Jimmy whispered to me, "Grandma said another bad word."

I ignored him. Grandma stomped harder on the gas pedal and centered the car on the highway to hog the road. The police car's brake light came on. I yelled, "Stop!"

The line had slowed abruptly to make a left turn. Grandma slammed on the brakes. The Rambler skidded. I threw myself on top of Jimmy in case we crashed. The cars behind us swerved. I heard screeches of tires burning rubber. When I looked out the window, I saw the two cars chasing us were in opposite ditches.

Grandma followed the sheriff who followed the fire trucks onto a side road. We were nearly stuck in sand until the tires caught gravel, a rat-a-tat pelting of stones underneath us, and we lurched ahead.

"Lookie there!" Grandma said, pointing to a cloud of swirling black smoke to the west. Together, the smoke and the early sunlight tinted the sky ahead a dull, dusky peach. As we drew closer, the fire appeared to be beyond a stand of jack pine, around which the road likely wound.

"Are trees on fire?" Jimmy asked.

"Smoke's too black. It's a house or a barn," she said.

As we rounded a bend, sparks and embers swirled and glowed orange red, fading in and out of the smoke. Grandma was wrong about it being a house or a barn. Both a house *and* a barn were burning. The firefighters didn't seem to know where to begin. Three were unwinding a heavy canvas hose while two others struggled to connect its nozzle to the water truck. By then, ladders were pointless. So too, was the hose.

I half-expected her to jump out of the car to pitch in, but she sat immobilized, staring out of the windshield. "Jesus, Mary, and Joseph, this is Jasper's place," she muttered. "You boys stay here. I'll be right back."

"Let's get out," Jimmy said as soon as she left.

"No! You heard her."

Pouting, he clambered over the seat to get in the front. I did the same, onto the driver's seat, accidentally kicking him.

"Ow!" he said.

His "ow" was fake, insincere, pretending I'd hurt him when I had only bumped him. I kicked him again, for real.

He got away from me, leaned against the side of his door, and poked his head outside.

The rest of his scrawny body followed. The windshield had heated up. Whiffs of smoke seeped through the dash. I caught sight of him passing the sheriff and Grandma together. Neither of them seemed to notice. Solely, I was responsible for stopping him. I jumped out of the car and ran after him. They noticed me, being of a more trappable size than Jimmy. The fire roared. Jimmy stopped and stared, much too close to the side of the barn that was burning. I ran faster than I ever could before. When I reached him, the timbers were about to burst. They crackled apart and split. The entire structure shuddered as the roof began to cave in.

I grabbed him with all my might, catching him off guard, and dragged him backward as fast as his little feet could pedal. I didn't look back when I heard a loud poof. We stumbled and fell to the ground. A cloud of hot air, embers, and smoke rolled over us. When it cleared, we were covered in soot on a carpet of sparks. I wiped my eyes. Grandma and the sheriff stood in front of us.

"Don't you ever pull another stunt like that!" Grandma scolded.

Her words were directed at me, not Jimmy, which stung me. He'd started the trouble and I'd saved him, and nobody thanked me.

"Go home, Aggie," said the sheriff. "I have work to do here. You've seen all there is to see."

"Tell the guys, beers on me tonight."

"How 'bout me?" the sheriff pretended to whine.

"You too, silly."

"You know I'd never miss your fish fry."

She smiled and batted her eyes. Even here, she seemed to be flirting.

"It'll be a big night," he said in warning. "There'll be a lot of talk about the fire."

"Let me know if Jasper's okay," Grandma said, and ordered Jimmy to sit in back, and me to sit next to her in the front. I was so mad for being blamed for not stopping Jimmy sooner but took satisfaction to see him alone in the back, looking like he was being hauled off to jail.

"I'm sorry," I said to Grandma, afraid she would send us back to Chicago.

She stared at me a long time, then said, "I am too."

Grandma didn't speed on our way back to town, even after Jimmy said he was hungry. She must've had her fill of him. She said to me, "There's gum in the glove compartment. Give him a stick. Take one if you want."

Between a comb and brush and copies of *Woman's Day* and *Family Circle*, I found a pack of cinnamon-flavored Beemans next to a small pearl-handled gun. In Chicago, we chewed Wrigley's Juicy

Fruit, which tasted nothing like fruit. I took a stick of Beemans and closed the glove compartment as fast as I could.

"Did you find the gum?" she asked.

"I did," I said and handed the stick over my shoulder to Jimmy. "Do you want one, Grandma?"

She shook her head.

Aware of a pistol within my reach, I stared at the latch in the glove compartment, trying to imagine why she'd need a gun. To protect herself, and from whom? Did she have enemies when everyone seemed to love her? Or was it to stop somebody from robbing the Tap?

As we rode into Friendship, I found myself curious to touch the pearl handle but knew I'd be afraid to touch the trigger.

Chapter 5

That afternoon as I sat at the bar eating lunch, people began to drift in. Most of them were talking about the fire, but one fellow named Bert, a friend of Joe's who'd arrived as soon as the bar opened, spoke loudly about a bulletin that the *Friendship Reporter* would soon release.

"I know something nobody here knows," I overheard Bert say to Joe. "They're saying Jasper's dead."

I didn't know where the old drunk would've heard that other than from a loose-lipped reporter or someone who'd been at the fire. As the tavern filled, new stories grew into rumors, some mean. Not only was Jasper dead, but someone said he'd burned down his own house and barn for the insurance money.

Gossip and the lack of facts exploded into rumors as fast as a fire until a new version took hold. Grandma asked me to help in the kitchen. She had two friends who worked Friday night to help with the fish fry, the busiest night of the week. Now, with the rumors about Jasper, the place filled faster than usual with more unfamiliar faces.

She introduced my new partners to me. "This is Mrs. Johnson." Mrs. Johnson's lips were as red as a rose. "And this is Mrs. Schmidt..." whose lips were a hot pink like a little petunia. Both were large, but less so than Grandma. Their faces were as colorful as Grandma's dresses. Mrs. Johnson's eyeshadow was green, Mrs. Schmidt's, orange. In the hot kitchen they looked like they were crying black ink.

Before Grandma left, she told me to check on Jimmy whenever I could. I wondered why she thought I could be in two places at once. My partners eyed me up and down. "Aren't you the spitting image of your mother," said Mrs. Johnson. "Sure is," Mrs. Schmidt lisped. "You can call us Johnson and Schmidt."

My job was to drop fish filets into a shallow pan of cornmeal where Schmidt would roll them around before dropping them into the hot bubbling vegetable oil. Johnson watched the vats to assure the fish were fried to perfection. As they worked they updated each other on the local girls who had been "knocked up." Was this one keeping the baby? Would that one's mother raise the kid? Seniors who had graduated a month and a half ago had had a wild party on Rattlesnake Mountain but had run off when a crazy woman started to shoot at them. The weekly crime report in the newspaper announced that eleven drivers in the county had been ticketed, four for drunk driving. A good week for the sheriff.

"And then there's poor Rosie..."

"Shush."

"What about her?" Did they think I wasn't listening? "I'm Mike," I reminded them.

"Forget it," Johnson said. "Your mother's a sweetie."

"She's a sweetie, that one," Schmidt echoed, her lisp making me feel sorry for her.

When Johnson brought up Jasper's love life, Schmidt joined in.

"Who knows?" Said with a side glance.

"Berniece never got him under the sheets."

"To think," Schmidt said, shaking her head, "all those fine ladies wasting their time on pies. Only them, gettin' fat."

Johnson handed me her glass. "How 'bout you get us refills?"

"Wash your hands first," Schmidt said, which I did promptly. As they chugged the last of their beer, they looked like regular guys made up as women.

I found Jimmy at the bar being entertained by firefighters. He was newly famous for almost dying, it seemed. I said excuse me as I butted in and told Jimmy to go upstairs. He could watch TV. I'd be right up. I knew Grandma would want me to take him upstairs so I dragged him away from the bar.

An old Zenith TV sat on a low table, facing Joe's bed. It was nothing more than a box with a greenish semi-rectangular screen and a couple of knobs below. A plastic half-ball with a flat base sat on top. Two slim rods were extended at opposing angles, their tips wrapped in aluminum foil for reception. People called them "rabbit ears," I knew. I played with the angle of its ears. When the static began to clear, I told Jimmy he was in for a treat. "You can decide."

Jimmy jumped on Joe's bed and yelled, "Yippee!" The mattress and rumpled sheet smelled like smoke and old sweat. Joe didn't need the bed right now. I'd heard Grandma tell him to tend the bar all night.

A page from the TV Guide program listings was taped to a side of the TV. *Leave it to Beaver* started in five minutes on Channel 5

Fire Conditions

out of Wausau, according to a fuzzy commercial for used cars. *Rin Tin Tin* started at the same time on Channel 27 out of Madison and had better reception. Jimmy chose the dog Western.

We sat on the bed and waited for *Rin Tin Tin* but, instead, *Broken Arrow* appeared. The introduction opened with an arrow being broken, followed by a pipe being smoked, and then, whoopee, peace was made.

"Where's the dog?"

"The dog's not on."

Jimmy threw himself on the mattress, dramatically, pounding as he pretended to sob. I held his shoulder until he fell still. I explained, soothingly, why summer TV was different from the regular season. New shows appeared, others vanished, starting times changed, repeats were run. I offered to change the TV to Channel 5.

"Will there be dogs?"

I shrugged.

"Nice ones and big? Not like Grandma's?"

I had memories of sitting with Dad on the floor and eating popcorn as we watched *The Lone Ranger*. I remembered what my father had told me about Westerns, how TV shows and history books had it all wrong. Even *The Lone Ranger* was flawed in his view, inaccurate he'd say, not like things really were. He was harder on other TV Westerns, and on big screen movies which he said were worse, except for being in color. What saved *The Lone Ranger* for him was that a real Indian played Tonto, not a white man. It was ironic, he told me. "Tonto" meant "stupid" in Spanish, so on Mexican

TV Tonto's name was changed to "Toro," the bull.

He never told me how he knew these things but I believed him. He laughed when a character in one episode said American Indians and the white man didn't always see eye to eye. "What an understatement," he said. I was pretty sure what he meant. But the most fun was when the show ended and together we shouted with the Lone Ranger and Tonto, "Hi-Yo Silver! Away!" as they galloped off to a new adventure.

"Can't we watch this one," I suggested to Jimmy. I told him I had watched this show with Dad. I hoped we'd have a good time but I needed to interpret what was happening. He sat up and began to watch the show. All of the shows were about a white man and a band of Apache who'd made peace. Tonight's episode was about a bad guy with a name that sounded like Coochy-Coo. Coochy-Coo stole dynamite meant for Cochise. He wanted to give the dynamite to Geronimo to keep the Indians fighting each other. The last we saw of them was Agent Tom closing in on Coochy-Coo when a blizzard of static blew in.

The fact I forgot was that after the show ended my father would go his own way and I'd play with Jimmy. Eventually he stopped watching with me altogether. He might've been bored. I always hoped Dad would find another show. I would've watched it if he'd found one he liked.

I expected Jimmy to throw another fit because of the static, but when I looked back, he was asleep. I carried the lunkhead across the hall to our room. I tucked him into bed, then found where I had left Tom Sawyer's adventures. It had been days, and I had to reread

Fire Conditions

what had happened. What followed left me wondering what I liked about the story to begin with. Tom was a troublemaker, which I liked when what he did was funny, but not when it was done at the expense of a friend. His crush on Becky Thatcher made me cringe. When Tom hid outside her bedroom window and imagined dying for her, I could've puked. I put the book down.

With nothing to do I went downstairs. Half-way down, from above the crowd, I saw Grandma sitting with the sheriff at a table far in a corner. I didn't know what to think when they began to tickle each other's nose, their lips parted, possibly cooing. I smiled at first, but the longer I watched them, the weirder I felt.

I had never been to a tavern on a Friday night, or, for that matter, ever. The loud voices, the music, and the stale, smoky air was a world wilder than those of Mom and Dad's parties. I stood off the side of the bar where Joe was too busy to see me. The jukebox set a new mood with each tune. "At the Hop" gave way to "The Stroll" to "Get A Job." Someone plugged in the next nickel and replayed "'Sha na....get a job,'" until a voice in my head repeated vague expectations of me. I thought about what my job would be. Maybe I would be like Dad, writing a big paper to get a job teaching at Northwestern, a few blocks from our house. Dad would be proud of me. Mom would too; but prouder than he was because I was her son.

When the lights suddenly dimmed, no one seemed to care. The only motion I saw was an occasional flash of a cigarette being lit. From the jukebox I heard a woman's voice, the saddest I could have ever imagined. She sang about walking after midnight, alone, and I couldn't move. She walked in the moonlight and searched for miles to tell someone she loved him. There was a highway and a weeping willow and being lonesome and crying. She could've been Mom on the shore of Lake Michigan, walking in daylight. But in a dream of mine she wasn't alone. Jimmy and I were right behind her.

"Mike?"

Johnson was waving at me from a table. Schmidt sat beside her like a sidekick. As weird as it would be to kill time with them, they had to be more interesting than lying awake in bed. They stopped drinking beer and changed to smaller glasses that held a yellowish-brown liquid and cherries.

"Call us The Madams," they said with impish grins.

"That's what Aggie calls us when we goof off. But don't get us wrong. We have hubbies. We don't fool around. We just like to have fun."

Well, I liked to have fun, too, but was confused by why calling them Madams would give me the wrong impression. They were already fun but were still Johnson and Schmidt to me.

"Look who's coming!" Schmidt said.

I turned to see who it was.

"He's a famous Hollywood star." Johnson giggled in awe.

I sat up straight in honor and anticipation of meeting someone of unknown fame. A lean, muscular man about my parents' age took the last chair at the table. He looked at me and smiled. "Well, who do we have here?"

"I'm Mike Calloway."

"I'm Beau. I knew your mother way back when."

Fire Conditions

I could never have guessed that Mom would know someone famous.

The Madams were giddy vying to buy him a drink. A Pepsi would do, he said, and Schmidt won by reaching into the top of her dress and pulling out a dollar bill. Up at the bar, she barked at Joe. "Give the man a Pepsi."

While Schmidt was gone, I began to notice a patch of skin above Beau's left cheekbone that appeared to have been polished smooth. Other areas of his face were rough. I wondered whether he'd had bad acne when he was young. Yet, all in all, he was good-looking.

Typically, I felt uncomfortable when someone took an extra interest in me, but I managed to say, "I never met anyone named Beau. Except, maybe a dog."

He laughed. "I've been called a rare bird, but never a dog."

Schmidt returned with a drink for Johnson and her and the Pepsi for Beau. "Did I miss anything?" she asked as she sat down.

Yes, you missed me, I thought, but I was just a kid.

After a few swigs Johnson whispered secretly to me that Beau had a lot of names. "Aliases, a California thingy."

He tilted his head, obviously, to show them his humility. The Madams, gaga, peppered him with questions. He could've been Eisenhower. When would he go back to California? He aimed for August. He had offers from studios but didn't know which role to take. The role he wanted was in a Western still under development, now delayed by a major script problem. He hoped filming would begin in September. The title of the movie was *The Hangman*.

"Who's the big star? Tell, tell," said the Madams.

Wasn't he the star? I wondered

They didn't know yet, he said. "They," whoever "they" were, were still casting the lead. John Wayne or Gary Cooper, probably. I asked him which one he would want to be. All he knew was that he'd play a bad man and get hanged halfway into the show.

"Wow!"

He smiled.

"What's Hollywood like?" I asked.

"Perfect weather all year long."

"Do you have a sweetie?" asked Johnson.

Well, he said sadly, there were none in the picture. He aimed to marry a rich famous actress. One who took to stuntmen. Afterall, stuntmen, everyone knew, were the best in bed.

The Madams snickered like two naughty girls.

I didn't know but had ideas what it meant to be best in bed, or why the Madams made light of it, but I planned to find out.

"Who are your friends?" I asked.

He chummed around with all kinds of people, he said. Nils and Tab were his best pals, always fun to hang out with.

"Is that Tab Hunter?" Johnson asked.

"No, no." He waved her off for being silly. "Tab Carter. He and Nils do stunts like me. They taught me the ropes."

"What kind of stunts do you do?" I asked.

"All kinds. Whatever they tell me to do."

"What's your best?"

My simple question triggered a long story. When he'd arrived

Fire Conditions

in Los Angeles, he wanted to be a star, he began. He used the name "Roger Hughes." He'd always liked the name Roger and thought people might think he was related to Howard Hughes. He paired the first and the last names together; but none panned out like he wanted. "They told me I sounded like a Midwest hick and looked like a choir boy when they needed a villain. They said to come back when my voice was done changing."

He paused as if to reorganize his thoughts and then continued.

He got his break when a talent scout spotted him putting a stop to a purse snatching near the corner of Vermont and Sunset. He bashed the thief in the face, pushed him down, and retrieved the old woman's purse. After the thief ran off, the old woman handed him a dime, and the talent scout tapped his shoulder. In that amazing moment, the talent scout told him that he looked like James Dean in *Rebel Without a Cause* and handed him a business card. "And the rest is history."

"So, what's your best stunt?"

He raised a hand for me to be patient. He was more of a body double than a stuntman, he said. His looks were important. On the streets, people would stop him and ask if he was the guy that fell off horses in whatever movie they remembered.

"It was little ol' me, I tell 'em."

What was his best stunt? I asked again. Was it being pushed off a building? Did he fall on a mattress or trampoline?

"Depends."

"On what"

"How high up I am."

"Was your best stunt getting thrown off a horse over a cliff? Or from the top of a skyscraper?"

He grinned, and I realized I was amusing him, and that he liked me.

"How 'bout getting run over by a car or hit by a train? Or, your parachute doesn't open when you get shot down by Nazis?"

He laughed.

"Or maybe you just catch fire?"

He hesitated and was quiet for a while. The Madams, too, seemed to have noticed a change in his mood. I knew it was because I'd pestered him.

"Hey, kid, don't be glum. Everything's cool."

Relieved, I listened.

Schmidt asked whose bodies he'd doubled for.

"Rock Hudson?" Johnson gushed.

"Gregory Peck?" Schmidt's preference.

What I knew about Rock was that he was good-looking to women, and that Gregory was a "thinking man's cowboy." A kid I knew in Evanston was a fan of Gregory and had told me that he had a new movie coming out; not the one Beau would be in.

He took a deep breath, and continued his story, a part of which he'd never told anyone in Wisconsin but was well-known to his circle of friends out west.

In early 1955, he'd played Godzilla in a cheap Japanese horror movie. The monster had horns on its head, unlike the spikes on the back of the American version. If you took a good look when you saw a dog, and you checked out its tail, some had long ones, like a whip,

Fire Conditions

then there were ones without any, like a bulldog. The monster's tail was like one of the dogs without a tail, or a stub of a tail that hadn't popped out yet.

We laughed. The big thing about the movie, get this, he played the monster! He stomped around on toy army men and tanks while blowing fire out of his mouth at mosquito-like airplanes. Being a Godzilla-like monster was a dream come true since he'd been a kid. The shoots and reshoots, like when he tripped, his big green feet tying him up, causing him to fall and wipe out all of toy Tokyo, made him laugh. The Japanese told him not to worry about the tripping. He was a good monster. He'd be great once he learned to walk. They had a sense of humor for pipsqueaks, he said. They asked him to be in the sequel.

His best stunt turned into his worst two days before filming was supposed to end. He might've tripped around a lot, but tripping made the monster more real (he claimed). It became a joke that he hadn't burned down the studio yet. Whenever he wanted to blow fire, he pressed his chin against a button on a canister of accelerant. He'd done this about fifty times. An airplane on one of the wires caught his eye. Burning airplanes were more challenging than a town that didn't move. Even people didn't move, being plastic. Today set up the final scene for the next day when he'd get to do what stars did, which was die dramatically. Hit by an atomic bomb, he'd twist and turn in pain and throw his monster body flat on the ground so everything could be moved out of the studio on time. He was about to take off his head when he spied a Zero. In a tangle of wire, he'd overlooked the last toy plane to burn for the day. His canister, low on accelerant, forced him to press his chin on the button again and again, harder. Instead of shooting flame out of his mouth, it backfired. The fire was put out fast. The fireproof jelly on his face kept him from being burned worse.

He paused to let us imagine the scene, for us to feel how awful it must've been. This, I understood, was why he had been reluctant to talk about his best stunt. I wondered how many times he'd told his story, and who'd listened. The accident was three years ago. He looked pretty good now.

He continued telling us about the years he was having surgeries to fix his scars. He was lucky enough to find work. Friends knew he was a good dancer, and he picked up parts in movie musicals as a body double for stars who didn't know how to dance. He made their feet look good. The directors didn't need his face. They needed feet that put people in awe. The studio's insurance along with his foot jobs covered his surgeries and paid for his day-to-day expenses. He'd be back at his regular gig in August, if the Western went through.

I wanted to cheer as he ended. If there was a sequel, he would be in it. The monster's head would cover his face. But if he didn't want to be a monster again, there was always a new Western in need of a double.

"Well, well, well," came a familiar voice, "who have we here?"

I sank onto my chair as Grandma's hand came down on my shoulder. "How was *Rin Tin Tin*?"

"It wasn't on."

She raised her chin skeptically. "What did you watch?"

"Broken Arrow. Jimmy fell asleep. I put him to bed."

"And then you came down here."

An observable fact. "I brought my plate to the kitchen. To be helpful."

"Hmm," Grandma grunted as the Madams fidgeted to avoid her gaze. "Beau, you can stay."

Grandma's sheriff friend stood watching from a short distance. "Henry," she said, turning, "you'll remember my grandson." Then to me: "This here is Adams County Acting Sheriff Henry Tuttle."

Henry came forward and acknowledged me with a nod. I said, "Hi," thinking he didn't look much like the real Sheriff Matt Dillon on *Gunsmoke*.

"Is Jasper really dead?" Johnson asked.

"Well, Hilda," he said, "we're just starting to investigate. I'm sure you and Trudy will be the first to know."

"Hilda! Trudy!" Grandma clapped at them like they were her dogs. "Get back to work. There's lots of cleaning to do." As she turned to me, she said, "Don't ever let me catch you down here this time of night again. Right, Henry?"

"Right, Aggie."

Grandma gave me a soft kick in the rear end when I stood. "Get moving," she said. She looked at the Madams. "You too. I don't wanna see any mess in the morning."

When I looked back, I saw that Grandma and the sheriff had sat down with Beau and they were all laughing.

Chapter 6

Now that I was in Adams County I couldn't stop thinking about Grandpa Calloway's lake house and how close it was to the Tap. Dad's side of the family gathered there two or three weeks in July, depending on schedules or issues in Chicago. I didn't know until I was old enough to understand that hanging out with people you didn't like was what went on there every year. The other thing I didn't understand then was the reality of lake people and town people not mixing. My mother's family was never invited, but they probably wouldn't have come anyway. My parents and others referred to the lake house as the Compound and that it could have been a prison with Grandpa the warden.

The group at its largest typically numbered about thirty but appeared to be fewer due to the size of the house, the woods, the long beach, and the cold, sparkling lake. Some of them stayed into August, but not us. Two weeks with them got under Dad's skin, particularly with his father. I, too, had someone to bully me, and that was Horace.

The first time my older cousin Horace tied me up, he stuffed me in a closet for what felt like forever. Other times he'd pull my hair, tug back my head and, once, sat on me and poured wine down my throat until I gagged. I was dizzy and sick to my stomach later that day. Another time he tied me to a tree in the woods and walked

Fire Conditions

away. A poacher found and freed me. Horace developed a habit of blind-siding me in front of our boy cousins. He'd punch me open-handed and cup me below the belt. I would double over breathless each time and ache between my legs the rest of the day. Whenever he did this, he would yell, "Squirrel!" laugh, and say, "got your nuts!" My boy cousins would laugh, and if any girl cousin came around, he would leave me alone, knowing the girls would tattle on him.

    I didn't know why no one noticed what he was doing. Not my parents, his parents, BeBe? None of them. So, I took matters into my own hands. My first act of revenge was to put random cat poo from the downstairs litter box under his pillow; the second, days later, I filled his tennis shoes with his own dog's poo. The third time, a few days before Dad's and Grandpa's last fight, I helped Grandma BeBe bake blueberry muffins and, without her knowing, filled one row of the tin with batter into which I had mixed Grandpa's castor oil when she wasn't looking. I sneaked into Horace's family's suite and set the special muffins on the table next to his bed, with a note that read, "Enjoy!" I signed it, "Love, Grandma BeBe."

The last time we stayed at the Compound, three years ago, I learned that Grandpa had found out that BeBe was paying my father's tuition for the last two years without Grandpa's knowledge. Mom had told me this when I ran into her at the kitchen. She was drinking what they called Mai Tais with other women who'd married a Calloway. Jimmy was running around outside on the beach. Downstairs in the game room I found Dad sitting far away from a few Calloway men. He motioned for me to come to him and

I sat down beside him.

"Are you okay?" I asked. When he didn't answer, only stared across the room, I asked him again.

That night I listened to my father and Grandpa through a vent in my bedroom. They were in the game room, I knew. Grandpa was slurring and swearing at Dad.

"Phoebe's been covering for you. I want you to know it's a loan, not a gift."

"I wouldn't have it any other way."

"You're wasting your life." The vent rattled as Grandpa's voice grew louder. "Get a real job. Like John!"

John was my father's younger brother. He worked for Grandpa's real estate firm. He was also Horace's father.

There was a lull in the conversation, if anyone could call it that. I expected Grandpa to continue, and he did. "I live an honest life."

"And I don't? I'm glad not to be like you. A racist."

"Oh, don't give me that crap. Get off your high horse and get real."

"Are you proud you bought this land? Built this castle?"

"You and your civil rights crap. How much will you earn when you're done with school?"

"None of your business."

"Your boys need a better home. I wouldn't have bought this land if I knew you'd marry trash."

Something glass shattered.

"Rose and our boys are the best thing that's happened to me."

"You didn't like her as much as your pecker did."

Fire Conditions

The vent stopped vibrating. A few minutes later Dad appeared in our suite. I crawled back from the vent. Jimmy was asleep with Mom in the other bedroom.

The next morning we left and never went back.

Chapter 7

Jimmy and I were playing Slap Jack at the bar Saturday morning when someone rapped at the door. Since the tavern didn't open for another two hours, Grandma peeked outside and eventually opened the door and signed for a special delivery. She carried a rectangular box and a padded envelope our way. They had to be presents for us, I hoped. She slowed, then quit altogether and scowled. She tossed the packages in front of us with an extra oomph of disdain. She hovered over us as we opened the gifts. My box contained a James Nagy's Learn to Draw Kit that included pastel-colored but mostly black and gray sticks of chalk, a book of instructions, a pad to soften the shades, and high-quality paper. Jimmy's envelope held comic books that he'd already read. So, naturally, he turned his attention to my kit.

Absorbed in our presents, I didn't notice Grandma's eyes tearing up until she turned away and hurried into the kitchen. The return address in Lake Forest told me everything I needed to understand her tears. Either BeBe or my father had sent them; though on second thought, my father would never have taken the time to buy and ship our gifts special delivery.

I went into the kitchen and asked Grandma Flowers whether our presents made her sad. She wiped her eyes and forced a small smile like nothing was wrong. To my knowledge, my grandmothers

Fire Conditions

had never met. If they had, it would've been at Elizabeth's funeral. I didn't know what to make of that; but I'd never thought about it until now. But certainly, they must know about each other somehow.

Jimmy rushed into the kitchen to join Grandma and me. "Mikey," he said, "there's a friend here to see you! Gertie's brother."

I met Roscoe outside. When I asked him what was up, he told me that Will's mother had said it would be okay if we visited today.

Grandma gave her permission for me to go, since Mr. Wyler was apparently Reverend Wyler, the Lutheran minister. "You behave there," was all she said. Curious, but uncertain what to say to a boy who had been so sick, we set out to the Lutheran minister's house.

As we walked, I asked Roscoe whether Will had been in one of those iron lung contraptions. He knew that people in iron lungs often died. Since Will was alive, and there had been no funeral for him, Roscoe's answer was, "He probably wasn't in one. But he came back from Madison in a wheelchair with his legs in braces. My mom says it's a shame they didn't have the vaccine then."

The Wyler's house was directly across the street from the Lutheran church and was two stories tall with a fresh coat of gleaming white paint and red window trim. Peonies were in full bloom. Despite the ramp that wound up to the porch, the house was the loveliest I had seen in town.

Mrs. Wyler welcomed us. She said, "Will is waiting for you. I'm grateful you've taken the time." She smiled and I smiled in return.

Like the house, she was dressed to perfection; but unlike the house, her blouse came with fancy pink sleeves and white collar, and with a long dress, and two large blue bows tightening the sides of her blond hair. She looked like the mother of Little Bo Peep.

She led us up a broad staircase and knocked on the door at the end of the hall. "Will, your guests are here. Do you need help before they come in?"

"I'm okay, Mom," came a faint voice.

She turned to Roscoe. "If he gets tired, let me know. I'll be in the kitchen." She sighed. "I don't expect he'll be able to play long. Please mind the time."

We would, Roscoe said and we went in.

The bedroom was dark, but not darker than Jimmy's and mine at twilight. Ours smelled of smoke and stale beer, whereas his held a harsh medicinal smell from what I imagined to be from a lingering, feverish past.

When Roscoe introduced me, Will responded, "I know who he is already," which Roscoe took in stride.

Will was sitting on the floor by his bed near a portable toilet. "I'm sorry we don't get more light in here."

Two crutches lay within his reach. The metal bones of two braces hung over the back of a chair. A folded wheelchair sat in a corner, vaguely noticeable from where I stood.

"Like what you see?" he asked. "I'm almost out of my diapers."

His words were sad and embarrassed me, but I found no fault in them, glad not to be him. Roscoe suggested we play a game.

"I don't wanna play Monopoly," Will said. "It's too boring.

Fire Conditions

Everything's pretty much that way." He scooched crab-like across the floor on his butt and extended his withered arm to me. "Shake," he said. I didn't hesitate. What I felt was a soft weakness run down the length of his arm, although his grip was strong enough to convey a hint of appreciation. In spite of his pale face, his mouth and blue eyes made him look handsome.

He looked at Roscoe. "What have the guys been up to? What have I missed?"

"We've missed you."

"Oh, geez. Sit down. Both of you."

We joined him, cross-legged on the floor. Roscoe updated him on our club meeting three days ago. "I like being a Big Fish person," Will concluded. To me he said, "What's it like to live in a saloon?"

I shrugged. I had no reason to let him into my world. But he persisted. Did I have a sister? She died, I told him bluntly. He paused. "Sorry to hear that," he said.

"Will's sister is older than us," Roscoe said to keep the conversation going.

"She acts sweet," said Will, "but she can be mean. Like the witch in Snow White, who got mad at the mirror for telling the truth." His appalling comment was aimed at me to shock, to test, to learn how I would react. But I gave him no satisfaction by being as ambivalent as Roscoe.

"Can you play chess?" he asked.

I nodded.

He raised his good arm and pointed his elbow to where the chess set would be. I crawled across the floor and found books and board games. The chess set was the farthest from reach, on the other side of his bed, out of sight until I found it.

Roscoe paid attention to Will and me as we played. Occasionally he would ask how pieces moved. His interest clearly showed he was pleased to see us hitting it off. As I closed in on Will's king, I sacrificed a knight to set up a checkmate, and then I gloated, my competitive side coming out.

I determined we were well-matched, and he could hardly wait to beat me. Beating a cripple was against my instincts, but winning was fun. To be fair I asked him if he wanted to play again tomorrow.

He said, "It's Sunday."

"We have church all day," Roscoe explained. "My older brother used to skip out. I'd never do that. Besides, I like the choir."

"Oh, another day then," I said. "We'll teach Roscoe to play."

A moment later Will doubled up, his arms hugging his belly tight. "Get his mom!" Roscoe said.

I hurried downstairs thinking I could not live with myself if by beating him at chess he'd die. I found Mrs. Wyler in the kitchen rolling pie crusts. Her blue apron read, "Stubborn Norwegian Lutheran." When I told her about Will she dropped the rolling pin and ran upstairs.

Alone, I did not know what to do, other than pace in the hallway. I knew I couldn't leave but had to do something. What I wanted was for Roscoe or Mrs. Wyler to come downstairs and tell me that Will was all right.

The silence unraveled my nerves and set me pacing again. In the living room I found ornate glass vases with tulips on end tables.

Chairs and a davenport matched the rose-colored drapes. A framed print on the wall near a side door drew me to a picture of a white rose and a red heart in its center, overlaid by a religious cross. I was drawn to and also perplexed by religious symbols but wanted to see what was behind the closed door.

As I was about to enter, I heard the front door open and someone walk in. I expected the Reverend but was caught by a stranger. I tried not to appear guilty. She stared at me from the hallway. "Who the hell are you?"

Her voice sounded at odds with the tone of her mother's kind words. She was dressed like her mother, even in the heat, in pink and white, and smacked of defiance.

I coughed out my name.

"What are you doing here, little Mike?"

"I'm Will's friend."

"Oh, I know who you are," she said. "You're the kid with the cowboy shirt everyone's talking about. Butch says you and your kid brother made fun of him. Like you think you're a big deal."

I tightened up, not comprehending my fame or infamy in town. I didn't care what she thought about me. Who was she to make fun of my shirt when she looked like an overdressed shepherd girl who'd pissed off her sheep?

I told her that her mother was upstairs with Roscoe. Will was in pain. "But why are you still here?" she asked.

"Will's in our club," I said, feeling awkward. "We want him to know all of us want to still be his friend."

"He can't be in any club. He can't walk."

"When he gets better," I clarified.

"Good luck with that."

I wanted to say something smart-alecky, but it didn't feel right. I said, "He wants to play chess with me again."

She studied me like she would a spider, a snake, or anything creepy.

"Why are you talking to me like this?"

Her face tightened from brow to jaw. "You guys are dumb nerds," she said.

"So, what if we're nerds? We're not dumb." I was unsure about Squirrel.

She stammered and sucked her lip. She couldn't stand the sight of me. The spider she would like to squash. Which didn't bother me. There were people, mostly kids, I didn't like, and didn't care that I didn't like them. I knew how to be invisible to them, to stay quiet, and careful.

She sneered at me as she tried to storm her way out of the house. She slammed the door after her, but it bounced open. She peeked at me. Part of me wanted to give her a little wave to say "hope you find your sheep" to mock her, but it would probably make her laugh. She shook the doorknob with a fierceness that looked like she wanted to shake down the house. In the end, when she attempted to slam the door shut, the intended sound was like a puff of air.

As soon as Roscoe returned, I asked him about Will. He whispered that Will's mom said it was "constipation," a word he must've thought was a swear.

We stepped outside into the muggy heat and began to walk to the Tap. I asked him the name of Will's sister.

"Sarah," he said. "Why?"

I told him what had happened between us.

"I'm not surprised. Will told you about her. She's fifteen, you know." I knew she was older than me, but not by two grades.

"Do you wanna know something funny?" he asked.

"Yeah."

"Her name Sarah means 'princess.'"

"How do you know that?"

"Reverend Wyler talked to us about names once when we were waiting for our confirmation lesson. Isn't that funny, princess? Go figure."

As we waited for traffic to cross, I told him my grandma had an idea about where we could build a fort, then teased him by saying, "Guess where!"

He laughed. "Tell me!"

"Rattlesnake Mountain."

That was far away, he said, but he wouldn't rule it out until after Grandma and I had been there.

Jimmy sat at the table near the jukebox, where I had left him, and Joe had joined him. They were drawing together, and Joe was smoking.

"Hey!" Jimmy said when he saw me. "Come see." He held a handful of pictures he'd drawn. Joe did the same once he saw what Jimmy was doing. "What do'ya think?" Jimmy asked as he handed pictures to me.

I glanced quickly at each of them. They were of different monsters. I said they were nice, and I would send them to Mom. He beamed.

I didn't know what to make of Joe's pictures. I asked what one of them was.

He blew a puff of smoke. "That's Aggie," he said.

She looked like a beach ball with eyes and a beard. When I asked him about a different picture from his collection, he said, proudly, "That's you."

I looked like a fish. "You're a regular Picasso," I said.

Chapter 8

On Sunday morning I mopped the bar room floor and cleaned the bathroom spic and span. Saturday night had been busy. When Grandma approached me, I expected that I'd overlooked or forgotten a chore. Instead, she asked me whether I wanted to visit Lena with her.

"It's Sunday," I said. "I thought you went Wednesdays."

"I close the Tap Sundays if I feel like it. I want to tell Lena about Jasper's death."

I reminded her that my friends and I wanted to know whether the woods on Rattlesnake Mountain would be a good place to build a fort. She said, "Good luck with that."

Despite her doubtful words, I was hopeful. I wanted to be the one who found the perfect tree. I wanted to be popular, basically. To be liked by my fellow club members, although I was already their friend. I studied the territory as Grandma drove toward the top of the bluff. The branches looked good for nothing but matchsticks. The road leveled off slightly after a sharp turn. Signs for hiking trails began to appear. On each sign was an arrow that pointed to a trailhead and gave each a name. Timber Rattler. Diamond Back. Snake Pit. Not at all what I would've wanted. But how could I be disappointed when I should've known? The place was called Rattlesnake Mountain. The trails wouldn't be called

Strawberry Lane, Deer Run, or Santa Claus Way.

We arrived a short time later in a cloud of dust at a rusted house trailer set on cinder blocks. "A home in a can," BeBe might say. Clusters of jack pine surrounded the trailer. Their needles appeared dry and brittle and smelled like Christmas. Their limbs limped in the heat.

As we climbed out of the car a voice from inside the trailer bellowed, "Who's there?"

Grandma trounced toward the trailer. I held back.

The voice inside shouted, "Go away!" When the trailer door flung open, an old woman with a shotgun stormed out. She looked like a scarecrow in need of straw. I froze, thinking I should get Grandma's gun from the car.

"Lena, it's me!" Grandma yelled.

The scrawny old woman leaned forward and squinted. "Aggie? Oh," she said, and lowered the gun. "What the hell! I could 'a shot ya! You got your days mixed up. I wish I'd 'a knowed you was comin'."

Grandma flicked her hand, no offense taken. "Happened to be in the neighborhood. Thought we'd say hi."

Lena looked at me. "Who's that?"

"Rosie's boy," said Grandma.

Lena squinted and then dropped her jaw. "Oh my," she gushed, "if this isn't a treat. I'll fetch us a beer."

"How do you know her?" I asked Grandma.

"My oldest friend. We dropped out of school together. She's a bit of a cuckoo." Grandma chuckled and circled a finger around the side of her head.

We waited in the driveway for Lena's return. When she arrived, she carried two sweaty bottles without labels, a signal that Bert, Joe's friend, had explained to me could hold illegal hootch disguised as beer. Tucked under one of her arms was a plush-covered book that looked like a squashed pink pillow. We followed her behind the trailer. Her backyard was large enough to hold an entire trailer park. I figured she spent more time out here than in her living room, being more spacious, maybe cleaner, and probably smelled better. A canvas shade on thin rickety rods protected a cluttered card table where two flimsy aluminum lawn chairs sat. From there a foot path led to a rocky peak, on which an identical third chair sat facing west. She said, "Be a honey and fetch that chair for yourself."

Before I returned, I paused to look at the bluffs, big and small, and the boulders and forests that stretched westward. We would never be able to build a fort here. Plus, it was too far from town.

I set my chair where Lena told me to go, between Grandma and her. They'd been discussing the big fire and that Jasper was probably dead. To boot, Grandma added, people were talking about a safe full of money, which Henry discounted as bull.

Lena flexed her gnarled fingers, swept off the table, and opened the pink soft-colored book, titled "Memories" in large silvery letters. "I have pictures to show you," she said.

Grandma, I noticed, looked as eager to see as the pictures as I did.

The first page held six pictures mounted in corners. All were of animals; two individual skunks, the rest chickens, and a goose. The skunks' names were scrawled beneath their pictures, Sister Mary Casimira, and Sister Beatrice. The rest weren't named.

"Let's skip these," Lena said, flipping pages. Grandma stopped her at a page labeled September 30, 1944. I recognized Grandma in one of her large flowery dresses, the photos a faded dull brown. Grandpa Frank stood beside her. He was middle-aged then, it appeared, burly and friendly looking, dressed in a suitcoat. I wondered whether he'd fought in the war like my father had. If pictures were meant for memories, I had no memory of him. But my mother had to have remembered her father. All I knew from her was that he'd died the month I'd turned five.

"Do you think he looks like her?" Grandma asked.

"He has her eyes," said Lena, looking at me so long that she made me nervous.

"A Flowers, for sure," Grandma said. "Jimmy's more Calloway. And to see them now..." She wiped a tear. Lena touched the back of her hand, and in that gesture, I saw the depth of their friendship.

"I remember feeling Mike kick," Grandma continued. "Rosie let me touch her belly when she got bigger. One time I felt something like a ripple under her skin. Rosie said it was a foot because the baby kicked her so hard she wanted to kick it back." I smiled in a kind of wonder to know that the ripple was me.

"The priest wouldn't marry 'em," Grandma said, "so I wrote off the Catholics on account of that. Wyler might've done the job, if not for his reputation being so damn important."

While I pondered what was wrong between Catholics and

Fire Conditions

Lutherans, Lena flipped the pages to my parent's wedding pictures in mid-March 1945. My father stood on crutches recovering from his war wound. My mother gave birth to me two weeks after their wedding. Lena told me that Uncle Mike took the pictures and she'd taken care of the marriage vows. "Such a happy time then." Lena turned the page. She was in the picture, dressed in a long dark hooded cape with a long chain at the end of which was a large pentagram pendant.

"The solstice is coming," she reminded Grandma. "How're your pups?"

"Eating me outta house and home." Grandma took a swig. "You can't call 'em pups anymore. I gotta get rid of some." Her eyes filled with a new notion. "You want one? Two? I can bring the best of the litter Wednesday. I'll bring dog food too!"

"Your dogs are the nippy-yippy foo-foo kind I can't have."

"You're more a skunk woman."

Now that I had seen pictures of her animals, it was an observable fact that the women loved their skunks.

"One more?" Lena asked, raising the empty bottle. Grandma nodded but sat too tight in the chair to bother standing. When Lena returned, and was comfortable, the women tag-teamed telling me the history of each of her skunks.

They had picked them up when they were babies from a farmer outside of Baraboo. Each took one and had its stink glands cut out by a veterinarian in Mauston. Jimmy and I had had our tonsils out together in Chicago, a twofer Dad called it. I wondered whether the skunks were put to sleep and felt no pain. I squirmed at the thought of them having two glands alongside their buttholes. When my tonsils were taken, despite the smothering ether, having them removed was better than having glands cut out if there were any down there.

The skunks were frisky, they continued, and played together until they got older and grumpy. They had named their skunks after nuns they didn't like. Sister Mary Casimira belonged to Lena. Sister Mary was a good skunk, overall. One day she didn't return. Lena looked all over the bluff until she found what was left of the good Sister near a barrel for visitors' trash. She had been mostly eaten, defenseless against a bear or cougar without her glands. Lena didn't bother to bury her, being only fur and bones and portions of rotting flesh swarming with flies.

By then Sister Beatrice was already dead, shot by Grandpa Frank in the woods after she tried to bite him at Thanksgiving dinner. Fortunately for Grandpa, Beatrice was defenseless because she'd been spayed.

As I rode down the mountain with Grandma I felt as if I'd visited a distant world where everyone was happy. But what had happened to change that? Of course, my baby sister had died and had made all of us sad. But now I would have friends waiting for me at Roscoe's house this coming Wednesday, and I was proud to be one of the Big Fish People.

Chapter 9

Jimmy and I arrived at the Larsen's toy-cluttered yard and found everyone playing outside except Roscoe. I had thought we'd be late, but apparently, we were not. Confused, I watched my friends. Jimmy laughed when Badger, kicking a rubber ball with Goose, struck a doll hard enough to knock off its head. Squirrel tossed a softball high in the air and would run to catch it, only to twirl, stumble, and fall.

Eventually, Roscoe rushed out of the house to greet Jimmy and me while flashing the manila folder in which he kept the club's business. "What's going on?" I asked.

"Dad's working in the basement today. He told me to meet somewhere else. Do you have an idea where?"

I suggested my grandma's house. "We can all talk to Pookah," I said. "She's our mascot."

Roscoe sighed in relief. He called the guys over and explained the situation. When Jimmy heard the news, he jumped up and down. He might as well celebrate his birthday with Pookah. Squirrel asked if there'd be cookies and I said no. Badger asked if he could kick the ball around more and Roscoe said no. Goose said having an animal of the Sky Clan would bring us good fortune. I knew I could count on Goose for common sense.

We marched from Friendship to Adams. Roscoe and I led the

procession. The others trailed behind us. Roscoe complained about his father. "He pretty much works all the time at the car dealership. When he isn't there, he's working on the house. Pretty much, I don't see him."

"Mine's like that, too," I said, though I understood our fathers were different. I recalled that at the last meeting mention was made of a missing kid. "Any word on him?" I asked.

He shook his head. "We have a prayer circle for him."

I had never heard of such a thing but it did sound like a good plan. "Do you know his name?" I asked, "to be sure God knows who you're praying for?"

Roscoe smiled. "He knows. It's Gary."

As we proceeded, he offered a copy of the agenda to me, which I needed no time to skim. It read:

June 11, 1958

Agenda

1. Fort
2. Will
3. Next Meeting

"Looks good," I said.

Behind me I heard Jimmy talk about Pookah. He didn't know what he was talking about but no one questioned him. "Pookah's as big as an eagle," he said. "She eats mush made from dead animals. Rats and mice. If you put your finger in her cage, she'll bite it right off. And she's really smart. She talks to me. She likes me best."

Grandma had left the front door unlocked, as I had expected she would. She trusted people, it seemed, or perhaps she didn't have anything worth stealing. Or perhaps she hoped someone would steal her dogs as the answer to them eating her out of house and home.

As soon as I opened the front door, the dogs began to yelp. Badger and Goose were drawn to the clamor. "Don't open that door," I warned.

They backed away and drifted around the living room. Goose took an interest in Grandma's large hutch, which stood against a wall. Badger joined him, saying, "Look at all this stuff!"

An assortment of plastic and plaster ponies crowded the countertop. On display above the pony-themed counter, behind a panel of glass, ran shelves of exotic-looking bottles of liquor. One was designed as a spaceship, another a hula girl; bizarre trophies that brought to mind athletic awards gathering dust outside our school gymnasium.

I glimpsed Jimmy leading Squirrel toward the kitchen, saying, "Pookah's in here! I'll show you."

I grabbed Jimmy's arm. "You can play with a pony," I told him.

"Can I have one?" Squirrel asked. I handed him a cow instead.

I turned to Roscoe, my eyes pleading to begin the meeting, but he didn't notice. He stood strangely transfixed by an old gray La-Z-Boy recliner within reach of a small stand on which sat a radio. "Would you hand these out?" he asked as he sat in the comfort of his cushy chair and handed his manila folder to me.

As I passed the agendas, I saw we were short two places to sit. I told Jimmy to stay put, to stay standing, and I left for the kitchen, where I found two extra chairs. When I returned, bumping my way through the swinging door, Jimmy asked whether I had said hi to Pookah.

I lied to cover for Jimmy's exaggeration. "Oh yeah. She was eating dead mice."

Badger and Squirrel sat on a small couch that was patterned in faded flowers with a fake leopard's fur draped over its back. Neither paid attention to Roscoe, even as he kept changing the tilt of the chair and kicked the chair's foot extender up and down.

Goose sat off to the side of the room on a rickety wooden chair. I didn't understand why Grandma would keep such a chair, since she could never sit on it without falling and hurting herself. I motioned for Jimmy to switch chairs with Goose, who looked pleased, if not grateful to be closer to the rest of us.

Roscoe kicked back his legs, sounding a thud. Before he could call the meeting to order, Badger interrupted him. "Hey," he said to me, "my grandma says she talked to you!"

"We work together," I said patiently.

"Your grandma's cool," he said.

"So's yours."

"Are you done?" Roscoe asked, annoyed.

We stopped chatting.

Roscoe cleared his throat. "Now, number one. The fort." But he stopped abruptly. "Crap, I forgot my gavel."

All of us laughed as he regained his composure. He apologized for not having time to look for a place to build a fort and asked whether any of us had something to offer.

I raised my hand, which caught everyone's attention as my

Fire Conditions

hand was the only one in the air. I told them I had been able to scope out Rattlesnake Mountain because my grandmother happened to have taken me there.

"Did you see a rattlesnake?" Goose asked.

"I didn't."

"But did you find a good place for a fort?" asked Roscoe.

I shook my head. "The trees there can't hold a nest of squirrels."

Squirrel shot a pointed glance at me. "Watch your step, buster."

"Now, item two," Roscoe said. "Will."

I sat quietly.

Roscoe told the others about our visit with Will. Aside from his constipation all was good. I reported that I'd played chess with him. Only Roscoe knew what chess was but he didn't know the rules. He read comic books and watched us play without seeming to mind.

"Last item," Roscoe announced. "Next Meeting."

"What about Pookah?" Jimmy shouted.

The "elephant" in the kitchen awaited us. We stood in unison and began to march. Before I pushed open the swinging door, I laid down the rules. I was chief of the zoo, I said, and Jimmy would decide who talked to the bird and when. He looked happy. I couldn't have done any better than if I'd handed a jar of cherries to him.

"Where's the bird?" asked Badger.

When I heard her wings flap I led them to the nook where Pookah's cage stood and announced, grandly, "Hereby I present you with the 1958 mascot of the year, better than anyone's in Adams County."

The guys jockeyed with each other for a glimpse of the bird. Right away Pookah's head twitched, short and snappy in synch with its blinking eyes, exactly as when Jimmy and I had met her. She started to stutter-step side-to-side on her perch. The guys gawked at her, a bird housed in a golden cage, and with a magnificent bright orange beak, a rarity anywhere.

"Make it talk," Badger said.

"It's not your turn," said Jimmy. "Raise your hand if you wanna talk."

I grinned, proud of him for following the rules. "Choose someone," I told him.

He looked at me and stepped up to the cage. The room went silent. Jimmy lifted his head and said, "Hi Pookah." He looked like he'd fallen in love.

"Hello, Joe," she replied.

"I'm Jimmy."

"Nice to meet you, Joe."

"I'm not Joe, remember?"

"I'm a chicken."

A smattering of giggles followed.

"I'm Jimmy." He looked forlorn and forgotten. "Can I make you smart?"

"I'm a chicken."

More giggles.

He looked at me, helpless, while everyone else looked amused, yet oddly impressed. I stepped up to the cage. I leaned to Jimmy. "Remember," I whispered, "you're in charge. Call on someone."

Fire Conditions

I took my place with the group.

"Who wants to go?" Jimmy asked.

Everyone's hand shot up. Jimmy looked at me and frowned. He was like me, I knew, afraid to make a mistake. I encouraged him with a gentle smile. His eyes wandered over the upraised hands, each vying for his attention, but he finally honored the last kid I would have chosen.

"Him," he said, pointing at Squirrel.

"Say your name," I said.

"Should I say my club name or Franklin?" he whispered back.

"Up to you. But say, 'Hi Pookah' first."

He walked to the cage. "Hi Pookah."

"Hello, Joe."

"Hi. I'm Squirrel."

Roscoe and Badger went through the same drill. After each said his name, Pookah would say, "Hello, Joe." She wasn't as smart as I had hoped, except for when she responded to "Goose" with "Gachoo." We laughed and urged Goose to repeat his name. Each time, Pookah answered, "Gachoo," as if she had a bad cold.

As we returned to the living room, Roscoe said, "Too bad we couldn't teach her anything."

"Maybe next time," I said, though I doubted we'd meet here again.

We returned to our seats in the living room to discuss our next meeting. Our presence triggered the dogs to riot behind their door. On the couch, Badger and Squirrel were talking about Rattlesnake Mountain. Badger's brother, Randy, and his friends were shot at up there.

"There's a loony old lady with a gun running around. She'd kill you as soon as she'd shoot a squirrel," Badger said, laughed, and punched Squirrel in the ribs.

"Not funny."

"Let me have that blanket."

"It's mine."

"Order!" Roscoe called to be heard over the dogs. "Last item. Next meeting!"

"Can you get the dogs to shut up?" Squirrel asked me.

I wanted to say, "If you two would quit fooling around, the dogs would, too," but, not to be offensive, I said plainly, "They'll calm down pretty soon."

"Okay," Roscoe said, fed up. "Any more business?"

Badger was holding something in the air he'd found between cushions. "Wow, this is neat," he said.

"Ick!" Squirrel scooted as far away as he could from Badger, and whatever Badger held, shielding himself with the leopard fur. His prize appeared to be a bone. Not any old bone. It was shaped like it had come from either a small leg of lamb or a large ham. The dry-hardened grizzle and bluish remnants of meat that clung to it provided no clue to its origin, only our personal knowledge that it came from between two cushions of my grandma's couch.

"Can I take it home to Manfred?" he asked.

As the rightful owner, I should've been ashamed. "Go ahead, it's all yours."

Then I had a brilliant idea, sparked by Grandma's telling Lena

Fire Conditions

about the dogs eating her outta house and home and needing to get rid of them soon. I opened the door. The riot spilled quickly into the room along with the dank smell of a kennel. The dogs' nails pecked the floor as they ran. The chaos caught everyone off guard. Four of the seven dogs attacked pants cuffs and ankles, two scuffled on the couch, and one scampered back and forth on the edge of the fray, the poor animal too afraid to join in.

The two scuffling brown fluffs on the couch took turns snarling and nipping each other over an inch of upholstery. Their noses moved like vacuum cleaners over the fabric. When one gained the advantage, it dug at the crack between the cushions, sniffing and snorting frantically to where Badger had uncovered the bone.

Two of the four remaining dogs nipped at Jimmy, being the easiest, most panicked of prey. He repeatedly nudged them away with his feet, gently at first, until one's teeth cut through his sock and into his ankle. He gave the dog a firm kick but not hard enough to hurt it. The dog lifted its eyes at him and barked like he'd hurt its feelings.

"If you want, you can take one home!" I called over the melee.

"I'll take one," Goose said, raising his hand.

"Don't your people eat dogs?" Squirrel asked.

Reflexively, Goose formed a fist. "We eat squirrels. They're tastier."

"Really?"

I slapped my forehead.

"Do they have names?" Badger asked.

A fair question. I clapped my hands and called, "Ginger,

Penny"; the names of the two dogs that had attacked Jimmy the day we'd arrived. None of the dogs perked its ears. Ginger and Penny were either unbothered by voices or didn't recognize their names to begin with.

"Take any dog you want," I said to Badger.

"I'll take two," he said.

"How about those?" I pointed to the two on the couch, who'd given up the fight, but were still pointlessly sniffing. "They're having fun together," I said.

"I'll take them!"

I patted him on the back. "They're all yours."

On picking up the scent of the bone, the dogs caught wind of Badger. They leaped off the couch and ran to him, and jumped up and down on his legs, trying to outdo each other. Badger wore the look of a boy in seventh heaven, unknowing their source of affection.

I looked for another taker. I ruled out Squirrel, which left Roscoe. "Want one?" I asked.

He shuffled in place. I could see he was interested but needed time to decide. In the end, he said, "I can't. I have too much to take care of already. Besides, Dad doesn't much like little dogs."

I understood.

He hung back with Jimmy and me watching whether the animals would bond with their new owners. Goose carried the cuddliest, the one on the fringe scampered around like he or she wanted to join in, while Badger teased his two doggies homeward by dangling the bone he'd found in the couch.

Squirrel vanished, likely to wherever he lived.

I lured the remaining dogs into their room by scattering what Grandma called "treats." I thought I should take them outside to take care of their business but didn't want to risk them running off on their own.

Roscoe and I walked to Lion's Park, across from the Tap. Jimmy tagged along and played in the sandbox.

"I have good news," said Roscoe. "Will's mother says it's okay for you to go to the hospital with them to play chess with Will."

"Me? Are you going too?"

"Naw, Mom needs me at home. His appointment's next Monday. Do you think you can go?"

"If Grandma says I can." I found it incredible to think that only a couple of weeks ago I hadn't known Will, or the Big Fish People. Or that I hadn't seen Grandma in years until we got off the train.

I assumed Grandma would permit me to travel to Madison with the Wylers unless she wanted me to watch Jimmy that day. I lowered my voice, not wanting Jimmy to hear me. "I might have to stay with my brother," I told Roscoe. "Do you know anyone who could take him?"

"He can stay with me. What's one more?" he said. "He'd be a big help with Gertie."

"Are you sure?"

"Don't worry about it."

"Thanks a lot!"

Chapter 10

"Can I help you with something?" I asked Grandma. It was early, the day after our club met. She sat at the bar eating pancakes smothered in maple syrup and butter. Jimmy and Joe were still sleeping. I had tried to sound cheerful, but my question drew a sharp glance that made me reluctant to say anything else.

Even so, I asked her if I could get her more coffee. She shook her head. She might've come out of an ice box for the chill she gave off.

"We'll talk when I'm done eating."

I waited out of her sight. When she finished, I quickly picked up her plate and coffee cup and carried them into the kitchen. She followed, asking me to fetch a chair for her from the back room. Her bunions were killing her. When I returned, I knew to pull a three-legged stool for myself.

We'd had good chats in the kitchen, but I didn't necessarily expect a good one, considering her mood. I couldn't read her today. Something must have been bothering her.

"How was your meeting?" she asked.

We moved our meeting, I told her, and that we couldn't stick to Roscoe's agenda. But overall, the meeting went well.

She found it funny. "You have agendas?" she asked. "Did you tell them about Rattlesnake Mountain?"

Fire Conditions

I told her I had.

"Where did you meet?"

She was playing with me, I realized. She had figured out my surprise. I sat upright, eager to hear her appreciation. I had already imagined the event. I would become a family legend, known as "Mike's Great Giving Away of Grandma's Dogs."

"Why are you smiling? You were in my house yesterday."

"We couldn't use Roscoe's basement," I said. "We didn't have any place to go. I didn't think you'd mind."

"Penny, Ginger and my little Namby were gone when I stopped to feed them last night."

The tone of her voice told me that I'd been mistaken. I should've told her what I had done when she got home. What a Bozo I was!

"What did you do with them?"

I gave little Namby to Goose, I said. Goose had a quiet, sensitive side to him, like little Namby, but not the dog's timidity or skittishness. A good match, I thought.

"And Penny and Ginger?"

"Badger took them. I know his grandma's your friend," I added. I hoped Badger's family would be pleased. Those two bratty gold diggers would inherit old Manfred's kingdom upon the hound's death. Another good match.

"When were you planning to tell me?" she asked, anger edging into her words.

"Last night," I said. "I thought it could wait."

"Don't you know I stop at the house to let the dogs out before

I come to the Tap?"

It had never crossed my mind. I was in her house twice; the first, when we arrived, and yesterday when the club met. She never mentioned when she would feed the dogs.

"I clean up after them too," she added.

Then why would the house still smell like a kennel, I wondered but didn't dare say what I thought.

"What got into your head?"

"I wanted them to have a good home."

"They had a good home already."

I could have disagreed but decided I'd better not. Instead, I reminded her that she had told Lena they were eating her out of house and home and that she should take two. "I thought you'd be pleased."

She tipped her head, baffled, until her words must've echoed back at her. "I still wish you'd talked to me first," she mumbled. "I would've thought one, maybe, but you took three."

"I was afraid for them," I said.

"Why?"

"Because you'd have them shot. Like Grandpa shot your skunk."

Her eyes widened. She slouched on her chair like the wind had been knocked out of her. "I would never have any of 'em shot. Beatrice tried to bite Grandpa."

Well, I thought, her dogs bit Jimmy.

"Remember," I said, "you complained about the cost of dog food." My voice cracked as I said, "I'll get them back, okay?"

Fire Conditions

She sat quietly for more than a minute staring at me. "You don't have to do that," she said finally. "Think about what you're saying. It'll make matters worse. My friends will be upset. So will your friends. What's done is done."

"I'm sorry."

"Oh, Mike. So am I." She shook her head, teary-eyed. "Come here."

I went to her. We hugged as we had before in the kitchen when there was a need for forgiveness. Relieved, we started the morning over with another round of hugs as if an evil spell had been broken.

There was no better time than now to ask for a favor, one that had been on my mind. When I asked, she said, "Shoot."

"Can I go to Madison with Will Wyler Monday morning?"

She mulled it over long enough that I held my breath.

"I could ground you, you know," she mused, "but I'll talk it over with Esther."

Surprised and nearly too grateful, I expressed "my eternal thanks" to her; something I had heard on TV once that sounded appropriate.

She raised her eyebrows and scoffed. "Eternal? How 'bout you just behave."

Chapter 11

Grandma informed me the next morning that she now needed a favor. I told her just to ask. I didn't want to risk not going with Will to Madison on Monday and knew I'd do whatever she wanted.

Her favor felt like penance or punishment; either way, she charged me to do whatever Joe told me to do to help at the Tap. Even though the tip of my tongue wanted to protest. My fate was sealed.

I finished my chores about two hours after she left. Joe took time to serve his early regular drunks and while they were drinking he showed me a trap door in the floor of the gambler's den where deliveries were stored. He mumbled too much for me to understand a lot of what he was saying. When I would ask him to repeat himself, I could usually understand. My job was to bring various types and brands of liquor upstairs. Not an entire box, he said. At least he recognized I could carry only one or two bottles at a time up the wooden ladder and that I had to reach simultaneously to pull the string to turn the light off or on.

This, I realized, when I finally descended the ladder to the bottom of the chilly, dark space, was what Grandma had called the "crawl space" in case of a tornado. Against two walls, cardboard boxes of liquor were stacked on lines of wood pallets. Somewhere down there something smelled like a dead mouse.

Fire Conditions

When Joe was distracted by his friends, about two o'clock, I roused Jimmy from a comic book and said, "Let's get outta here!"

Soon we were marching along Main Street. Jimmy peed behind a tree near the courthouse. We laughed. At Friendship Pond we skipped stones until they were scarce. We decided to follow a dirt road out of town. We sang as we went, "To see what we could see, to see what we could see," a loud, shrill version of "The Bear Went Over the Mountain."

I spotted a kid on a bike coming our way a short time later. Too small to be Butch. He stopped in the road and asked us who we were. He looked to be Jimmy's age. When we told him our names, his eyes opened wide, and looked at us like we were right out of *Leave It to Beaver*.

"Oh, I know you!" he said excitedly. "Your grandma gave us a dog!" He had to be Goose's kid brother. They had the same brown eyes, though the kid's cheekbones weren't as high or his jaw as sharp as Goose's.

"How's Namby?" I asked.

He paused, confused. "You mean Miwak?"

"I guess so."

"What's your name?" Jimmy asked.

The boy smiled. "Joseph."

"Not Joey?" I asked.

"No, Joseph. Like the famous chief." He glanced at the clouds. "Do you know what time it is?"

I checked my watch and discovered I'd forgotten to wind it. "Sorry," I said. "I don't know."

We chatted a minute; where we lived, that sort of thing. He lived outside of Cottonville, which meant nothing to me, as Evanston meant nothing to him.

"I gotta get home," he said. "It's pretty far."

"Say hi to Goose for me," I said, and the three of us said goodbye after he thanked us again for Miwak.

"I wish I had a bike," Jimmy said as he watched a potential new friend disappear.

Next, we walked back to town to the library. I figured there'd be fans to cool us off there. I reset the watch to two-twenty by the clock on the library. I tried to check out books for Jimmy, one easy for him to read, with pictures, but was denied a library card. I needed an adult companion to sign for me. So, we sat at a table, and Jimmy read the books I couldn't check out. I skimmed magazines; *Look*, *Life*, and *National Geographic*, which was known to have pictures of naked women. This issue didn't. One article was about a desert in Mongolia, another about what's under the ocean.

I discovered a *Friendship Reporter* hanging on the newspaper rack, hardly anything size-wise compared to the *Tribune*. A right-hand column, first page headline seized my attention: "Finnegan Fire Update." I sat beside Jimmy and spread open the paper.

I read that the sheriff's department and medical examiner's office had issued a joint communique about Tuesday's fire. Arson hadn't been ruled out. A suspicious wound was apparent in the autopsy. Jasper was known to have been seriously ill leading up to the fire. The next paragraph lauded his generosity to municipal projects as well as to churches and private endeavors, citing the

Fire Conditions

Boy Scouts of America and the Lions Club. The last paragraph informed the readers that the funeral hadn't been scheduled, pending notification of next of kin.

The other article of interest was the area's fire conditions. They were high. The newspaper reminded readers of last year's forest fire, the one Grandma had mentioned on our way to Jasper's, and the one she had said had burned down the 4-H building and had threatened the town.

Chapter 12

Grandma surprised me when I got home. I was relieved that she seemed to have forgotten my responsibilities to Joe. She had talked to Esther Wyler, she said. I could go to the hospital with Will.

I was on my way to Madison the next Monday, June 16. Grandma handed my duffel bag to the hired transport driver. She had packed extra clothes in case of an overnight stay and had given me a key to the tavern.

Will was asleep in his wheelchair, snoring, already strapped into the back. The driver rearranged the Wylers' luggage to make room for my duffel bag rather than place it on top of theirs. In the process he repositioned the box with Will's chess set to a secure place where pieces wouldn't spill if he made a sudden stop; leaving pawns under the wheelchair, and possibly a queen lodged between one of the chair's large side wheels and the footrest, which had been folded inward.

Grandma hugged me. Be careful, she said, and do what Mrs. Wyler told me. I would, I said, and thanked her for letting me go. The driver watched us, waiting, while holding the door open. I kissed Grandma goodbye after telling her not to worry. She loved it that I loved her, which, in turn, made me love her more.

"Take good care of him," she called, sticking her head into the van. Mrs. Wyler, already sitting in front, called back that she would.

Fire Conditions

As Grandma stepped away, I climbed into the van and took my place behind the driver's seat. To my horror, I found the dreaded sister sitting smack dab beside me, behind her mother.

I had never imagined, dreamed, she would be here with me, inches apart. I slid away, fearing one of us might accidentally brush the other. Cooties, I thought. If we were alone, I would have told her she had them. I looked out my window to avoid any chance of making eye contact. I tried to put myself in a calm place in the back of my mind. I reminded myself I was here for Will but should've known she would be here too.

Reverend Wyler didn't accompany us, otherwise he might have driven the family to Madison. Roscoe had mentioned a Spring Pastor's Conference of the North Wisconsin District of the Lutheran Church, Missouri Synod. The conference had been canceled in May and rescheduled to begin today.

While the van rattled toward Madison, I wondered if Reverend Wyler regretted being unable to drive his family himself. Mrs. Wyler must've found herself in this position over the years, I suspected, and by now had grown accustomed to hospital visits and clinic appointments without him.

Through Sarah's window, I watched the bluffs of Rattlesnake Mountain pass by. Certainly, on Wednesday, Grandma would tell Lena the story of what I'd done with her dogs. I imagined Lena, a strong non-believer, would have a conniption to hear that Grandma had let me spend the day with Lutherans.

Sarah caught me watching the bluffs. I knew, right away, she thought I was looking at her. If I were a toad under her gaze, she'd be a snake and have me for dinner. I squirmed, resentful that she had the best view. My window offered scrawny pine trees, run-down barns, and dry fields, hardly a pasture, with an occasional cowherd.

The van rattled louder as it gained speed. She said, "It's going to be a long ride."

I watched for cows.

"Why are you in Adams?"

A hard question, one I didn't want to answer in detail. "Just visiting."

"For how long?"

I shrugged, looking back at her.

"You don't know?"

"A month, maybe. Could be most of summer."

"That long! Doesn't your mom care?"

"She cares," I said in defense of my mother.

"Mine knows where I am, all the time," she complained, lowering her voice a decibel.

I glanced at my window, finding the scenery unchanged.

"Never see a cow before?" The snooty sound of her voice was clearly intended to hurt me. I shifted my gaze to where she could see the back of my head. I made motions with my head to make her think I was looking aimlessly around, not watching cows anymore. Her eyes, if sharp, would have seen I now had trees to look at.

"You should've worn your cowboy shirt," she said. "Get it, cows? Cowboys?" Her condescension drew out a prick of anger in me. "People notice you if you dress like that. I just wanted you to know."

I wanted to laugh. I could've said to her that the first time I saw her she looked as if she'd stepped right out of a fairy tale. I would say to her, "You looked like Little Bo Peep. Where I come from, people would laugh at you. So, you know!"

I chose not to be mean because I liked her mother. Today, they'd dressed like they'd bought their clothes at the five-and-dime store.

"How old are you?" Sarah asked.

"Fourteen," I said for no reason, adding a year to my age.

"Can you stay home by yourself?" She sniffed at me like one of my Lake Forest cousins would, a girl Jimmy's age, who'd get uppity with him; the one who lost her cake to the dog after I tripped her.

"Just curious," I said, "how do you know Butch?"

She blinked. The corner of her left eye began to twitch like she had a tic. "You don't need to know about him."

"He's a bully, you know."

She refused to continue.

Okay, be that way, I thought.

We sat at an impasse as we entered the Dells. The backseat was bench-like, like the one in our car at home; the kind on which you'd pretend to draw a line between you and your kid brother, and when he crossed the imaginary line, you'd punch him.

Downtown Wisconsin Dells dazzled me as the van merged slowly into traffic. Like a carnival, families crowded the sidewalks, happily wandering in and out of Cowboy and Indian souvenir shops, queuing at stands to buy popcorn, sno-cones, and cotton-candy, and carrying luggage into and out of motels, and sacks of leftovers from restaurants. The only thing missing was Jimmy to see this with me.

Eventually the main street crossed a tall bridge suspended above a gorge, where traffic fell to a crawl. A large road sign rose from the gully to beg travelers to escape into the Enchanted Forest and Prehistoric Land. Below, to tantalize, two dinosaurs were visible. A bright blue T-rex was bowed to take a bite out of a fading orange triceratops as the triceratops aimed its horn to rip out the meat-eater's guts. These popsicle-colored beasts stood unmoving as kids ran around and climbed on them. Two boys in cowboy shirts, like Jimmy and me, sat on the plant-eater.

"What are you looking at?" Sarah asked.

"Dinosaurs. Really cool ones!" I said. These were unlike the skeletons in the Museum of Natural History, where you couldn't sit on them, their bones brittle, yellow, and gray.

"Will liked them, too, before he got sick," said Sarah. "It looks different now. Like they're not real."

"Could Will come here with Jimmy and me?"

"That's not going to happen."

She was right, I knew.

"I wish you hadn't mentioned Butch."

"You said you didn't want to talk about him." A gentle reminder.

"School's small," she said. "All of us have known each other since we were little. I'm going to be a sophomore. He would be, too, but he's still a freshman. He was held back in fifth grade."

"Why? Because he's a bully?"

Fire Conditions

Suddenly Mrs. Wyler asked the driver to roll up his window, the traffic's tailpipes were downright poisonous. Over her shoulder she asked Sarah to peek at Will.

"He's sleeping," she said softly. "His chest's moving. I wiped some drool."

She brushed my upper arm with what might've been her breast when she turned back to her mother. A hot prickling sensation like pins spread across my cheeks. My mouth hung open. She looked at me. Her eyes held me within her power as if she were trying to open my mind to parts known and unknown. She didn't appear to be embarrassed in the least. Why did she brush my arm? Was it intentional? To tease me, I was sure, by the gleam in her eyes.

The van was rolling down the highway again, toward Baraboo, roughly halfway to Madison.

"Did you know your grandma came to our house?" she asked. "About you coming today."

"I didn't know that," I said, genuinely surprised.

All I had known was Mrs. Wyler and Grandma had talked, perhaps the first time, or the first time in years. After I learned I had her permission, I didn't think more about how they had worked out the details.

"They talked a long time," Sarah said. "When I came downstairs, they were still at it."

I hadn't appreciated the courage it must've taken for Grandma to step into the Wyler's house. All on my behalf. Wanting to please me. Now, days later, I could almost feel her touch my heart, which added to my jumble of feelings, prominently including my lingering internal buzz by Sarah's touch.

After Baraboo we headed toward Sauk City and Prairie du Sac, twin towns like Adams and Friendship. I tried to imagine Grandma's and Mrs. Wyler's get-together. Grandma entering the Wyler's well-ordered house with its fine furniture, vases, and pictures, compared to Grandma's sparse, disordered, animal habitat of a house. A baked cherry pie would be waiting. Sitting at the mahogany dining table, each with a slice. Sipping tea that Grandma would rather dump in the sink. Uncomfortable, but cordial. Asking and answering questions about Will and me. Both good boys, we were almost angels. No hint I could be a problem.

Mrs. Wyler would say, "You must love him a lot, like I love Will. Mike can come with us if you let him."

And Grandma would say, "Oh, thank you! This means so much to him. And me, too."

The embellishments of my mind were of comfort as we approached Madison. "Okay," Sarah said, as if she'd resolved a tough decision. "You asked about Butch. His dad beats him."

"Oh," I said, unable to find any sympathy. "I can understand."

Neither of us said anything to the other for the rest of what was now a much shorter ride. When we arrived at the hospital, Will looked groggy as the driver lowered boy and wheelchair out of the van. I grabbed the chess set before the driver could lock in our luggage.

I said, "Hi."

Will managed a weak smile to see I had brought his game. His mother and Sarah kissed him lightly on the cheek. A young woman

Fire Conditions

accompanied by a younger Black man greeted us. She was a nurse in a white dress, taut in the middle, and a white cap folded back with a button-down crown. He was an orderly, also in white, not as nun-like in appearance, and in short-sleeves with a top too baggy for his thin frame. Each was handsome in their own way, and projected smart, knowing kindness. The near unearthly look on Mrs. Wyler's face told me the hospital people were angels.

The doctor greeted Mrs. Wyler and Will in the waiting room. Sarah and I held back. After they conferred a short time, Will was wheeled away, his good arm raised, waving backward over his shoulder at us.

Mrs. Wyler took a seat near the door through which Will disappeared. Sarah motioned for me to follow her. We headed away from her mother to a table of magazines off near a corner. Mrs. Wyler had brought a satchel of yarn and prepared to spend time knitting. She had learned to prepare, I suspected, out of long hours of waiting for word of her son. I watched her hands as her needles moved frantically, like scissors. At times she slowed to poke and twist a strand or two. Once she stopped altogether. She slashed at her handiwork with her needles out of frustration. When she lifted her eyes to the ceiling, she stared for nearly a minute. Watching her I began to wonder whether she was talking to God. When she finished, she went back to her needles and yarn.

While I had carried the box with the chess board and pieces from the van, Sarah had carried a white hand purse with lace. She rested the purse against her thigh as she sorted through the magazines. She chose one with Elvis Presley on the cover, his fringe-sleeved arm reaching out to readers and appearing to say, "Look at me."

"Do you want to play chess?" I asked, opening the box to show Sarah the pieces. She looked at me like I was offering her a chocolate.

She shook her head and flipped the pages to something of more interest. The magazine's name was *16*. I would have bet a gazillion dollars that I wouldn't find a copy of it in her minister father's house.

"I can teach you," I offered.

"Here, you can read this." She handed *16* to me, for some unknown reason, and picked up a copy of *Teen*. I wondered whether she ever knitted with her mother, or shared an activity like a boy would with his father, say baseball. Tentatively, I opened the teeny-bopper rag, glancing around, ready to toss the magazine if I caught anyone watching me. The picture on the cover was of Pat Boone and his bland wholesome smile, inviting the reader inside. Her mother would approve of *Teen*, I thought, when Sarah was older.

These magazines carried advertisements at their end, similar to how comic books were arranged. Rather than a boy on the beach getting sand kicked in his face and transforming himself into Charles Atlas, *16* allowed me into the minds of teen-aged girls and enlightened me through the advertisements about facial creams and ointments that prevented pimples, glossy pin-ups of rock 'n roll stars, and a collection of "well-known" books on etiquette that stressed the importance of manners in a good marriage or when hosting a party.

"I'll be right back," Sarah said, and crossed the room to her mother. The time was already after twelve noon. No wonder my stomach was growling. I straightened the pile of magazines and watched Sarah and her mother talk.

At one point they appeared to be disagreeing about something Sarah said. Her mother set down her needles and glared at her. After more brief exchanges, they settled the matter. I was amazed by how quickly they came to terms. Grandma and I would string out our issues heart-to-heart in the kitchen, and put ourselves through an emotional wringer until we reached a clean resolution.

"What was that about?" I asked as she returned, grinning.

"She gave me a dollar for us to eat."

"You looked like you were mad at each other."

"Not really. She's upset, not knowing what's going on."

"And you?"

She put a hand on her hip and harrumphed at me like it didn't matter. "I'm not always easy."

And didn't I know it?

She sat and opened her white lace purse, producing a pen and piece of paper, and scribbling before returning pen and paper from where they came. "Let's go," she said, and waved goodbye to her mother.

I followed her to the lobby like a puppy. She told me to stand back, then stepped to the reception desk. If she planned to ask directions to the cafeteria, she led us the wrong way, based on an arrow pointing down a different hallway. I stood back, well-trained to watch from a distance, thinking she had been here before, and should've known the right way to go. Then, I realized she hadn't been here in years.

When she returned, I said, "We made a wrong turn."

"No, we didn't."

"Aren't we getting lunch?"

"Yes, silly." She laughed. "Do you think we're staying here? We can if you wanna eat cold hash with old people."

Befuddled, I didn't know there were options.

Outside, immediately, the heat came at us, thick and sticky, full of the damp scent of manure to fertilize grass. She led me around the hospital and onto a steep, graded side street toward a library. Large granite buildings hovered alongside us, providing stretches of shade, while the street shimmered, and the concrete beneath our feet had baked earthworms earlier. We turned abruptly, crossing the street, westward, onto a long mall where there was no traffic other than shoes, sandals, and bicycles.

"Is the restaurant close?" I asked.

"We're going to a place better," she teased.

I shielded my eyes from the sunlight. My shirt clung to my back and arms. Beads of sweat covered my brow. I blinked. The sun was more brutal than any day since I had arrived in Wisconsin. I had heard in the Tap that animals sometimes died in the fields from the heat. The lower central part of the state was roasting. Rain had fallen in the west, but here, the heat was merciless.

"This is it!" she announced. We'd reached the Babcock Ice Cream Store, a part of the on-campus dairy farm. "Ice cream is better than hash," she said. "Do you agree?"

I nodded, envisioning melted ice cream oozing over my hand from fingers to wrist.

She ordered a strawberry cone and I chose vanilla. About this, she said, "You're such a plain kid." Then she added, "That's good."

We joined a small group sheltering under an awning until more people crowded in. Sarah pointed to a cluster of trees in the distance. "There's a bench there. In the shade," she said. I followed her, licking the crown of the cone around and around. When we reached the bench, we found a young man and woman already sitting there on "our" bench, their backs to us, enjoying "our" shade.

Sarah approached. I followed a step behind. The bench I saw was built of sturdy wood. Its back was carved with the initials of couples who'd professed their love through their vandalism over the years. For some reason, out of being a little giddy with her, I decided to think of the couple as Hansel and Gretel.

She took hold of my wrist and led me trotting around the bench like a tethered poodle to meet Hansel and Gretel.

"Hi," she said; too cheerful, I thought. Like a good friend who was a transparent phony. Nevertheless, I stifled a laugh.

Hansel's reaction was precious. His left hand had been resting on Gretel's right knee, but he tightened both hands reflexively into fists. Did he think we planned to push them into an oven? Neither of them was lean, nor ready to be eaten, if we were a hungry pair of witches.

"Mind if we sit while we finish our ice cream?" Sarah asked.

Gretel turned to Hansel. "Can you slide down a few inches?

Give them a little room?"

Hansel showed himself not to be the kind Hansel from a fairy tale. He bared his teeth and his nostrils flared like he was a big bad wolf.

By coincidence, the four of us sat aligned in order of height; Hansel the tallest, me the shortest, with our two friends in between. Any passerby behind us could easily believe we were one happy family.

"I want to be Alice in Dairyland," Sarah announced out of nowhere, loud enough for all to hear.

I knew about Wonderland Alice but had never heard of one from Dairyland. "Who's she?"

"There's a contest every year," she said. I saw Gretel looking curious. "The girl who wins gets to travel all over the state. You meet farmers. You tell people about milk, cheese, and all of things they make out of them. You get to be on TV. On *Farm Hour*! I saw the last three Alices riding in parades. They got to throw candy to kids from a convertible."

From a distance I heard Hansel mutter, "Let's go." Either Gretel hadn't heard him, or had ignored him, which appeared the most likely. Regardless, they stayed where they were.

Sarah continued to study me. In the happy lines of her face, I saw she appreciated their extra attention. "What do you want to be?" she asked. Now it was my turn on stage.

The problem was, I hadn't given thought to who I wanted to be, specifically, as she had. "I like science," I said. "And arithmetic. But I like to read. I've tried to write poems…" Which was close to an exaggeration; my only poem was what I had composed in my mind based on a Burma Shave sign. "I think writing stories would be easier."

"Have you thought about acting?" she asked.

"Not really."

"Don't you want to be famous?"

I gave little thought to this. "Well, famous with a small group of friends. People I trust."

"How 'bout you kids get outta here," Hansel cut in.

Sarah stared at him like an innocent lamb for Gretel to witness in case of a slaughter. "We've been here a while," Gretel pointed out to Hansel. "Why don't we let them take their turn?"

"Oh no!" Sarah said, turning bluntly to matter-of-fact. "We'll leave. We have to get back to the hospital. My brother has polio."

We surrendered the bench and tossed the soggy remains of our wafer cones, their bottoms all mush, into a nearby trash can. Looking back, I saw Hansel and Gretel on their feet, in each other's faces, arguing. I thought about how amusing Sarah could be.

"How was lunch?" Mrs. Wyler asked, greeting us on our return.

"Ice cream cones," I said.

Sarah's eyes shot arrows at me. Her mother shook her head, as if Sarah were just being herself. More than an hour passed before Will emerged, grinning victoriously as he walked into the waiting room in an upgraded brace and crutches.

The nurse who'd met us accompanied Will and the attendant, who pushed his empty wheelchair. The nurse asked Mrs. Wyler to stay behind to give her instructions on managing his brace.

While they talked, I pulled two end tables together and Will, who had sat again, and I started to play chess. Soon we had to stop. From his wheelchair he couldn't reach the board and his pieces. Frustrated, he said he was sorry. I told him we would play sometime this week at his house. He told me that he had been seen by four doctors, and other people who'd tested his breathing and had taken measurements of every part of his body. He'd spent a long time in a gymnasium-like area, practicing how to walk with his new equipment, and was now worn out.

"They put me through the wringer," he said feebly. "But I'm lucky. Nothing's as bad as being in one of those iron lungs that breathes for you. Some kids are stuck in one for more than a year. Some die in them. I was only in two weeks."

The nurse wheeled Will out of the waiting area while the attendant carried his crutches and brace, plastic, lighter than the metal contraption he'd been wearing. Mrs. Wyler walked beside the nurse, Sarah and I slightly behind them with the attendant. Mrs. Wyler and the nurse talked loud enough for us to hear. Will would return in December. Apparently, symptoms of polio could return at any time in a victim's life. He'd also need more frequent "postural drainage," to which Sarah sighed wearily.

"What's that?" I asked.

She whispered, "I pat his back, chest, sometimes his side until he coughs up his slime. If I don't, he could choke to death."

"You do that?"

She nodded and rolled her eyes. "Yeah, when Mom's busy."

"Wow," I said, amazed.

Fire Conditions

We ate in the cafeteria. After a few bites of macaroni and cheese, Will fell asleep. The transport driver was late picking us up. By the time the van arrived, we were all tired. Mrs. Wyler slept.

Sarah and I, in our same seats, rode northward in silence as the night fell into deep darkness, a scattering of stars breaking through. I didn't realize I'd dozed off until I felt Sarah's hand on mine and heard her whisper, "Are you awake?"

I flinched. "No, I mean yes."

She smiled. "On the Fourth of July, let's see the fireworks together. Wear your cowboy shirt if you want. I won't mind."

Was I her boyfriend? I wondered. I felt like I might be, kind of. Was what I felt like Tom Sawyer's feeling for Becky Thatcher? I would have to reread that part to understand why I had wanted to puke back then.

"I'll have to bring Jimmy," I said, rapidly calculating the days until then. Eighteen days. We'd probably still be here. Would we?

"That's okay. I hear he has a cowboy shirt, too."

If I'd kissed her that moment, quickly, I was aware that the strange tingle below would get out of hand. And then what?

She said, "Save it for the Fourth of July."

Chapter 13

The van dropped me off at the Tap after midnight, last, after unloading the Wyler family. The driver had made frequent stops to smoke cigarettes. I crept quietly into the kitchen so as to not wake Grandma, who was sawing wood on her cot in the gambler's den. I hung the key on its hook and headed upstairs, dragging myself to the bedroom. I expected Jimmy to be asleep, but in the hallway light that slanted into the room with me, I saw him sitting cross-legged, his sheet balled in his lap. He burst into tears when he saw me.

"What's wrong?" I asked, disturbed. I tossed my travel bag aside and sat beside him. He sounded frightened. Or was he sick? If someone had hurt him, I would make that person pay. His lower lip quivered. I put my arm around him. "Tell me. It's okay."

"Dad's coming!" he said.

Was that all? I didn't want to see Dad right now either. My mind was on Sarah. But why be upset? Unless it was because something worse had happened between Mom and him.

"How do you know he's coming?" Grandma didn't have a phone.

He wiped his nose on a sleeve of his pajamas. "I heard Grandma tell Joe. She said to keep it conversional."

"Confidential."

"Yeah that."

Fire Conditions

"I think it's tomorrow."

Which was today. Shocked, I was too tired to wake Grandma. I'd talk to her in the morning.

As I lay down, he peeked at me timidly across the space separating our beds. "Can I sleep over there?"

I patted my mattress and slid over to make space. He quickly grabbed more than half of my sheet, leaving my backside uncovered. I took my sheet back when he was asleep, the satiny soft end of the sheet in his mouth. He looked like a baby, sweet and innocent, his eyelashes like pixie dust that would let him fly someday.

With the first light of dawn, I willed myself into waking. The streetlight outside my window was still bright, illuminating an ice truck making deliveries. I hurried downstairs in my pajamas. Grandma was already at work; I heard clinking of utensils and plates in the kitchen. She had her back to me as I walked in. She was bent, stretching into a low cupboard for what turned out to be a fry pan. Turning as she stood, she was surprised to see me, but recovered to greet me with a cheerful "Good morning!" She slathered a slab of lard onto the pan and turned on the heat. "Can you fetch me a chair?" she asked. "And fold up my bed, please, since you're here?"

I went into the gambler's den and did as she'd asked. The bed folded easily, and when I returned with her chair, she asked whether I would fix her a cup of coffee. Her order: Folger's coffee crystals, hot water, and three spoons of sugar. "Are you hungry?" she asked, stirring the melting lard.

I told her I wasn't hungry. Between Sarah and my father, my stomach was too balled up to eat.

"When did you get in?"

I told her after midnight and thanked her for giving me the key.

"You must be tired." She suggested I go back to bed, saying, "Why would you want to beat the early birds when the worms will still be around later?"

I didn't quite follow what she meant but it sounded like her kind of wisdom.

"I talked to Jimmy," I said.

"He was awake?"

"He was upset."

"Oh?"

"He told me Dad's coming."

My words must've put a bitter taste in her mouth by her change of mood. "That little scamp. How did he know?" She plopped on the chair, avoiding my eyes. Her cheeks turned pale. "Let's talk," she said.

All ears, I let her start.

She blew the steam from her cup and took a sip before she began. It was true our father was coming that afternoon. She didn't know what time. She hadn't talked to him directly, she admitted. His message had come from the woman at the five-and-dime, who took calls for her from time to time. She paused, then said, "I'm not happy about this."

I wasn't happy either, but I didn't want to dwell on our feelings. I wanted facts; what else did she know and hadn't mentioned? Her silence continued, and before I could pressure her, she turned teary-eyed. I found a napkin for her. She dabbed her eyes, but when I believed she had recovered, she wept.

"He better not take you away from me!" she cried.

My eyes settled between her and the wall. I saw nothing as I tried to absorb the gut-punch that my father might take us home. A big deal: Jimmy and I could be taken to Evanston, where we'd be with both our parents. What was worse? Being home with them wouldn't be any better than before, or we could end up with Bebe in Lake Forest?

"Is Mom coming too?" I asked. I considered praying to stay here and wondered whether any prayer from me would be heard. I would get Roscoe to pray for us, Will and Sarah too; the three of them talked to God. And then, my mind went to Sarah completely (sorry God), and to our Fourth of July plans. I expected to kiss her, more than once, if it worked out that way. And her expectations? The same as mine, I hoped.

Grandma and I sat quietly face-to-face in thought. I had grown curious to know how she knew to pick us up at the station. When I asked her, she admitted my mother had sent her a letter.

I pondered this and concluded she had mailed the letter days before she sent us to Friendship. If she hadn't, we would've been left on the platform, Grandma unaware we were there, while we watched the train head to St. Paul. Now Dad was coming today, and I hoped Mom would be able to come with him.

"Read the letter if you want," she said. "It's in there." She pointed to the three-drawer file cabinet near the door to the gambler's den. "Top drawer."

Out of curiosity I had searched through the cabinet soon after I'd arrived. The top drawer held her business files; one file thick with tablets of columns and numbers, another stuffed with receipts and an unmarked envelope that held unused coupons for the Red Owl. I was now more careful, with no reason to be afraid of being caught. I found a slim folder marked PRIVATE between the thick ones, essentially an invitation to open. All I found inside was an envelope in Mom's handwriting, postmarked Chicago. With my back to Grandma, I unfolded the letter and read:

Dear Ma,

Mike. Jimmy. Coming June 3. On the 400. I know you will take safe care. Thank you. Sorry, too. A letter soon.

Love, Rose

Not quite a letter. Had Grandma received the promised second letter? Apparently, she hadn't. I didn't know what to think. I heard the lard begin to sizzle and saw smoke rising behind her. Any moment we'd have a fire. I startled her as I dashed past her and turned off the gas. I grabbed the pan's handle with two thin potholders, burning my hands, and quickly dropped the smoking pan into the sink.

That was a close call. My nostrils stung from the smell of burnt animal fat. Grandma was on her feet by then, waving a towel over the smoke. "Oh, my," she said repeatedly. "I don't know what I'd do without you."

I didn't know what I'd do without her, either, I said.

Chapter 14

I ignored Grandma when she suggested I get some sleep before my father arrived. My long day with the Wyler's (like a year ago) and being woken up by Jimmy in bed with me drove me to lie down for what I planned to be a few minutes. When the noon whistle jolted me awake, I couldn't believe it was afternoon.

I told Jimmy to get up. He rubbed his eyes. "Is Dad here?"

"Grandma says he's on the way."

"How does she know?"

I shrugged.

We didn't have many clothes, and those we'd brought hadn't been washed in weeks. Grandma didn't have a washing machine in her house, and there was no room for one here.

We changed into the least stinky clothes that fit. Why not? It didn't matter to me if we would look poor. I found a T-shirt without yellow pit stains and put on the jeans whose zipper slipped open with hardly a tug. Since we had little choice, I handed two mismatched socks to him, one red, the other green. He scratched his head. "It's not Christmas, is it?"

For an afternoon, a surprising number of people occupied the bar. Bert, our regular, was already there. Joe poured glass after glass of beer for him. A group of men were shooting darts. The only person I recognized was Beau. I'd never seen him this time of the day, being more of an evening guy. The Madams Johnson and Schmidt sounded tipsy as they chatted with Grandma, who'd changed out of her morning muumuu and was now in a dress the color of mushrooms.

She looked like a pauper, except for a small blue purse I'd never seen. Other than its color, it resembled Mom's tiny red purse that she carried to special events, such as gallery openings, weddings, Bar and Bat Mitzvahs, or parties hosted by someone believed to be important.

A dart player called to Beau, "It's your turn."

"I'll catch you later," Beau called back and sat at the bar.

"Who's that guy?" Jimmy asked.

"A movie star."

He stared at Beau then shrugged, unimpressed.

I wanted him to like Beau because I did. "He's Captain Kangaroo," I said.

"No, he isn't," Jimmy shot back.

"Do you know about body doubles?"

He shook his head.

They were like stuntmen who looked like movie stars, I explained, and went on to describe the stunts Beau had shared with the Madams and me.

"You're fibbing," he said when I finished.

I stared at him, thinking of saying, "You're getting too smart for your britches." Instead, I said, "You're right. He isn't Captain Kangaroo. He's Mr. Green Jeans. Remember the show when he rescued the chicken? That was Beau."

Fire Conditions

No chicken ever needed rescuing, as far as I could recall, but he said "Wow!" like the episode was fresh in his mind.

I led him to the bar and took a deck of cards from Joe. We played War, Jimmy's favorite. I let him win in ridiculous ways. Sixes took sevens, the same with queens beating kings, giving him reason to gloat.

Whenever the door opened, I turned to see if Dad had come in. I was surprised when I saw Henry. His uniform told me he was on duty, not just stopping by. Grandma left the Madams and hurried to greet him.

I headed over to say hello to Henry too, but paused when I heard him say, "Look at you, all gussied up," which made Grandma giggle. "He'll be here in about ten minutes."

How did Henry know Dad would be here so soon? Sure enough, a brief time later, a long black car cruised past the Tap. Not blue, and not our Chevy, yet familiar somehow. Because of its length, color, and slope of its fins, it dawned on me the car could be Grandma BeBe's Cadillac. Before I could confirm my impression, the car had disappeared north.

Jimmy and I went to the big window at the front of the building and sat on stools as we waited for Dad to come back.

"That was him, right?" Jimmy asked, jiggling a foot.

"If he's driving BeBe's car, it's him."

I wasn't sure I wanted Mom to be with him. They'd have to be together like they were before they got crazy. When the Cadillac reappeared, crawling south, I saw the front license plate, black numbers on top of white tin and read Land of Lincoln. He parked across the street alongside Lion's Park. He must've finally seen the sign for Aggie's Tap and stopped. Jimmy jumped up and down to see Dad step out of the car. People began to murmur. Someone said, "He's here."

I counted more than fifteen people now waiting to see my father. Grandma told us to go upstairs, but I wasn't about to go to our room. As Henry watched us, he took Grandma's wrist gently, and I heard him say, "Aggie, don't you think he wants the boys to go with him? He's their father, after all."

"They need their mother."

Dad paused at the crosswalk and looked both ways before he approached the tavern. His stride was purposeful, but he still limped slightly from the wound he got in the war. He wore the tattered tan suit coat he wore when he taught a class. He double-checked the Tap sign. The right place. Jimmy and I peeked at him. He fastened his eyes on the door. Cautious, he crept in like the soldier he must've been in Europe when he crossed into enemy land.

Everyone at the windows except Jimmy and me retreated to the bar as our father entered. Jimmy broke from me and ran to him. Dad lifted him into the air and swung him, his legs kicking, laughing like he would when we played Tickle. I felt oddly alone. Fresh from reading her letter, I wondered why Mom wasn't here.

Dad put Jimmy down and looked at me. "Aren't you happy to see me?"

Aware of the spectators, I said politely, "It's nice to see you," though the spirit of my next words seemed to ring hollow. "Where's

Mom?"

Had he heard my question? He looked uncomfortable, probably because he was surrounded by strangers.

"You!" he said on seeing Henry.

"Do you know each other?" Grandma asked.

Henry grinned. "We're acquainted. I pulled him over a few minutes ago for speeding."

"I never speed," Dad said, and he should've stopped there. He was driven to add: "I've heard about two-bit, small-town sheriffs, but I never expected to run into one."

Henry shrugged. "I'm the County Sheriff. You best hold your tongue. Show some respect."

"Or what?"

"I'll tell my deputies to run you out of town."

Grandma laughed as she slapped her thigh.

"You wouldn't…"

"Try me," said Henry.

Dad studied Grandma a moment. "I don't want trouble, Aggie. They're my boys."

"They're Rosie's, too." Grandma's voice cracked. "Where's my daughter?"

"Where are their clothes?" Dad asked. "I left you a message. I talked to a friend of Rosie's. She gave me a number to call. Someone from a dime store. She was supposed to tell you I was coming."

"Well, I didn't get the message."

She was lying, I knew, because she admitted it that morning, and Jimmy had told me he'd heard Grandma and Joe talking about our father coming today.

"What's up with Rosie and you?"

"She's sick."

I knew what he meant. For a long time, I'd seen her down in the dumps. He should've noticed her sadness sooner. I'd been living with her longer than he had in months.

"Too sick to be here?" Grandma asked.

"She's getting the help she needs. You don't have to worry," he said. "Now boys, where are your suitcases?"

"Upstairs."

I didn't like how people were beginning to talk. Couldn't they sit down and be nice? I couldn't predict what it would be like if we went home with him now. Probably the same old thing, or worse.

I knew he'd leave us at BeBe and Grandpa Calloway's house during the day. BeBe could be nice, but only her maid gave us cookies and played games with us. The most dreadful thought came to me suddenly. What if Horace would be at the house while we were there?

"They have a pool," Dad reminded me. "You won't have to go to the park, where you could get polio."

Don't tell me about polio, I thought. I made up my mind then and there. I squeezed Jimmy's hand and he squeezed back, which I took for trust. I looked at our father and said, "We're staying here."

"Oh no, you're not." His words were surprisingly sharp.

"What if I don't wanna pack?" I said.

"I don't want any lip from you. Get moving."

I felt like I'd been slapped. I wished he knew how I felt once in

Fire Conditions

a while. I didn't want much. But even if he'd hugged me or given me a kiss within recent memory, I still wouldn't have changed my mind after he talked to me like that.

"I came a long way," he said to Grandma. "I don't believe you didn't bother to tell them I was coming?"

"I forgot."

The crowd went quiet. Jimmy and I squeezed hands. I caught a glimpse of Beau at the bar. By the kind way he looked at me I knew I'd found another good friend, only older than Roscoe and the rest.

"Jimmy, come with me." I didn't let go of my brother's hand. Dad clenched his jaw and turned red, grabbed Jimmy from me and headed toward the stairs. I watched Jimmy wrap his arms around Dad's neck, his eyes wide open on me.

"Oh, for crying out loud, who's in charge here?" some drunk shouted.

"I am!" Grandma stepped forward, flustered and furious. She fumbled open her purse and pulled out the stub-nosed pearl-handled gun she kept in her car.

I couldn't believe what I was seeing. Nor could other people, who gasped.

"You want to shoot me in front of my kids?"

Henry stroked her arm gently like the horse whisperer we'd met at the dude ranch a few years ago had stroked a wild horse's snout. "Be careful, Aggie," he said. "Don't make a mistake. Give me the gun."

"Let go of him!" she shouted, ignoring Henry. Her hand shook as she aimed the gun in Dad's general direction.

"Aggie, stop! You're not a good shot."

Dad set Jimmy down and I went rubbery with relief.

Henry grabbed Grandma's gun and emptied its chamber of bullets into his hand. He slapped Grandma lightly on the butt. "Bad girl," he said. The Madams laughed.

Dad froze a moment and then lost his balance. The knee of his damaged leg buckled when he took a step downward. I rushed to him as Jimmy watched where Dad fell to the barroom floor. Henry and I helped him up.

"Are you okay?" I asked, afraid and guilty for my role in our family fiasco.

"I'm not well," he mumbled.

He wasn't himself, I understood. Could he be as bad off as my mother?

"It's time for you to leave," Henry said, "if you can drive."

"They can leave their clothes, for all I care," Dad said. "I'll buy more in Chicago. Come on, boys." To me he said, "Don't start in again. We'll have plenty of time to talk in the car."

"Will Mom be there, waiting for us?"

"She's sick. I already told you."

"So, she's not at home?"

"No. She isn't!"

"She said you left us. Is that true?"

"No, not actually." He stared at me a long time before he told me that I was a disappointment. I stared back at him in silence, daring him to tell me which of us was more disappointed in the other.

Fire Conditions

"I'll be back," he said. "I have resources."

"Bring Mom," I said. She was the only resource I needed.

People lingered in the bar after he left. Shock at the spectacle still hummed in the air. The eyes of solemn, sad faces kept me in sight. I hugged Jimmy. He looked at me and I saw he must've felt battered inside.

Grandma apologized to us for bringing her gun.

Beau came to me and put a hand on my shoulder. He asked whether I was all right. "Yeah," I said. I liked the steady feel of his hand.

"How 'bout I help you guys with your fort? Glad to do it."

"Really?"

"I'm serious."

I gave him a half-smile, doubtful, afraid of being let down.

"You have a lot on your mind," he said, "and I have a lot of work on the farm. I'll swing by Saturday night, and we'll make a plan."

Chapter 15

Saturday was the day of the summer solstice, four days after Dad had come and gone. Grandma had decided to join Lena's summer festivities on Rattlesnake Mountain. It was clear she was trying to put my father out of her mind. She had arranged for the Madams to run the tavern. Joe was supposed to take orders from them, which I assumed he resented. I was supposed to chip in, too, with the dishes.

Before the Tap opened, I updated Roscoe on Beau's intention to help us build the fort. As I predicted, Roscoe was delighted. I expected to see Beau after Grandma was gone. That would give us plenty of time to plan and hang out for as long as we wanted.

Henry sat beside me at the bar as Grandma finished dressing in the gambler's den. Jimmy was upstairs, supposedly watching TV. He had a hard time getting over Dad's visit, whereas I did not.

Soon Grandma sashayed out of the kitchen, thighs shifting side-to-side, tight in a pair of floppy blue jeans. She wore a long open-front coat in the pattern of a universe with various colored planets, yellow suns, and full white moons winking. She approached Henry, smiling and fluttering her eyelashes, and earned applause from the early evening customers.

"Now aren't you something else," he gushed.

"I could've dressed like a witch, but it's not Halloween. Besides

Fire Conditions

there'll be old hags who're real witches there. I don't want to put them to shame."

Henry laughed. "I suppose you'll dance naked all night in the woods."

Girlishly, Grandma giggled. "I'll keep my dress on."

"Even what's underneath?"

She poked the nearest fleshy part of his arm she could reach. "Silly old man." Then, noticing me, she shushed him for talking bad.

"What did you do with the gun?" he whispered, not escaping my ears.

"It's in the car."

"Good. Don't touch it."

Grandma considered this in a way that told me he had given her the same advice before. When she waltzed away from the bar, her patrons gave way, out of respect, it seemed, or because she was too large in life to let anyone stand in her way. Grandma tossed acknowledgments of their respect like candy as she walked by. "Thank you ... Yes, I've been needing a break ... You're so sweet ... Don't burn the place down (wagging a finger), you old scallywag." After she blew a kiss back to Henry, she was gone, and after that Henry departed.

In the kitchen the Madams let me in on something they'd overheard. Two off-duty deputies had been grousing about Henry's ways of scheduling their time compared to the sheriff-on-leave. How come they got stuck with more weekends than everyone else?

"And do you know what Henry said?"

"What?" I asked.

"Boys will be boys."

That wasn't the kind of gossip I expected. They had to be hard up.

Who would've believed Aggie Flowers was my mother's mother when I could hardly believe it myself? Mom was petite, Grandma was, well, large. Mom took after Grandpa's side in looks. She resembled Grandpa's brother Mike in a grainy, old photo Grandma kept in her house. Mike, Grandpa Frank's honorable brother, was young in the picture, slim, with deep eager eyes like Mom's. I knew already from Lena and Grandma's talk that I looked more like Great Uncle Mike, my namesake, than Jimmy did. Jimmy was pure Calloway, based on pictures of my father at Jimmy's age. I wondered whether the resemblance was the reason BeBe liked my brother better than me. For at least a year I wanted to tell him he was adopted, but never got around to it, which was ultimately good. If I'd told him, I would've been in trouble if Jimmy asked Mom whether she was his real mother.

"Hey little man," came a familiar voice on this magical night. Beau appeared, as I had begun to worry whether he would show up. He ordered a beer from Joe and a Shirley Temple for me. He led me to a table under the bear's stuffed head, where we would have privacy. His first sip left a line of foam across his upper lip, which, when I pointed this out, he wiped away and laughed.

He apologized for being late, which he wasn't. "The soybeans," he grumbled. "The heat." Yesterday he had irrigated part of the field. He had to go to the well and hope the water table wasn't too

Fire Conditions

low, or that the pump wouldn't lose pressure. "Some days I'd jump off a building onto a mattress," referencing his stuntman days, "than work on a farm."

He raised his glass. "Here's to the fort!"

"To the fort!" and we clinked our glasses and sipped.

I was aware that Grandma had told Beau that the Big Fish People were having problems finding a place for their fort. We had ruled out Palmer's Woods and Rattlesnake Mountain already, and she was at a loss to help us.

An impish look crossed Beau's face. "I have two ideas," he began. "The first is to find a good tree on your Uncle Mike's land. It's in walking distance from the farm. The land is posted, meaning private and all ours, protected by a legal barrier to prevent the Gophers from destroying your work. And here's the best thing, the farm is close to town."

That was a reasonable option, I thought, and asked him, "What's your other idea?"

It was farther away, but we wouldn't have a problem with that, he said. He would drive us to and back from the location. I asked him how far away it was. Ten miles, more or less, he said, on Castle Rock Lake. That would be unrealistic. I couldn't picture us crowded in the back of the old truck. If he was unable to drive us, their parents would likely be unable to drive all of us at the same time.

For some reason he didn't want to give up on the Castle Rock Lake site. Along with what I'd seen as practical problems, I had my own issue with the location. It was too close to Grandpa Calloway's house and bad memories, and that the family's presence could coincide with our work. He continued by describing the qualities of the land and the lake like a used car salesman trying to save a sale. The area was more beautiful than any area around. The trees were taller and greener than any in the county.

He stopped. He saw he was wasting his time. Yes, I knew the magnificent lake. I'd swum in its water. "What if you get a part in that movie?" I asked. "Then where would we be?"

"I'm not going back to L.A. anytime soon," he said after a pause. "And I'm kinda bored, to be honest. The crops will be fine, and it'll be fun to help you guys, besides. I got the old truck running better than ever. With the truck we can haul lumber, tools, shingles if we need 'em."

I pointed out that we would need the truck regardless of where we would build it. "The farm's better," I said, "for all of us."

I saw he was considering me as he thought it through. Soon he saw I was right. At last, he said with enthusiasm, "The farm it is!" We raised our glasses and clinked them again.

When would we start? He suggested next Tuesday—the day of Jasper's funeral, I remembered. I had planned to tag along with Grandma if she would go to the service. I doubted she'd entered a church in years. I hoped to get a glimpse of Sarah. She was in the choir, as was Will. The service was in the Lutheran church for reasons I didn't understand, Jasper being Catholic like Uncle Mike.

Wednesday would be the better day. We would start the meeting at Roscoe's house at one o'clock. Could he talk to us about our plan?

His enthusiasm returned. "How 'bout I pick you all up and take you to the farm? We can go to the woods after your meeting. There's a tree I think you'll like."

"Did you like my mother?" It was the very question that had been on my mind for a while.

"She was wonderful," he said, subdued. "I bet she still is. Has she ever mentioned me?"

"Once, I think." My lie was well-meant, and I knew he wanted to believe it.

When he paused, I wondered whether he was thinking about how awful my father had been in the Tap. Everyone in town was still talking about him. Poor Aggie, poor boys, having that man in their lives.

We caught sight of the Madams waving at us. With Grandma up on the mountain with Lena, I had a lot of time to spare.

"Let's say hi," he said. "Get in on any new gossip."

I followed him to their table, relieved not to talk about my parents anymore.

The Madams were technically my bosses tonight. They were in charge of the tavern. Being Saturday night, the place was jammed. Sweat dripped from Joe's forehead into some of the drinks. I didn't look forward to washing the dishes. My hands would be sore and red while I dried them and put them away.

I wanted to check on Jimmy sometime later. Ever since the showdown with Dad, I was concerned about his moping around, shuffling in and out of our room, not speaking, not eating. He'd turned into a sad sack, lost and alone. But for now, I enjoyed my companions.

Beau and I sat across from each other, hemmed in by the Madams. "How are you doing, sweetie?" Johnson asked. And so it began, her words curling like a spider pulling me into the web of her gossip.

"Have you heard the latest about Jasper?"

"The priest won't bury him with the Catholics. No man more virtuous than him."

"Gives me a reason not to tithe."

"Aggie has to be proud of you," Schmidt lisped.

"I bet you're proud of Bucky too," I said.

"What's with your father?" asked Johnson. "Aggie sure got under his skin. But what's up with Rosie?"

I tuned her out. She wouldn't be able to understand how I felt. I looked at Beau, felt the tenderest nerve we shared.

Beau told the Madams not to trouble the boy. They raised their painted eyebrows, which crinkled their makeup.

"I have to check Jimmy," I announced, relieved to have saved this reason to escape. I sent a smile around the table to let them know I was leaving. Beau stopped me, raised his glass, and said, "See you Wednesday, Roscoe's house, then to the farm."

I shouldn't have left Jimmy so long on his own. As I walked upstairs, I expected to find him on Joe's bed, either watching TV or sleeping. I caught a whiff of what smelled like a blown TV tube. Jimmy wasn't there. The screen showed the off-the-air logo around a storm of static. I felt the top of the TV with the flat of my hand. The plastic-like wood was warm but nowhere near hot. I turned off the TV, just

Fire Conditions

in case.

The air smelled different in the hallway. There was a sharp biting odor, heavy and having teeth. I knelt down and sniffed what were whispers of smoke curling from under our door. My heart jumped and my breath quickened. If the door was hot, upon opening it, fresh air would rush in, turn into hot smoke, and suffocate us. Once again I reminded myself of Dad's rule that we were not to open a door without feeling it first. Our bedroom door was now warmer than the TV.

I risked death to save Jimmy (and myself) when I opened the door. As I entered the room. I covered my nose and mouth with my sleeve and saw that Jimmy's blanket was on the floor, smoldering. He cowered on his bed, coughing. His eyes were watering. Packs of matches were strewn across the room. A few single matches were spent on the floor. Each pack bore the black on red logo with the words "Aggie's Tap." He wouldn't have known that if the mattress caught fire, the entire town could've burned down.

I went about gathering the packs of matches and as many singles as I could. I freed one hand and picked up the blanket which I stuffed under my arm. The fabric smelled like burnt wool.

"Freeze," I told Jimmy. Immediately he stiffened. Freeze tag was one of his favorite games. I reminded him of the rules. "I mean it now," I said. "Freeze!" He morphed into a little dog, his mouth wide open to catch a ball.

"Stay like that," I said.

"Where are you going?"

"Shh, you're frozen."

I soaked the blanket in the bathroom sink to drown the smell and any spark left alive. I ripped the matches out of their packs and flushed them down the toilet; it took three flushes. After each, I watched the water swirl and trickle back into the bowl to be sure the toilet didn't back up. If it did, I'd have another big mess on my hands, not remembering where I'd last seen the plunger.

When I returned to our room, Jimmy still hadn't moved. I kicked the stinky, wrung-out, still-damp blanket under my bed. I poked him and said, "You're unfreezed."

"No, I'm not," he said. Only his mouth moved.

I shoved him and he tripped and fell. "Now you are!"

He lifted his innocent boy's blue eyes at me and tried to kick me.

"I'll freeze you forever unless you promise to never start a fire again."

He picked himself off the floor. "Okay, okay, I promise."

"Say what you're promising."

"I won't start fires." His eyes hinted regret.

"Okay," I said. "I'll help you put on your pajamas."

Everything felt different in the peace of our bedtime routine. When we would slip under our sheets our world was made better. "Where's Grandma?" he asked.

"At something called 'the solstice.' It's supposed to be magic."

"That's dumb."

"Not really. How 'bout this? Because it's solstice tonight, I can read the future."

"Shut up."

Fire Conditions

"Listen! I know places where we'll go someday. Cool ones. Like Prehistoric Land."

"Like it has dinosaurs?"

"Yes," I said. "And you can ride them like horses. And they're all different colors. Like popsicles." I turned my fingers into claws and roared. "The T-rex is blue. Just like me! Grrr."

He laughed. "You're not blue!"

"I am too!" I said and tickled him to make him laugh harder.

"Stop!" He squirmed but was losing energy. I helped him into bed.

"I'll buy you a sno-cone, cotton-candy, and a hot dog," I said softly. "But if you play with matches I won't."

"I promise," he said, and soon his eyelids flickered and his lips parted in peace. I whispered sweet dreams to him as he fell asleep.

Outside the night at midnight was more of a dark gray than pitch black. Somewhere, Grandma was having fun. By then Jimmy had climbed into my bed. Quickly, he began to hog my threadbare sheet and twist it around his feet. He had kicked the blanket to the foot of the bed. There was no reason for a cover as hot as it was. The fact that he had already burned one blanket kept me awake, worrying about what I could do to help him other than watch over him more closely. He needed a kind of help I didn't know of or couldn't give. Not knowing made me afraid for him, and for me.

Chapter 16

I arranged to meet Roscoe early in the morning before Jasper's funeral. I told him that I had invited Beau to join us at our meeting and my reasons for doing so. He promised to get the word out to the other guys that a movie stuntman was coming as a guest visitor. Since none of us had telephones yet, he would ride his bike across town to inform Badger and Squirrel and then make the long-distance journey north to where Goose lived.

I met Jimmy and Grandma in the bar so we could walk together to Jasper's service. He had died officially on June 6, 1958, more than two weeks ago, it now being June 24th.

We were dressed as well as our wardrobes allowed. Grandma avoided a flowery dress in favor of a pair of black pants, possibly the ones she wore for solstice, that unfortunately revealed her true size below. Her bulky pink top made her breasts look smaller.

We stood rigid in front of her as she inspected us. Right off, Grandma spit on her hand and flattened our cowlicks. Though we'd combed our hair, the cowlicks had sprung back, like weeds, as Mom would say. She tugged our shirt collars in turn. Jimmy's buttoned easily, mine pinched my throat. She hadn't gotten around to the laundry, or I might've had a shirt that fit, apart from the cowboy shirt that would've made me look stupid. She had ironed our clothes, so at least we went wrinkle-free. If she hadn't thrown away

Fire Conditions

our bow ties, we'd look perfect.

In spite of the obituary in the *Reporter* yesterday, people kept Jasper alive through their gossipy rumors. That he was hiding out in the Dells was one of the longest-lived speculations. Others had him living in Chicago or Las Vegas, though these and various other versions lost their punch, and thereby interest, except as fading curiosities. The latest I had heard had been hatched by a certain Mrs. Billings, of whom I had never heard. According to the Billings woman, Jasper wasn't the crisp corpse in the coffin, but would arise in three days in the form of a glowing Angel of God to announce the end of the world. The Billings woman was also known for being an early heralder of the visions of Mary at the shrine in Necedah, and it was whispered she swore God talked to her through her cat.

The morning itself was bright with the threat of another sweltering day. Grandma cooled herself with a pink flower-patterned fan as she, Jimmy, and I walked the block and a half to the church. I had convinced her to let Jimmy join us because of my secret fear he could burn down the Tap if we left him alone with Joe. My reason for bringing him, I told her, was that he wanted to see the inside of a church.

The Roseberry Funeral Home people introduced themselves and were polite and welcoming as they greeted us at the church entrance. Two days after her solstice frivolities, Grandma had to have been thoroughly rested. She practically crept into the church, skittishly glancing around as if she might be struck dead as punishment for her all-night binge with would-be witches.

This would be my third funeral.

Thomas C. Malin

The first had been held in a Cathedral on a cold winter day when I was four and a half years old. All that remained in my memory were dim impressions of Elizabeth's tiny white casket, and the enormous glowing windows reflecting startling colors of light in which I lost myself to escape the sobs.

My second funeral was held in Adams-Friendship, but not in a church. Grandpa Frank was buried in a bitter wind. Mom had a hard time driving through snow on our way north. Dad was too busy to drive us, and Mom hadn't seemed happy. But I was happy to be alone with her and my six-month-old brother, asleep in a basket on the back seat beside me. Between the coming and going, I vaguely remembered standing near a hole in the ground and Mom holding Jimmy, and people I didn't know nearby. Earlier Mom had introduced me to the woman who was my grandma. She stood beside Mom. I tried to tickle the baby to play a game with him, but each time, Mom would turn away, and the big woman next to her would laugh.

Now I was attending my third funeral, this one in the Trinity Lutheran Church. Sarah stood in the choir box in a white and black gown with slender sleeves as additional choir members arrived. I couldn't take my eyes off her. As we proceeded with the mourners to pay our respects, Sarah caught sight of me shuffling along, and sneaked a wave and a smile, which I returned, hoping no one would notice. Outside of the box railing, alongside the choir, Will sat in his wheelchair, dressed in a black and white gown of his own. I waved at him more boldly than I had to Sarah, but he didn't notice. Grandma nudged me. I had slowed down the line.

Fire Conditions

At the casket, I took my moment with Jasper to take a good look at an old picture of him that sat propped on the coffin. He was a handsome young man with a gentle smile. He could've had brown hair, or perhaps the picture had faded. The longer I studied the picture, the more he seemed to be staring back at me.

"Sorry I didn't meet you," I whispered to the picture. I genuflected, made a sign of a cross with a couple of quick hand motions to cover the bases, and moved on.

The organist arrived, took her place near the choir, and placed her foot on the pedalboard. As I knew from playing cello in my school orchestra, she struck a chord in A minor, not dramatic, but soothing for such a large instrument. She paused, satisfied with the tone, and smiled at the choir to be ready.

We found available seats near the front of the church; the back rows were already full. Grandma immediately looked behind her to see who might be watching us. She jumped nearly out of her skin when the organist squared down like a pair of bricks on the opening note.

Soon Reverend Wyler came through a side door and stood near the altar. The church fell perfectly silent as Reverend Wyler began to address us mourners. First came a solemn, silent prayer for our dearly departed, Jasper Finnegan. I wasn't sure how to pray, or what to say, so I told God to say hi to Jasper for me, since I had already said hi to Jasper's picture. If my "hi" came through God, I was sure Jasper would get the message.

"A self-inflicted wound," Reverend Wyler began softly, "by a generous, quiet, and obviously complicated man who did good deeds in our world…" His words came like gentle drops of rain. "It's difficult to understand. But whoever can? A family can never bear the pain of the loss of someone young or of a person of any age with an unfulfilled life. Jasper was a man of God, which makes this act more difficult to accept. Yet let's not judge him personally." He lifted his eyes and took in the entire congregation, arms spread. "He robbed no family. He left no generations of children and grandchildren haunted by whatever reason he had. Or the emptiness he left behind for others to try and try and try to fill. We're his family. He touched us, all of us, throughout our town and county. So, in our grief, let us pray for his soul to find eternal peace in the arms of God, whose forgiveness is great and eternal."

His words moved Grandma and me. Jimmy yawned.

What I didn't know until later from Roscoe was that Reverend Wyler had agreed to perform the service after the Catholic church denied Jasper burial in St. Leo's Cemetery. Despite being a life-long Catholic, suicide was an unforgiveable attack on God.

The rest of the service was all praying and readings I didn't know. The best part was the choir. I envied their sound. I played instruments because my voice couldn't carry a note. Will surprised me with a falsetto range that had to have been difficult on account of his lungs. The choir softened their voices for Will to be heard.

Outside the church, I asked Grandma if I could stay behind to talk to Sarah and Will. I had to ask twice before she heard me. The heat was getting to her, and her hand fan was busy. "Go ahead," she said, finally, and took Jimmy in tow and headed back to the Tap.

The Roseberry people were loading Jasper's coffin into their hearse when Sarah came down the steps to greet me. I asked if she wanted to go somewhere to get a Pepsi, but she had to help the women who fed people after a funeral. A service of comfort, she said. I asked if I could help, but she said, "Women and girls make the food, silly. But don't forget the fireworks." She winked.

"I'd never forget!" I said, too loudly.

"Better not," she said with a teasing smile, and disappeared through a church side door, presumably to where females made food for sad people.

Initially, I stood on the sidewalk, thinking I should've gone home with Grandma and Jimmy. My internal response was not to go home, but to do anything else on my own. At that moment, Henry's police car pulled up. He rolled down the window and leaned out. "You sweet on the reverend's daughter?"

"We're friends," I said.

He winked, which I didn't take as coincidental; he must have caught sight of us winking goodbye. I expected him to drive away, and leave it at that, but he sat in the police car, cleaning his glasses with a handkerchief, and glancing at me to test his vision. "I got an idea," he said as he put on his glasses. "Do you wanna go on sheriff's rounds with me? See what turns up?"

"Yeah!" I said.

"Well, hop in."

I wasted no time and jumped in the car. Right away, my eyes were drawn to the dashboard. Noticing my interest, he reached into a holster strapped to the dash, and pulled out what looked like a ray gun from outer space. "I catch speeders with this." He returned the gun to its holster, and said, "This here's my two-way radio." He patted a box with knobs and dials apparently bolted under the dash.

"All righty then, you ready, pardner?" He didn't wait for my nod and wheeled away from the curb. "Today, you're my deputy," he announced grandly.

I beamed at him as we drove off, imagining that while Henry was an "Acting Sheriff," I was his "Acting Deputy."

Henry took pride in showing me the town, unaware of how familiar I already was with the streets, not that there were many to learn. From the sheriff's car, the town looked different. There were alleys here that I hadn't seen. In Chicago, I avoided alleys or anywhere bullies hung out. Here people stored junk in backyards, from rusted cars, their wheels on bricks, to overturned garbage cans and little kids' playthings. Henry traveled slowly, alert for mischief, the same as I always would, but without the car.

We eventually entered a neighborhood without an alley. The houses looked peaceful, quiet, and well-kept. He pointed to a healthy vegetable garden alongside one of the houses. This was where Bucky's grandma lived. She had raised six kids here, he told me. Bucky's father, the last-born, came a year before her husband died of mouth cancer, images of which were too gruesome to contemplate.

Suddenly, two little dogs scampered into the yard. They had to be Penny and Ginger. When Mrs. Schmidt tossed a ball out the door, they took after it. I was happy to see them. They looked happy, too.

Fire Conditions

At that moment, I knew that, by giving them away, I had done what was best for them.

We were sitting at a stop sign, waiting to turn onto Main Street, when Butch rode up on his bike and stopped on my side of the car. The moment was perfect for me to roll down my window and let him see me sitting beside the sheriff. The pimple-faced punk did a double-take when he saw me. Eye to eye, we stared at each other with spite. He flipped me the bird as Henry turned onto the street. I stifled my laugh. Henry responded, "Gesundheit."

Next on our rounds we headed out of town on J to the Mount Repose Cemetery, where Jasper's burial was underway. Empty cars lined both sides of the road. Henry drove slowly to study the cars. He focused on their license plates and would jot down the numbers whenever he found one from Illinois.

"Why are you doing that?" I asked, recalling that he had pulled Dad over for speeding because he was from out of state.

"There's a car been around," Henry said. "'A vehicle of interest,' we call 'em."

"Suspicious?"

"Exactly."

"Why's it suspicious?"

He took me into his confidence now that I was his deputy. "There've been three separate sightings of a strange car lurking around. The folks who reported it described it in a comparable way. The car was either black or dark blue. None could identify its model, nor did they have the brains to write down its plate number. All agreed there was a man inside. He would park, sit, and watch.

People were nervous."

We climbed out of the police car. He'd noticed two out-of-state plate numbers, one from Illinois, the other from Minnesota.

"Who do you think owns the car?" I asked.

Henry shrugged. "Could be someone who had business with Jasper. Or about his will. Or something else, having nothing to do with him." He frowned. "It's bugging me. Usually, I can put my finger on something this fishy."

We passed under the iron arch and into the cemetery. The land was flat and dry, like the graveyard in *Gunsmoke*. Mount Repose—without a real mount or tumble weed—was humbler than the acres of lush gardens and grass where Elizabeth's tiny body lay interred in the Calloway family mausoleum with dead ancestors I'd never met. In the distance, we could see a large group of mourners, which identified the burial site. As latecomers, and not as mournful as those near the grave, we stood back on a small rise while Henry scanned the gathering for someone he didn't know.

At one point, he removed his glasses. They needed to be cleaned again. Before he put them on, he asked me whether I saw anyone I knew from, say, Chicago. I said I didn't, and I also didn't understand why someone from Chicago was suspicious (about what? I wanted to ask, since Jasper had committed suicide), not when Jasper likely had no known link to anyone there.

The mourners' backs were turned to us. The only person I recognized was Reverend Wyler, whose outstretched hand rested on the lid as if in search of a heartbeat.

"Okay, let's wrap this up," said Henry.

Fire Conditions

Last on our rounds were the fairgrounds, down the highway toward Friendship, ten minutes away on the left. The gate was open, and he drove straight onto the grounds. As expected, there were patches of grass surrounded by acres of sandy dirt. Shuttered buildings lined the perimeter. A grandstand with a baseball diamond sat empty. Farther down, near a back fence, rows of maintenance vehicles were parked; mostly old trucks and antique-like tractors.

"Soon, they'll be shooting off rockets there." He pointed to a hut and stacks of wood platforms nearby. I assumed this was where the launching pad would be for the Fourth of July fireworks. "It's a big show. A whole lot of the county turns out."

My heart skipped a beat thinking of Sarah. We were little more than a week away from being together. An eternity. In the meantime, I could pass time building a clubhouse with my friends, starting tomorrow.

"Well, we're finished. I hope you had a good time."

I couldn't describe the extent of my gratitude. He made me feel special. Plus, I was now his deputy. I smiled and said, "Thank you. It was great!"

Finished with rounds, we made our way back to Friendship, crossing the fairgrounds to County J. Before we reached the road, however, the microphone crackled and spat out numbers of a secret code. He stopped the car and pulled the mic to his mouth.

"Ten-two," he said.

"Ten-twenty."

"Fairgrounds."

"Ten-thirty-two, vehicle of interest sighted going west, County F to Z."

"Dellwood for intercept," he ordered.

"Ten-four."

He shot me a glance after he hung up the mic. Whatever was happening took him away from me. I didn't want to go back to the Tap. I didn't know what I wanted to do. I didn't dare ask him to take me with him, despite being his deputy. My presence, I feared, could complicate his duties right now. I brought him back by asking questions.

"What's a ten-thirty-two?" I had already figured out that a "ten-twenty" was intended to request our location, and a "ten-four" meant goodbye.

"A thirty-two is a 'reportable situation,'" he explained, no longer impatient. "Everything you say after the code is details."

"What's Dellwood?"

"Little speck of a place near Castle Rock. Bernie, one of my deputies, spotted the car we've been looking for."

So, I wasn't exceptional. I wondered how many deputies he had, including me. "Heading west?" I asked in my husky deputy voice, wanting Henry to know I paid attention to business.

"Yup."

I knew that Grandpa's lake house was in the general direction the car was headed. I couldn't ignore the possibility that it was my father driving the car. Henry, I assumed, was of the same mind. I hoped we were wrong.

Fire Conditions

I was relieved to see that the Tap hadn't burned down while I was on sheriff's rounds. Apparently, Jimmy had kept himself busy without setting fires. The bar had filled early after Jasper's funeral. Grandma recruited me to help the Madams set up the kitchen while she greeted thirsty mourners. Eventually, I was able to go upstairs and watch TV with my troubled and troubling brother. The CBS Tuesday night lineup turned interesting at eight o'clock. *The Invisible Man* was followed by *To Tell the Truth*, one being invisible, the other about lying—both cool.

I helped Jimmy dress for bed around nine. He fell asleep soon after he lay down. I checked under my bed to be sure Grandma hadn't discovered the blanket. If she had walked into our room, she would've smelled the strong smoky odor. I knelt and peeked underneath the bed. Of course, both the blanket and smell were still there. I lay down. The sooner I found a place to get rid of the evidence of his tendencies, the better. And I worried about him.

I didn't know exactly when I fell asleep, only that the fire siren jolted me awake at three a.m., based on my Timex. I rolled on my side and looked at Jimmy. He was on his stomach, a pillow covering his head. We tolerated the sound of firetrucks chugging out of the station, the red flashing lights through our window, and Grandma's shouts to hurry up if we wanted to be first to the fire. We were too tired to reply.

We tried to get back to sleep when there was silence and darkness outside. Jimmy fell asleep fast. I was too alert to do anything but overthink and worry. My mind wandered into a fantasy kitchen fire caused by one of the Madams while the sound of the fire trucks leaving town was real.

When I got up, I heard Grandma snoring in the gambler's den. It was clear that the late-night fire had taken a lot out of her. While she slept, I buried the burnt blanket beneath last night's fresh garbage, nearly under her nose, and went upstairs to wake up my brother.

For a boy as young as he was, he sometimes was a little too smart-alecky for me.

I woke him up and told him we were going to clean the bar and the kitchen. "See those glasses over there," I said, "that fork on the floor, everything else that needs washing? You're going to take all of that into the kitchen. And when you're done, I'll see what else you'll do."

"What are you going to do if I don't?" he asked.

"I won't take you to the club meeting tomorrow. I'll tell Beau you've been bad."

"Oh," he said, no longer cocky, and immediately began to carry dirty utensils and dishes into the kitchen. I would mop the floor whenever Joe decided it wasn't his chore that day. After all of my practice, my arms and wrists knew how to handle my rag-topped partner. I was steadier on my feet. I could sling the mop's fully soaked head into the water, then wring it out after washing the floor, leading our dance without tripping.

I kept a close eye on Jimmy as I worked. Whenever he caught me watching him, he would grab a plate or a glass and hurry, pouting, into the kitchen.

We worked an hour, or at least one of us did. He kept busy by being slow, which he must've learned from Joe.

"Did you hear the fire siren last night?" I asked.

He sniffed. "Maybe."

Yet I caught him eyeing the bowl that contained the Tap's matches. Without a glance at me, he plucked a cherry that had been overlooked on the bar and popped it into his mouth.

"Did something burn down?" he asked, chewing.

"We'll know when Grandma gets up."

"I'll go get her!"

I grabbed his arm. "Let her sleep."

He pinched one nostril leaving the other open and tried to blow snot at me. I slapped him on the top of his head just as Grandma emerged from the kitchen. She wore yesterday's clothes rather than her usual muumuu. She was rubbing sleep out of her eyes when she spied me. She blinked twice, trying to focus. "What time is it?"

"Half past ten," I said, and reminded her that I, and I suppose Jimmy, would meet Beau at Roscoe's house at noon. Considering her condition, whether out of weariness or too many drinks, the reminder was needed.

"I'll make you some breakfast," she said.

I told her we had already eaten and waved my hand like a magician around the room to show her how clean and orderly the tavern was now.

"You did all this?" she asked, astonished. I told her both of us had cleaned for her.

"Rough night?" I asked.

"Kinda."

I helped her sit on a stool at the bar. She asked me to make a cup of coffee for her. I knew where it was, and that she liked her crystalized coffee piping hot with heaps of sugar.

When I returned, I found Jimmy and Grandma carrying on what sounded like a meaningful conversation. I handed her the coffee. "What burned?" I asked.

"Shh, she's telling me."

I didn't like to be scolded by anyone, especially my kid brother. Grandma told me she'd start over from the beginning on my behalf. With no context, she said, "Ye Olde Tapper burned down."

"What's an Old Tapper?" I interrupted.

She sipped coffee and looked at me. "Ye Olde Tapper is—was—an old tavern. Clyde Tapper owns the joint. Serves him right it burned." With that, she launched into the full story.

Grandma had opened the Tap after Grandpa Frank was laid off from the Powder Plant after more than twenty years of making gunpowder for bullets and shells. By then, the military no longer needed bullets when atom bombs threatened to keep people safe. By Grandpa's calculations, he had processed more than a hundred tons of powder. He should've gotten a medal.

They held the grand opening of Aggie's Tap in August 1948, and soon afterward Clyde Tapper sued them for infringement on his "Tapper" trademark. Sure, she admitted, Clyde's tavern had been around longer than theirs, but their business had boomed from the start. A lot of their success was due to the Tap's location, being in town on the corner of Main Street and Pine. Clyde's business, on the other hand, was in the boonies, south of the railroad tracks, past the pickle factory, and off a narrow side road into the woods. Although some locals continued to support the Tapper, it was nearly impossible for anyone from out of town to find, let alone know that it existed.

"It was no fault of ours that he failed," she complained. "We were having a great time. We made loads of new friends. People liked us. We took in Joe after Ethel, his wife, dumped him. He had his brain tumor by then, but it wasn't malignant, just a slow-growing mass. The doctors decided not to operate. He's been here since he went full gump."

I appreciated learning what had happened to him, though I didn't have much sympathy for him because he bossed me around. Jimmy, on the other hand, liked to hang out with him before the tavern opened.

Grandma's voice grew spirited. The good part was just ahead. "Clyde's lawsuit was named 'Tapper verses Tap.'" She slapped her knee when she recounted the time Grandpa Frank got in trouble with the judge. During testimony he called Clyde's place Ye Olde Crapper. "Boy, that got the bailiff laughing, and the judge to say, 'One more joke outta you and you'll get a hefty fine.'"

Jimmy and I laughed. Grandma seemed to take pride in us, like chips off the old Flowers block. "And do you know what," she said, "the judge tossed the suit, Clyde's claim being frivolous."

She hadn't mentioned the early morning fire but had enjoyed telling us the history. I imagined that the same people then now believed she'd had a hand in burning the Crapper. In my short time here, I'd never heard anyone claim Grandma carried a grudge. How would she start a fire while she was sleeping? When she tried to rouse us out of our sleep, she couldn't have known it was the Crapper. This morning, she sounded genuinely surprised. And gleeful. She confided that there was a long-standing rumor—certainly started by Clyde—that she and Grandpa Frank had burned their trailer for the insurance money to buy the Tap. I imagined the rumor could possibly be true, but I quickly let go of the thought.

Chapter 17

Jimmy and I met the guys at Roscoe's house at noon. Roscoe had told them already that Beau would pick us up and take us to a farm where there was a place good for a fort. As we waited, I told them about some of the stunts he had done without mentioning that when he played a dinosaur, he had set himself on fire.

When Beau pulled up in Uncle Mike's old Ford pickup, its muffler rattling, we were ecstatic to see him step out of the truck and lower the tailgate. "Okay boys," he said, "I'm ready for your meeting. Hop in." Then to Jimmy and me, he said, "You can ride in front with me." I said "okay," unhappy not to be with my friends.

I watched the road as we set out. It was familiar. I had gone this way with Henry on sheriff's rounds: passing the construction site for the new hospital, the fairgrounds, and, across the road, was Mount Repose where Jasper had been laid to rest. Beyond that I was in new territory. The trees along the road looked like those everywhere here; their limbs were too scrawny and weak to support a fort. Then, after a right turn, we came to a driveway. Unlike the trees along the road, the trees along the driveway stood tall and promising but the branches were probably too thin and not what Beau had in mind.

A farmhouse came into view as the driveway widened. Uncle Mike had lived in this house before he had to go to a nursing home miles away from here. The house appeared to be in meticulous condition. The barn and the fields, too, might've been in a picture painted and hung in the folk art museum in Chicago.

Beau parked the truck near where chickens pecked seed from the dirt, not far from their coop. Goats had free rein of the front yard. The guys jumped from the tailgate onto the ground and staggered like sailors fresh off a ship. We followed Beau up onto a wrap-around porch on which he had already arranged chairs for the meeting.

We took seats more comfortable than those in Roscoe's basement. Roscoe opened his folder and asked me to pass out the agenda. When I stood, about to distribute the papers, I saw only one item, "Fort." What a waste of paper. I passed the paper around in case anyone other than Roscoe wanted to take notes.

Roscoe called the meeting to order without his gavel. He laughed at himself for his forgetfulness. "Item one," he announced "I'm turning the meeting over to Beau."

Beau had drawn a sketch of the fort. The drawing was detailed. He took the paper from Roscoe and held it up for us to see. He pointed to tall poles supporting a rectangular wooden platform, reinforced by crossbeams. He would help us, he said, by attaching a cargo net to the trunk of the tree for us to climb up. He pointed to the woods beyond the soybean field. "That's where your tree is. Follow me."

We paraded through the soybeans to a tree line, where a swath of beautiful leafy trees like an orchard awaited us.

Badger whispered to Goose, "Wow, this is crazy cool." Goose

Fire Conditions

agreed. But I noticed something odd. When we reached the tractor path that ran the field's perimeter, an area appeared to have been carved out from the beans. The plants growing there looked like out-of-control weeds with slender jagged-edged leaves. I wondered whether I should point them out but decided he would probably get rid of them without being reminded.

"Hurry up, Mike!" he called, noticing me.

I took Jimmy's hand and followed the others into the woods. We had set out hot and sweaty, but the trail led us into the soothing comfort of deepening shade. He signaled us to stop. "Right there!" He pointed to a tall, majestic oak tree, like those in parks in Chicago, perhaps more than a century old. The oak grove was a haven from the scrub pine destined for pulp.

"This isn't Palmer's land, is it?" Roscoe asked.

"It's posted private," said Beau. "This land belongs to Mike's family." My head swelled to imagine owning Uncle Mike's land someday. My friends stared at me. I hadn't changed, though they seemed impressed.

We sat on the ground. "For now, this is our tree," Beau said. We could've been on a noble journey. "So, now listen up. We need to round up good pieces of wood for poles. Lumber would be even better, anything sturdy that can take a nail. Two-by-fours, planks, anything. Except, the wood has to be long."

"How long?" I asked.

Beau looked at Roscoe. "Hmm, maybe four Roscoes long." We cracked up.

"My dad has lumber," Roscoe said. "He's got a lot left in the basement. He's trying to finish a room. I can get nails, too, and a hammer."

"Terrific," Beau said, patting him on the back.

Roscoe's example inspired us to pitch in. Badger volunteered more hammers, and a handsaw he knew was sharp. Squirrel asked if it was okay if he just showed up; to which Beau lifted his eyes, smiled approvingly, and said, "It's important you do."

Goose was quiet and appeared not to know how to answer. "What would you like to do?" Beau asked.

Goose lowered his head.

"Hey," said Beau, "you look like a strong guy. I bet you're a hard worker."

Lifting his head, Goose said, "I am."

"I know," said Beau, earning himself a smile. "I can tell."

He made us feel important, part of a team. He had a way with kids, with people in general, it seemed; a man any kid would want for a father.

"What about me?" Jimmy piped up.

"You can tell me if something is wrong."

"Okay!"

I was at a loss when it came to my turn. As unskilled as I was, I didn't have much to offer unless it involved a mop and a bucket. But I was a quick learner. Beau said, "Don't worry. I'll teach you as we go."

The next morning, while the Tap was closed and dark, I found Grandma at the bar in her muumuu. "Good morning," I said. She

Fire Conditions

didn't seem to recognize me. "Are you okay?"

She patted the stool next to her. I sat down. "Something's happened," she said. I put my arm around her. Her pearl-handled gun rested on the bar alongside her small blue purse. She wiped her nose with a rag. "Someone has it out for me, and it's gotta be Clyde Clapper."

Henry stopped by the tavern and loaded one bullet into her gun. By then, Jimmy was up with us. Henry explained that an anonymous note had been left at the *Reporter*, and that it had stated, "Flowers has it coming."

"What's Grandma getting?" Jimmy asked.

Henry didn't answer. "But there's more," he said. "Someone wants the boys."

"It has to be their father," said Grandma.

I couldn't wrap my head around the fact that Jimmy and I were part of a threat. Was this about the Crapper or them? If the note was short and sweet, it wasn't my father's. He'd written hundreds of pages of his important paper and it still wasn't finished.

"Dad's not stupid," I said, realizing she still carried a grudge.

"He could have hired someone else to do this," she said.

"What's this? Get a hold of yourself, Aggie," Henry said. "Clapper's bar burned, not yours. If someone wanted to burn down the Tap, he made a big mistake. Think about it. His kids are here. He knows where they are. Why would he burn down the Tap?"

"Well, someone sure wants to hurt me."

I took Jimmy's hand while I should've covered his ears.

"Keep your gun close," Henry said.

Chapter 18

We started the real work on the fort early the next day with the goal of finishing by Thursday of next week, the day before the Fourth of July. Beau picked us up at Roscoe's house but recognized that picking us up there every morning could be a problem for his parents. By that time Goose arrived, a half-hour later, having ridden his bike from Cottonville, three miles away, he left his bike in Roscoe's yard.

Beau watched us pile into the truck for our first full day's work but didn't get into the truck himself. He looked us over. "Didn't you guys bring lunches?"

Duh, between the shrugs and dumb looks, no one had brought anything to eat or drink. I couldn't blame Grandma for not packing lunches when I should've remembered myself.

Beau groaned. "I'll get you some food."

He drove us downtown and disappeared a long time into the Red Owl. The guys on the bed of the truck sat on bales of hay beside our lumber and tools. Jimmy and I, inside the truck, sat quietly, listening to the engine rumble. When Beau returned, he carried two large bags of groceries.

There had been glitches even before we'd left Roscoe's. His planks were too long and hung over the tailgate, which required Beau to tie a red rag to the wood to alert drivers behind us to stay back. Badger had brought his handsaw, but had forgotten his hammers, and had wanted to go home and get them. The hammers could wait until the next day, Beau had said; he had plenty of them at the farm.

We reached the farm two hours after we had planned to start work. Rather than have us lug lumber and tools through the soybean field, Beau took a shortcut along the tractor path that separated the field from the woods. We needed three trips to carry and sort everything out on the ground in front of our magnificent tree.

Beau nailed his sketch of the fort to the trunk of the tree and gathered us together. "Listen," he said, then paused, waiting for Jimmy and Squirrel to settle down. "I'm going to tell you, then show you how we'll go about our work. I'll help you all I can but make an honest effort yourselves. Understand?"

We nodded in unison.

"First," Beau said, "we'll shape Roscoe's lumber into pilings, shaved to a pointed end to drive into the ground, and squared above to support a platform. They have to be sawed at the same length."

From there he continued: Four pilings required four holes to be dug at the same depth. The base of each piling's hole had to be filled with dirt and tamped down, leaving three inches flat from the ground. We would use Redi-Mix to top off the soil. Beau had a bag of it in the barn.

Those of us who'd paid attention looked at each other guardedly. I, for one, embraced the work, but worried if it would be too difficult for me. When those experienced with tools, Roscoe and Badger, looked up at the tree, they appeared eager to start.

"How high in the tree do you want to be?" Beau asked.

Not too high, I hoped.

Badger said, "Four Roscoes aren't too tall but high enough no one can wreck our place."

"Great idea," Beau said, "but promise none of you will fall. Especially you," he added, looking at Squirrel.

He told Roscoe to lie down in the grass alongside one of the soon-to-be pilings, with his shoe bottoms even at the end of the wood. From the top of Roscoe's head, Beau cut a mark in the wood with his jackknife and asked Roscoe to scooch down. Roscoe, being a big guy, and flat on his back, needed a hand to help him slide along. After the measuring was finished Beau helped Roscoe to his feet. "Well guys," Beau said, "the wood's only tall enough for three Roscoes, not four."

I was satisfied with three Roscoes, even though we wouldn't be as high as we wanted. But there was an upside: less of a chance of breaking a bone if anyone fell.

Next, he told us to follow him, which we did, for about a hundred feet before he stopped. On the ground within an area of tall grasses, where sunlight broke through the trees, lay a black tarp that covered a post-hole digger, two shovels, and a can of tar creosote. These, he had left last night, he said.

He showed us how to use a post-hole digger then gave Roscoe, Badger, Goose, and me opportunities to get a feel of the shovel. If we hit a rock, we should stop until the rock was dug out. Creosote

Fire Conditions

was a different matter. None of us were allowed to use it. If one of us touched the oily wood tar accidentally, without protective gloves, his hand could swell and his skin could burn. If he inhaled the fumes, they could tighten his throat. Beau made creosote scarier than a handsaw.

We broke for lunch around two thirty due to our late start. We sat on the ground beneath our tree as we ate, sheltered from the sun. Our togetherness made me feel like we were one happy family. Roscoe and Badger talked seriously about tools and how fast each thought we'd finish the fort. Goose sat at a distance from us, alone, eating in silence. I decided to join him. The inches between us felt like an ocean at first until I said, "Our brothers made friends."

"I know." He smiled.

After we finished eating, Beau gathered us together. He reminded us to bring lunches tomorrow. Tonight, he said, he would drop us off at Roscoe's house unless anyone needed a ride home. He knew where all of us lived except for Goose.

"Let me give you a lift. I hear you live a few miles away," Beau told him when we got to Roscoe's. But when Beau tried to help Goose put the bike in the back of the truck, Goose told him he would do it himself. Cottonville was off Highway 13, a few miles north of Friendship. I sat in back with Goose and his bike. I felt every bump and lurch of the truck hard on my butt. Jimmy sat happily in front next to Beau.

Goose rapped the back window to signal Beau to slow down. "We're close," he said.

A short time later, we turned into a trailer park. When we

jumped out of the truck, Beau let Goose handle the bike himself.

"How 'bout I meet your folks?" Beau asked.

"Not now," Goose said. "They're at work. Joseph stays with Grandma Chenua until they pick him up. It'll be late."

"Does that mean I can't see Joseph?" Jimmy asked.

"Maybe tomorrow."

Remember," Beau said, "I'm picking you up at seven. Don't forget your lunch."

Goose lifted his chin at him. "Thank you, don't worry. I won't forget."

By Sunday we'd made progress. Roscoe and Badger were unable to work on account of each's religions. Squirrel was out of town for Sunday dinner with family. Grandma had kept Jimmy back to draw pictures for Mom. Where Grandma would send them, I didn't know. Maybe no one did.

Goose and I had offered to work with Beau, regardless of the day. It felt good to be in the woods with the three of us. Beau took charge of the platform. Goose used Badger's saw, and I took Goose's weekday job of hoisting wood planks to Beau. Although Goose could take three in a hoist, I managed only one piece at a time.

Midday, Beau left us to eat lunch alone while he disappeared down the trail. Goose asked me if I would swap half of my ham and cheese sandwich for a handful of nuts and dried berries, which we did. "How long will you be staying here?" he asked.

"Maybe all summer." I shrugged.

"What do you like about being here?"

Fire Conditions

"You guys!"

"Even Squirrel?"

"He keeps Jimmy busy, so I don't have to," I said. "He's cool, for that."

Goose took a moment to rethink Squirrel, but when he spoke, he said, "You're friends with Will, I hear. I wish he could be here."

"Me too."

"I was thinking we could build a ramp for him," Goose said.

I let him know that I'd already asked Beau whether Will could join us somehow. Beau said it would be too dangerous. "What would we do if his wheelchair slipped off of the ramp or over the edge of the fort?"

Goose agreed. "Not a good idea."

"Have you ever been to Wisconsin Dells?"

"I've been there," he said flatly.

But I continued, not paying attention to the tone of his voice, and told him about my trip with Will and his family to the hospital in Madison, that we played chess when we could, but nothing about Sarah and me and our ice cream.

"Someday," I said, "I want to go with Jimmy to Prehistoric Land. You want to go with us?"

His eyes narrowed and he stared at me as if I'd turned into a stranger. "All the cowboy and Indian stuff there. It makes me sad. This place you call Wisconsin Dells was called 'Neesh' by my ancestors. I'm Winnebago and will be of Ho-Chunk nation when our tribe gets recognized. Like, you're what? What's your tribe?" when he could plainly see I was of European descent.

A moment later, he gave me a sly grin and I got his point. He was just teasing.

But there was nothing funny about my father's family. One of Dad's last fights with Grandpa came after days of putting up with his father's complaints and slurs of Jews, Black people, Asians, Mexicans and, on the day before we left the summer house for good, Grandpa had gone after Native people, the Ho-Chunk people in particular, because they were nearby. Although I was proud of Dad then, I didn't mention anything to Goose about my summers nearby.

I asked, "Is there anything cool we can do together?"

His eyes brightened as he said, "There's a Pow Wow in August. I'll talk to my father. He might let you come."

"I would like that," I said.

He smiled. "Pow is about a mistake. Wow is for being nice anyway. Together, it's cool."

We were very cool with each other at that moment, and we knew it.

When Beau returned, he brought us bottles of warm RC Cola to toast our day's work. The three of us sat in the grass, amazed by our progress as we stared upward. The platform was fully framed and firmly perched on the pilings. With all-hands-on-deck tomorrow, we'd work on the railings, Beau said, and possibly beat our Thursday deadline. The guys would be happy; we'd have more time to buy firecrackers, M-80s and other explosives before they sold out.

We called it a day and headed out to drop Goose off at his

trailer home. As we pulled into the drive, Goose's parents took quick puffs on their cigarettes before rubbing them out and rose from their lawn chairs. His father set a sweaty bottle of beer on the sandy ground, then wiped his hand on his overalls.

Although Jimmy and I had already met his brother Joseph, I was glad to meet his parents. Goose's entire face showed his pride in them, and cautious delight at our presence.

His father greeted us with "Haho," and introduced himself as Harry Wildgoose. He wore work clothes and sawdust from his job at the mill. Apparently, he'd worked a Sunday shift as Goose had. He shook Beau's hand, then mine. His grip was solid and rough like a piece of worn sandpaper. Overall, he looked older than I expected.

His mother stepped forward, offering a gentle smile, and told us her name was Flora. She looked twenty years younger than her husband. She had long, gleaming dark hair and had possibly the prettiest brown eyes I had seen. Goose had her eyes. She asked if we'd like something to eat, and we felt obliged to accept.

"Pinagigi," said Beau, meaning thank you, I learned later.

Her smile returned. Her lips reminded me of a small flower.

Joseph came out of the trailer, carrying Miwak, aka Namby. The tiny dog wagged its tail like a furry stick beating a drum. "Where's Jimmy?" Joseph asked.

"At home drawing pictures," I said.

He held Miwak out to me and asked if I'd like to pet her. "We thought she was a boy," said Joseph, "but she's a girl," which I hadn't known.

"She's sure happy." I let her lick dried sweat from my hands.

Goose asked his father if I could go to the traditional Pow Wow at Lac du Flambeau with them. His father lowered his head to hide his irritation. "I'll see," he told his son, which I knew meant no.

We looked at each other, disappointed.

Chapter 19

Late Monday morning, Jimmy ran to me shouting that a police car was coming. We were a couple of days from finishing the fort. I set down my hammer and called Beau. When I told him the news, his eyes narrowed, which tightened and smoothed the scars near his eyes. Henry appeared where we were working. His uniform attracted the guys like curious pests.

I wanted him to see the progress we'd made on the fort, and to be proud of me, but before I could point out our effort, he said, "I need you two to come with me."

Beau and I exchanged glances. We hadn't done anything to get in trouble as far as I knew, although neither of us could vouch for the other.

"Can I talk to my boys first?" Beau asked. "I don't want to scare them."

Henry and I stepped aside. The boys left behind were allowed to play hide and seek, tag, or kick the can while we were gone but no one could touch a tool, climb a tree, or be mean to somebody else. I told Jimmy to do whatever Roscoe told him to do or not to do. Beau made them promise to follow the rules. They said they would, even Squirrel, whose fingers were probably crossed because he'd lied.

"How long will we be gone?" I asked.

"An hour. A little longer, maybe."

Beau and I followed Henry down the trail from where the police car was parked tight to the back of the truck. As I climbed into the front seat next to Henry, I noticed the odd patch of weeds I'd seen last week. Either Beau hadn't noticed the weeds or he didn't care enough to remove them. After all, he had plenty of work to do.

When Henry turned onto County Road Z, I had a vague feeling that I'd been on this road before. Beau asked Henry where we were going.

"To Mike's house on the lake."

It wasn't my house! I was too surprised to ask why he would want to go to that dreaded place.

"Don't you know the way?" I asked.

"There are too many houses on the lake now. More built every day. I can't know whose property belongs to who anymore."

"Why am I here?" Beau asked.

Henry chuckled. "Everyone who's been around here a few years knows you dropped Rosie off at the house in summer. What was that all about?"

Although Beau was in the back seat, I knew he had to be squirming.

"I did her a favor."

"How many favors?""

"Two, three times a week, Julys, Augusts, over two years."

Wow, I thought, he must have really liked my mother. Did he ever try to kiss her? Would she have married him instead of Dad if

Fire Conditions

Beau never did favors for her? If so, I wouldn't be here. Nor would Jimmy, and there would've been no Elizabeth to die.

"Where did you drop her off?" Henry asked.

"It's about two miles ahead. Where there's a dead-end sign. I'd stop the car. She'd thank me, then jump out and disappear."

Henry pulled off the highway road and headed down the dead-end road. I knew this road! I remembered the area and the people from the time I began to stay here. The dead-end ran to the shore of the lake. Grandpa Calloway's land lined the road between the water and Z. His property was thick with mature poplars and maples and tall mighty oak trees deep in the woods, none of them as magnificent as ours. Across from Grandpa's land was a run-down trailer park that had mushroomed over the years, a small grove of scrub pine now shrouding the trailers. Once, I overheard my parents talk about a plan that Grandpa and some of the Calloway men had made to evict the "squatters," as they called his neighbors, to buy up their land.

I listened closely to every conversation the men had while shooting pool downstairs. My father knew more than I ever could, and I relied on my ears to listen to my parents talk after Jimmy fell asleep. The small marina directly across Grandpa's driveway was a major aggravation to him. He wanted to buy the Tickle-My-Tackle Bait Shop and Marina, valuable for being lakefront property. When we arrived the following summer, I learned that the owner of the marina had rejected all of Grandpa's offers. In response, Grandpa spread rumors at supper clubs that the owner sold more than lures and bait but also drugs on the side to defame him and drive him out of business.

The gate was closed, as I should've expected. I got out to push it open knowing that the seasonal caretaker occasionally left it unlocked. Beau jumped out of the car and helped me. Within a half-minute, Henry was driving us up the long curving road to the house.

My heart pounded as memories filled my mind, mostly all bad. The driveway ended in a circle in front of the house. Flat stones piled knee-high surrounded dry dirt, where BeBe's favorite field of sunlit daffodils should've been. I climbed out of the car and walked to the statue of naked David, where he was perched on a pedestal in front of the fountain, bone dry. He looked as strong as he had three years ago, and crack-free despite Wisconsin's weather.

Henry and Beau milled around the grounds gawking at the excess of the place. I stepped over the short stone wall and walked to the statue. I tipped David slightly—he was as heavy as a boulder—and reached under his feet to retrieve the key to the house.

"Hey!" I shouted, running toward them, waving the key. "Look what I have!"

They met me at the front door to regroup. I believed they were amazed. I led them into the vast hall to the main floor. "You must've had a lotta good times here," said Henry.

"Not really," I said, except for when I got revenge on Horace.

Not much had changed in the house. Without the Calloways, the place felt less like a prison. The interior was impressive, as they could see, and as their guide I felt duty-bound to feed them some of the house's short-lived, unremarkable history. They peeked into each of the four bathrooms on the main floor; and the library, with built-in bookshelves holding books that had never been opened, the den, and the dining room, fit for twelve adults, with a private side dining area for the kids, where we children ate under the hired help's supervision. The kitchen was twice the size of the Tap's, with nearby rooms to accommodate the help's stay. The appliances, counters, and sink looked like they'd never been used.

From there, I led them down to the lowest level. "This is where grown-ups have parties," I said. Henry was impressed by the fully stocked bar and Beau by the room with the pool tables and pinball machines. There were also plenty of places to rest, drink, and talk. Large sliding glass doors provided an exit to the lake and the beach. Most beaches here were covered with rocks and stones, whereas Grandpa's beach was pure sand for as far north as an eye could see.

We took the elevator to the top floor where my family stayed in the smallest of seven suites in a corner room across the hall from a cleaning closet. Our family referred to our suite as Siberia. Nevertheless, the cubbyhole where Jimmy and I slept served me well, being within earshot of our parents.

Now, as I ducked my head under the sloping ceiling, my mind filled with memories of Jimmy, his crib pulled alongside my bed at night. I pretended he was smarter than a baby, smarter than me. I knelt on the bed, reached over the rails, and aimed picture books at him of animals, fruits, and vegetables. I pointed to letters and told him what they were. When I grew bored, I made up silly stories that rhymed and made goofy faces to make him giggle and squiggle all over. Sometimes I tickled him just for fun.

"We didn't see the garage," Henry observed, finally suggesting his purpose for coming here; it had to do with the suspicious car, and its possible connection to my father, which was ridiculous. My father had vowed never to set foot in this house again. What he wanted was for Jimmy and me to be in Illinois with him and, if she were well, Mom.

I had seldom been in the garage over the years and now remembered that Grandpa had disliked kids running around when he worked. Sometimes he gave one of us a smack. We walked down one flight of stairs rather than take the elevator. In the garage, we found six spaces to park cars. Grandpa's classic Model T filled the space to our far left.

"Holy cow!" Beau said, making a beeline to the antique and climbed in. Henry busied himself by studying the storage shelves and a long woodpile that extended from the kitchen door to the end of the garage. Nothing caught Henry's attention, I noticed, until he began to pace the floor. He paused at the open space closest to the woodpile. He stretched his neck and lowered his head, sizing up what looked to me at a distance like a spot on the concrete floor. He grunted and turned to Beau and me. I expected he would tell us about what had caught his attention but instead he said, "Let's go."

He drove us back to the farm. At the fort we found the other kids lying around in the grass. We were later than we expected to be. There was no point in continuing our work.

Instead, we worked our tails off the rest of the week through Thursday when Beau proclaimed the fort was finished. We crawled up the cargo net that acted as our ladder and crowded the platform, giddy and proud. A heavy wind shook limbs and leaves and yet our fort held steadfast. We hugged each other, clapped backs, and slapped hands. I felt that my life had changed for the best.

Beau drove us to town to buy fireworks before they sold out. We agreed to hold a party at the fort the following week to thank Beau for his help. If we were lucky, after the parade we would have a war with the Gophers. Roscoe believed we would outnumber them, but Larry, a Gopher we wanted to be our spy, turned out to be a double agent, so we were outnumbered.

Later, I wondered, why a war? We made it sound like a game. My father didn't play war. He had been wounded. Friends of his had been killed. Sam and Rashid—my Illinois friends—we didn't play war, but watched a lot of cowboy and Indian shows on TV. Boys all over the country, probably, pretend-fought too.

But I had more on my mind than war. Sarah and me, tomorrow night. I didn't envision her as Miss April in Sam's father's *Playboy* for obvious reasons, but I liked Sarah for being a real girl who liked me for who I was. I imagined us kissing. We would time our kiss to coincide with the first rocket explosion. A bright red, white, and blue we would never forget if we kissed with our eyes open.

PART TWO: DANGEROUS TIMES

Chapter 20

The Big Fish People and Gophers went to war after the parade. I wasn't sure I wanted to participate, but I went along with my friends. Grandma, getting a whiff of what was up, kept Jimmy behind. We started by throwing firecrackers at each other and when we ran out, we switched to M-80s, although most of us, between both clubs, were chickens when it came to them. They came in small red tubes with relatively short fuses which left only a short time to throw one. They were touchy and could explode depending upon unknown, varying forces. Rule of thumb: throw the thing as fast as lightning, or don't light it to begin with.

I only had enough money to buy one M-80. At twenty-five cents a pop it felt like a rip-off. Regardless, I wanted one. I kept it in my pocket, which made me nervous, but also gave me the feeling of power. After both clubs ran out of ammunition, we moved the fight to neighborhood gardens and threw dirtballs at one another. Dirtballs stung, especially if rocks were packed inside them. Dennis, the Gopher's leader, hit me once and I hit him twice, my throws were more ferocious than his. Goose had more hits than all of us. The battle then shifted to Badger's grandmother's backyard. When one of the Gophers ran off crying to mommy, Mrs. Schmidt came out the back door with a baseball bat and threatened to call the sheriff.

We ran away and stopped in an alley four streets away to catch our breath. We laughed and clapped each other's backs, exchanging brotherly punches before we went home. If the war was not enough to make my nerves tingle, I felt charged with anticipation to see Sarah that night.

I showered as soon as I was back at the Tap. I groomed my cowlicks with dabs of Joe's Brylcreem while singing the jingle, "A little dab'll do ya..."

Duded up, I admired myself in the mirror. I sniffed my pits. They smelled good enough. The evening would be unimaginable. The kiss would be heavenly. An older girl who was pretty and interested in me. And smart about making pies and polio care.

I walked into the bedroom, towel wrapped around my waist, and told Jimmy to get dressed in his cowboy shirt. We would be cowboys tonight.

"Yippee!" he shouted, then asked what had I done to my hair?

"It looks good, doesn't it?"

"I guess so."

Grandma palmed me fifty cents after supper, and said, "For Jimmy and you," without knowing Beau had already slipped me a dollar. I felt as rich as I was happy. Sarah and I sat in the backseat of the Wyler's station wagon. Jimmy sat next to Mrs. Wyler, jabbering.

"Grandma says you eat real stinky fish. I got a Shirley Temple yesterday. Dad's real mad at Grandma."

Between the lutefisk and Dad's outburst, Mrs. Wyler showed no sign of shock or of judging him poorly. Rather, whenever she leaned toward him and listened, she smiled.

Sarah didn't wear blue jeans because her father, the minister, didn't allow them. She carried a purse out of which she pulled a tube of lipstick as soon as her mother drove home. Mrs. Wyler had given each of us a blanket. Sarah and I spread ours side by side, touching each other's. Jimmy's blanket was smaller and thinner than ours. Before my knees touched the ground, he asked me to buy cotton candy for him.

I searched my pockets to be sure the money and M-80 were there and hadn't slipped out during the ride. My search turned out to be successful. I gave Jimmy a quarter and told him to buy his cotton candy and come right back.

As soon as he left, Sarah and I laid near each other, without touching.

"Do you think about your future?" she asked.

"I do," I told her, but let her know the path to my future was already set by my parents. College, a job, an ordinary Evanston life.

She sighed. "Sounds boring."

I shrugged. "Yeah, it will be what it will be," I said. "And you?"

She smiled wistfully. "I told you, silly. Alice in Dairyland."

"Maybe I'll run Grandma's tavern."

She laughed.

A moment later the grandstand lights snapped, crackled, and popped on, flooding the grounds with a brightness strange and unreal. I turned to look for Jimmy but he wasn't to be seen. All I saw were people coming and going between layers of swirling smoke-like fog. Kids chased other kids in and out of the haze, throwing firecrackers at each other. Younger kids, around Jimmy's age, waved sparklers like magic wands in the air.

"You're cute," she said, her head tilted dream-like as if she wanted to be kissed. When I started lifting my mouth to hers, she swatted a mosquito. I pretended to cough.

"Get ready!" the loudspeaker announced. "Fireworks start in twenty minutes and counting."

I leapt to my feet. "I'll get Jimmy," I told her, then asked her if I could buy something for her, being the polite thing to do.

"A Pepsi. Thanks. Hurry back."

I searched for Jimmy at the food booths where cotton candy was sold for a nickel. The sleazy barkers rigged the games like Baseball for Basket and Stand the Bottle to rip people off. They told me to go away unless I could afford to play. I asked strangers if they had seen a boy in a cowboy shirt with a sticky pink face, as I expected he would have by now. Eventually I saw him sucking a cherry-colored sno-cone, a ten-cent expense, sharing a grease-stained bag of popcorn with Joseph, Goose's brother, as they watched a clown turn a balloon into a dog. I grabbed his arm and yelled, "Let's go!"

Startled, he lost a lot of his ice. Cherry syrup slopped on his shoes. As I dragged him away, Joseph called, "See ya later."

I bought Sarah's Pepsi after a long wait in a line that allowed me to keep a close eye on Jimmy. On the way back to our blankets the first rocket lit up the sky. Out of the darkness, silver, red, and blue streams of stars screamed overhead and sent the crowd into "oohs" and "ahs."

"I found him," I called to Sarah, and then I saw Butch standing over her, talking down at her face. "I have your Pepsi," I said, wondering what he was doing here.

"Thank you," she whispered but didn't take the soda pop.

I remembered her telling me that she had feelings for Butch. She'd defended him when I'd called him a bully. Was I supposed to feel sorry for him because his father beat him? I didn't care.

"I see your cowboys are back," Butch said.

Sarah looked at me. "Butch is just leaving."

"Who's leaving?" Butch asked. "I know I'm not."

"You are," she told him. "Let's talk tomorrow."

"I see. You're babysitting tonight."

I stepped around him and tried to hand her the drink. Before she could take the cup Butch shoved me, not hard enough to put me on the ground, but enough for the drink to splash on my hand and sleeve.

"Oops," he said and laughed.

Sarah stood, stiffened, and gave him a gaze that could scorch a T-shirt like Mom sometimes did. Butch flexed his hands into fists. As he was going to hit me, Sarah pushed him from behind and doused him with what was left of her pop.

His mouth opened wide but nothing came out. In his sopping wet muscle T-shirt he looked like my Evanston friend Sam's new dog the day it was spayed.

Butch glared a long time at her, then turned and punched me in my left eye. I stumbled; lights flashed. I could've been hit by a brick. What had I done to deserve this?

Butch hung around, lurking. Jimmy looked sympathetic, cowering nearby. For a moment, I mistook the red syrup on his shoes for my blood.

"Go away!" Sarah yelled at him as she came to my side. "I'm going to have my father call your mother!"

Butch shrugged, eyed me up, lowered a shoulder, and rammed into my ribs. I doubled up but didn't fall.

Sarah apologized to me, but it wasn't her fault. I could take care of myself. When Butch was gone, I turned to Jimmy and asked for a match.

He wore a devilish grin as he pulled a pack of matches out of his shirt pocket; the Tap's logo was prominently displayed on its cover. "Don't tell on me," he said.

I didn't say whether I would or wouldn't tattle on him, best to keep him unsure. I turned and followed Butch.

"Stay!" I heard Sarah yell, but I ignored her.

I was oblivious to the fireworks. They might as well have been noisy, colorful pinwheels spinning inside of my head. I wanted revenge, as I had with Horace, but without using poo. I came upon Butch with two other guys, one his own age, the other mine. They were smoking cigarettes and drinking bottles of beer. The kid my age looked familiar and soon I remembered him from our afternoon skirmish. He was the Gopher's chicken boy who'd run off to his mommy. They were too busy to notice me as I crouched between two porta-potties. I covered my nose, and, without thinking, I willed myself to step into their view. They looked like gunslingers. They called me nerd, spaz, and greaser, of which only nerd applied. Butch laughed and dared me to fight, which was what I wanted. I removed the matches and M-80 from my pocket-turned-holster.

Butch looked like a psycho ready for fun. Did he think I was stupid? My eye was throbbing. I was pleased to see how eager he was to hurt me more. He approached slowly, fists forward. I stood my ground and stared at him to draw his attention to my eyes. He continued to walk toward me until he noticed what I was about to do. I lit the fuse of the M-80.

"Catch!" I called when he was in range and threw my mother-of-all firecrackers at his crotch. He tried to dodge the blast, but my aim was off. The M-80 sizzled down his right leg and exploded an inch from his shoe. I didn't wait to size up the damage. I ran away but caught a glimpse of Butch on the ground cursing at me.

I caught my breath before I returned to Sarah. She was upset, I could see. "Where were you? You've been missing the fireworks."

"I went to the porta-pottie," I said.

She leaned close to me. I hoped for a kiss as proof she was no longer upset. Instead, she traced a finger under my bruised eye, which was proof enough that we were cool.

Jimmy tugged my leg. "Can I see your eye?" When he saw the damage, he said, "Wow. Grandma's gonna be mad."

"I'll tell her I ran into a door."

Sarah and I sat on our blankets. I stroked the back of her hand. Her fingers felt as light as feathers. When I opened her palm, I tickled her like I would a cat or a dog wanting its belly rubbed. She giggled and smiled.

Jimmy sat behind us, crunching old maids. I turned and saw a near-empty bag of popcorn in his lap. His eyes were on the dark sky and would light up with each burst of sparkling color. I couldn't imagine what he was thinking, the little pyro. If I knew his innermost thoughts, how his brain worked, I might not have to worry about him and his future. What I feared most was what he would do if I wasn't around.

Sarah pointed to a group of men in the distance who were readying the platform for the grand finale. We hadn't come close to kissing. My urge drove an electrical current through me. Her hand tugged my hand, and she whispered the words I longed to hear, "It's okay. Let's go."

"Don't go anywhere," I told Jimmy. "We'll be right back."

I didn't know if he heard me or not, but by then Sarah had guided me to my feet. We carried our blankets behind the grandstands, not near the porta-potties, but to a place much darker. We spread our blankets on the ground. She caressed the bruised area around my eye again. "He really hurt you, didn't he," she said and, this time, she leaned forward and kissed my bruise.

She seemed to be saying, "Kiss me!" so I aimed my mouth at her lips. She moved her mouth to mine. She smelled good, a pleasant flowery scent her mother might wear. Our lips all puckered, we kissed. Her lips were soft and sweet. Mine felt chapped. "Mmm," she sighed.

"Mmm," I sighed in return. We looked into each other's eyes and laughed. "Have you kissed anyone else?" I asked. "Not counting your parents."

Fire Conditions

"I've kissed my share," she said slyly. "You and me, it's our secret."

Instead of asking her how many boys she'd kissed, specifically, I asked, "Have you kissed anyone like me?"

"You're sweet. Maybe too sweet."

How could I be "too sweet" when I had so much to prove to her?

"You're a good kisser," she said. Her compliment felt like a consolation prize. I was too young, a puppy to her, but good to play games with Will.

When a series of explosions rocked the grounds, she said it had to be the grand finale. Before we stood, she wiped the lipstick off my mouth with a tissue. We held hands as we left the darkness behind the grandstand into the chaos of families packing their coolers, lawn chairs and little kids. In the distance, the platform from which the rockets were launched was now coughing smoke and sending sparks into the night where they'd disappear.

We made our way through the crowd and eventually reached the area where we'd left Jimmy. I was confused at first. Was this the right place? I'd told him to stay where he was. His blanket was here, strewn with popcorn; a full bag overturned, which puzzled me. We'd left him with a near-empty bag of old maids. He must've found money to buy a fresh bag. He couldn't have had enough left from the money I gave him.

Sarah appeared as mystified as I was. A creepy feeling crisscrossed my nerves. While I grew more furious with my brother, any worry I felt was fear. Who'd bought the popcorn for him? Goose or his parents? Unlikely. A kind stranger? Someone unkind? That thought made me shudder.

The missing boy, Gary, felt real to me in a new way. He was now more than a fading picture taped to an empty fishbowl at the end of a bar. I tried not to imagine my brother's face there. Someone had loved Gary as I loved my brother. Someone still had to have hope for the boy who'd vanished two counties away.

"Go ahead," I told Sarah. "Tell your mom I don't know where Jimmy is!"

"Not yet," she said. "Let's split up. We can cover more ground. We'll find him."

Fortunately, the grandstand's lights continued to shine for people to find the exits and for us to find Jimmy. A high tide of groups and families jostled me as I dove into the flow. I called Jimmy's name again and again. Adults often blocked my view of the occasional kid who could be my brother. I tripped and lost balance frequently. My head was spinning, and I tried to grab a kid who looked Jimmy's age but managed to stop myself before anyone noticed.

I wandered around asking random strangers if they'd seen a young boy wearing a cowboy shirt like mine. Some shook their heads or said, no. Others in a rush ignored me. The barkers told me to get lost. No one at the food booths remembered a kid like him.

I stopped to catch my breath. I was running out of ideas and didn't know what to think. He wouldn't know where the porta-potties were. He had a routine. He would need to pee soon. He'd find a dark corner or the trunk of a tree this side of the fairgrounds.

Or he went looking for me.

Swept into the last of the crowd, Sarah and I found each other. Neither of us had been successful. I asked her mother to call Henry. "You do have a phone at home, don't you?" She nodded.

I ran across the littered field, sand filling my shoes, and my legs growing heavier, to where the volunteer firefighters were dismantling the launch pad. I recognized some of the men from Grandma's tavern after the fire at Jasper's. Two of them recognized me as well and took time to help me look for Jimmy. They left no nook uncovered. The fire chief had access to Henry, and said he'd call him on my behalf.

"Are you with Aggie?" he asked.

"No. Mrs. Wyler."

"You're in good hands with her."

I thanked him and hurried back to the entrance. Sarah was pacing alone under an overhead light that had attracted a swarm of a variety of bugs. She ran to me when she saw me.

"Did your mom get hold of Henry?"

"She can't get home. She has a flat tire." Sarah shook her head miserably. "The car's just up the road."

I hung my head, afraid, and needing time to be still. If the memory of Gary's face taped to a fishbowl didn't trigger dark thoughts about Jimmy, nothing would.

Mrs. Wyler appeared at the entrance. Sarah ran ahead of me to meet her mother. As they spoke, their frantic movements confused me. They soon came running toward me. Mrs. Wyler ran barefoot, carrying her shoes to keep up with Sarah. Mrs. Wyler crouched down and hugged me the way my mother would have if she were here. Sarah squeezed my hand. Together we walked to the gate.

This was my fault, I believed. I wanted to die, but not really when I thought about it. At least I'd kissed Sarah, but at what cost? I'd still lost my brother, and I had to find him.

Down the road, coming out of Friendship, I heard the sheriff's car racing toward the fairgrounds, siren blaring. One saving grace was that apparently the fire chief had reached Henry, while Mrs. Wyler's car sat with its flat tire. The squad car skidded to a stop, swerved, tossing gravel, and blocked the entrance. Henry jumped out of the car. Although he mostly moved at a leisurely pace, he ran faster to us than I thought he could run.

The last thing I remembered was Henry picking me up, my tears, and my scream, "We can't find Jimmy!" before I passed out.

Chapter 21

I heard Grandma crying when a man said, "It's understandable. Do you need something yourself?" I didn't hear her answer. The man directed his voice at me. "This won't hurt," and with his words, a sharp needle pierced my arm.

I felt a haze descend upon me. With nothing to see or hear, or to rise to in my life, I lost consciousness.

My mother was with me.

"How are you, Mikey?" she asked.

"Sad about something."

"Elizabeth-sad? Where's Jimmy?"

"He's here, silly Mom. He's under my bed. He's waiting for me. Do you have your kaleidoscope?"

"I do."

"Can you see Jimmy?"

"Let's see."

We tumbled through colors to find him. Steel gray, then ice blue like the sky over Lake Michigan; then, a heavenly gold gave way to a silvery glow that turned the lake into an ice rink, and we skated together. We held hands to keep each other from falling but I fell over and over until I couldn't get up.

"Can you see him now?" she asked.

"No. He's still under my bed."

I came out of my dreams when I heard church bells ringing. How long had I slept and had they found Jimmy? Outside it was bright and traffic on Main Street was slow. I found my watch on the side table. Strangely, it had stopped at nine.

I held the handrail firmly as I made my way downstairs. People were talking softly and the Tap was dark. Being Saturday, the tavern should've been open. Could it be Sunday? If so, I had spent a day and a half in a place between hope and hell.

"Boys his age who want to run away don't have the courage to go too far," I heard Henry say. "We'll find him."

Grandma sniffed. She could've been at the tail of a good cry. Joe stood behind the bar. Even in the shadows he looked sad. And what would Beau think when he heard what had happened? What would the Wylers and all of my friends think when they learned the truth, that I'd lost Jimmy for the sake of a kiss. They'd send me away, like Mom had.

Grandma wiped her eyes when she saw me and leapt from her chair. She swept me into her loving arms as I let loose a torrent of tears.

"Where's Jimmy?" I asked.

Henry led me to their table and suggested that Grandma sit down.

"Who gave you that shiner? he asked.

"Butch."

"Why would he do that?"

"For fun, I guess."

Fire Conditions

"Do you think this Butch could've scared Jimmy away?"

"That kid?" Grandma interrupted. "I know him. He's a bad apple. I'm goin' right over to his ma's house and fix him right now. That, and his no-good father if he isn't in jail."

For a moment I wanted to pin what had happened entirely on Butch. But, deep in my heart, I knew he didn't deserve the blame but deserved to be punished for being a bully.

"I can't let you do that, Aggie," Henry said reasonably. "You can't go and knock someone around. Please stay put." He turned to me. "Did you see anyone—a stranger—hanging around, watching you two?"

"Everyone was a stranger," I said, "except for Goose's kid brother. They were at the food booths. Someone could've seen him."

"Who's Goose?" Henry asked.

"Joshua Wildgoose. His brother's Joseph. Goose is one of us Big Fish People." If Henry's intent was to give me hope, his questions alone were gentle distractions. I asked him if people were searching for Jimmy.

"Listen," he said, "we're doing our best."

He told me that, since Friday night, his deputies had formed search parties and were out now looking for Jimmy. Already farmers had brought bloodhounds. One dog was an experienced evidence-sniffer. When he paused, I knew he meant "dead bodies," but said "evidence" for my sake instead. The law enforcements from Waushara, Juneau, Sauk, and Columbia Counties were on alert.

"Yesterday, your grandmother circulated Jimmy's photo and

description to taverns and grocery stores and posted them on telephone poles around the county. The Wylers and Roscoe, this moment, are distributing flyers to people coming out of the Catholic and Lutheran churches. Highways in and out of the state are being monitored," Henry continued. The State of Wisconsin would be filing a formal request to the FBI for assistance, if necessary.

By the time he finished, I felt hopeful. With all of the people searching there had to be someone who'd seen him eventually unless he was dead. I blocked the thought, refused to believe the worst. And I felt alone without him. Where was Mom?

Early that afternoon Beau stopped at the Tap. He'd stopped yesterday, too, I learned.

"Hey," he said, lightheartedly, "how 'bout we go see the fort? Make sure it's still standing."

He was being kind, I knew, but he didn't have to be. Like Henry, he wanted to make me feel better, but I felt conflicted about leaving the Tap. I said, "Maybe we can go after they find Jimmy."

The thought never crossed my mind. Was it possible? The farm wasn't far from the fairgrounds but it was too far for Jimmy to go at night. If no one had taken him, and I prayed to God no one had, it was possible he was at the fort. But first, I asked, "Didn't you check for him at the fort already?"

"After I got up, then I came right here."

"Didn't you check for him yesterday?"

He hesitated. "Didn't think of it then." Why hadn't he thought of it? I would have. "Hey," he continued, "don't you want to get out of here? For a short time? I'll talk to your grandma if you want."

"I can talk to her myself." I went to the kitchen and told Grandma that Beau was here and that he wanted to take me to the fort.

She looked worn out. "Go, it's better than sitting around here fretting all day."

Chapter 22

Beau was pleased to hear I could go with him. He was upbeat as always as we climbed into the truck. The day could've been like any day he drove us to the fort, if not for Jimmy. The country air was cool and fresh on my face. The sight of the farm, chickens pecking the ground, goats nibbling grass and glued labels off cans, lifted my spirits.

He parked at the head of the path that led to the fort. I saw that he'd removed the weeds. The fort was more than remarkable. My friends were too. Beau told me he'd put grapes and a sandwich out for Jimmy before sunrise yesterday in case he showed up, which I knew was unlikely. How would a boy Jimmy's age find his way to a vaguely specific place far away? Where would he have slept? If anywhere, he might've found his way to the Tap.

"Let's look," Beau said as he helped me climb the net. I couldn't imagine Jimmy being able to make the climb on his own. My first step on the platform felt solid and when I saw that most of the food was gone I could've jumped for joy.

"It's gone," I shouted.

But when Beau reached the platform he looked down at the food and said, "Those racoons mustn't have been hungry. They only ate the grapes. I left chocolate for Jimmy. They didn't touch it."

We hesitated, wondering whether there was anything else we

could do but eventually we crawled down to the ground. "Hey," he said, his eyes twinkling. "I have a crazy idea. Let's go to your grandpa's house!"

The idea was crazy. Jimmy would never go there; at least not on his own. But reconsidering, I opened my mind to the possibility that he could be at the house, safe with our father, and then the nightmare would end, especially if Mom was there too.

I decided the idea wasn't entirely crazy and said, "Let's go!" Maybe my father *was* there with Jimmy, or they were on their way to Illinois. At least Jimmy would be alive.

On our way, we passed Henry going in the opposite direction. He wasn't in a hurry, and I suspected that he had been at the lake house and had found nothing of interest. I was sure that the Calloways had learned of Jimmy's disappearance by now. When we arrived, there were no cars, trucks, or boat trailers parked randomly along the circle drive and no cousins in the yard messing around. Sometime soon they'd arrive.

Beau parked the truck and turned off the engine. The muffler stopped rumbling. I took the key from under David. We walked to the door and went in. The place smelled vaguely different from the last time we were here. I caught a whiff of burnt grease in the kitchen, like the smell Friday nights at the Tap. One downstairs toilet hadn't been flushed, and I took care of someone else's business. The hired help's room smelled. Someone had recently smoked a cigar in there.

We went upstairs where Jimmy would likely be if he were here. Already what I had seen and smelled would have reminded my father of his intolerable times here. Inside my family's former suite, I called Jimmy's name as I walked around checking for him, or for a sign of him. He was not under the dormer where we'd slept or the closet where my parents had hung their clothes. There was nothing amiss in the bathroom and I gave up.

I suggested we go to the garage and reminded Beau that Henry had seen something unusual on the concrete floor. Henry hadn't called our attention to it, and it was probably nothing. But still, I was suspicious.

I led Beau through the kitchen into the garage. He spent time caressing the antique car. I motioned for him to quit messing around and follow me. I led him across the otherwise spotless concrete, and we came upon a murky brown stain, two by three inches in size. Henry would have acted differently if his "tiny" spot was this big.

As Beau knelt and ran a fingertip over the stain, I caught sight of something moving in the woodpile. I jumped, but whatever it was, was gone.

"It's fresh," he said, and stood.

"Does it smell?" I asked.

He looked at the ceiling without answering. Of two gizmos that opened the garage doors, one hung directly over our heads. He craned his neck at different angles as he looked up. I assumed he was watching for a drip of oil to appear.

"We'll have to tell Henry," he said. "Let's go."

Before we could move, the gizmo above us lurched. Its motor kicked into a fast whir, its cables clacked, and the door rose like a stage curtain. We stood in the spotlight.

Beau cussed, grabbed my arm, and led me running toward the door to the kitchen. I saw a face, indistinguishable, through the windshield looking toward us. The car's bumper and grill had emerged. The car was either black or dark blue, similar to the suspicious car we'd been looking for.

"Do you think he saw us?" I asked when we paused in the entry way to the kitchen.

"If he didn't," Beau said, lifting a window shade, "he sees the truck now!" A moment later he yelled, "Oh crap, he's getting in!"

I poked my head under Beau's arm to see for myself what was happening. The man with his butt hanging outside of the truck was hunched over on the driver's side, rummaging like a bear in a garbage can.

"One of your relatives?" Beau teased.

I laughed despite our situation.

Appearing to have found nothing of interest, the man turned toward the garage, where, for a moment, he was easier to see. He wore a suitcoat and looked a little like a hunchback, the one of Notre Dame. From a distance, the back of his head seemed to be square.

He disappeared into the garage, the door still wide open.

"Should we make a run for it?" I asked, my heart racing. When he didn't answer, I tugged his arm.

He said, "I have an idea."

Where had I heard that before?

"Don't you want to find out who he is?"

"Not really," I said.

"What if he knows where Jimmy is? What if he's hiding Jimmy here?"

I hesitated, but I knew he was right. Finally, I said, "I'm with you."

"I'm with you too."

The garage door suddenly started to rumble closed. Soon we heard footsteps in the kitchen approaching us. My knees shook like loose doorknobs. Beau, being a stuntman, stood with ice in his veins.

"Who's there?" a voice bellowed.

"We're in here," Beau called back.

"What the...?" I started to ask, but after a glance at Beau, kept quiet.

The man came face-to-face with us. We studied him, and he studied each of us, like dogs getting a scent of the other's worst end. Inside he appeared more like a fat but compact gnome than a hunchback. His face was pocked and ruddy. His nose looked like a red crabapple. I noticed a bulge underneath his suitcoat, possibly a gun. In one hand he carried a bottle of what Joe had taught me was either brandy or bourbon.

"Who the hell are you?" the man said.

"Name's Henry," Beau began, folksy as a hillbilly telling a lie. What a hoot. I could almost hear Henry laugh. "And this is my boy, Casper. Like the friendly ghost."

I rolled my eyes.

"What are you doing here?"

Beau didn't balk. "My boy and me, we're checking the place for the owners. It's what we do for summer people here before they arrive."

"Find anything wrong?"

"Nope. It's A-okay. What's your business here?"

"None of your business, Henry."

Beau raised his hands to show how harmless we were. "Casper and I'll be on our way. Sorry for any trouble."

Every stranger I saw now was a kidnapper. Beau could poke fun at him, but I needed to be sure he was not just a stranger, but the person who'd taken my brother.

"Excuse us," Beau said, overly polite. "We gotta get to our next job."

The guy couldn't have cared less.

In the truck, Beau started the engine but didn't shift into gear. He let the truck run in neutral and left the parking brake engaged. He stared at the garage door, thinking.

"Why aren't we going?" I asked. Grandma would already be worried.

"I've gotta find a way to get back inside," Beau said. He had to be crazy. I listened to him talk about having another opportunity. He would go into the house, then to the garage, and get the car's license plate number.

"Why do that?"

He explained that license plate numbers help police catch criminals. If someone knew the number, the state could tell who owned the car. "It's important. If this guy's up to no good, we have to find out."

"Shouldn't we tell Henry?"

Beau shook his head. "The guy could be gone by then."

"I see," I said, understanding now why he'd left the truck running. But the plan wasn't good. "How 'bout I get the number?" I volunteered.

He stared at me. "Out of the question."

I didn't want to stay in the truck, I said. I could manage myself. I wasn't very good at sports, I told him, but I could outrun every kid in my school. Beau studied me for a moment, then opened the glove compartment. He handed me a pencil and a piece of paper from under a small clear sack of his dried-up weeds. I didn't know what they were and didn't care right then.

"If he sees you," Beau said, "tell him your father left something in the garage. That I asked you to fetch it for our next job. Tell him I'll beat you if you don't get it. Then write down the number and get out as fast as you can."

"What is the 'it' I should find?"

"Anything handy. Make up a story. If you take too long, I'll break down the door if I have to. If you get afraid, get out of there, and we'll take off."

I climbed out of the truck. The thug was watching us from a window. I rang the doorbell, intending to catch him off guard by being polite. I didn't necessarily think he would open the door, but he did. Immediately he laid into me with swears interchangeably in English and a language I had never heard. I tried to explain my contrived dilemma, but he wanted nothing to do with me. "Get lost," he said.

"But—"

"You deaf?" He cut me off and took a drink straight from the bottle. When he raised the bottle again, I slipped past him. He spun clumsily and lost his balance.

"My dad forgot something!" I shouted. "Don't worry! I know where it is!"

A dark blue Buick was parked above the oil stain, alongside the woodpile. I knelt in front of the car, aware of how little time I had. Rushing, I fumbled the pencil under the car.

"What the f**k you doing?" The thug stood in the doorway, the bottle still in his hand as he tried to tiptoe down the two steps into the garage.

"Dad left the thing right under here!" I shouted. "Where your car's parked. Can I get it?"

"I didn't see nothin' when I parked."

I took a swipe at the pencil, but it had rolled too far from my reach. I stood. The thug grunted when he successfully planted his feet on the concrete. I circled around to the back of the car to put distance between us. The rear plate should've been higher, easier to read than where I'd knelt in the front. Unfortunately, a clean rectangular area, where the plate should've been, was covered with dirt like the rest of the car.

The thug followed me. "What's your name, kid?"

"I'm Casper. Dad told you."

I recognized real danger when his eyes narrowed. I scooted between the woodpile and the car's front left fender. The driver's door was too tight to the woodpile to open completely. I was trapped, although being skinny and sober gave me an advantage. Instead of squeezing into the car, I crawled under it. The pencil was still out of reach. I kept an eye on his shoes as I crawled. I skinned my elbows while stretching my fingers. I bumped my head. A trickle of liquid ran down the back of my neck. When I wiped the smear, I found it was oil.

I watched as his shoes circled the car, opposite the woodpile, where he fit in the wide-open space of the rest of the garage. I heard him grunting. He sounded like he was out of breath. When he stooped to reach for me under the car, he planted a hand to steady himself, but wobbled and buckled and went sprawling. "Get outta there!" he shouted, managing to position himself to paw at me blindly.

I felt the tip of the eraser but quickly lost touch. Struggling, I glimpsed something stirring in the woodpile. A rat or a mouse moved differently. This was a snake, shadowy brown, slithering down the wood and lifting its head when it reached the floor.

Movement more than sound drew a snake's eyes; I had learned that from *Wild Kingdom*. I lay still, but nearly gasped when it flicked its tongue and lifted its head. It hissed, suddenly, its eyes not on me, but aimed at something moving behind me. I felt the thug paw at me to catch my ankle. The snake darted past me. The thug screamed. I scrambled on my belly but froze when I saw a second snake slither between me and the pencil. This one was longer than the first, at more than six feet of slippery skin.

I found myself standing in the open space, not far from the

thug and the snakes. The thug stumbled backward to the Model T, maintaining a grip on his booze. Both snakes, heads swiveling, kept lunging, snapping at him. When he tried to pull the gun from under his suitcoat, he dropped the bottle. Glass shattered, sending liquor pooling across the floor. Its only effect was to propel the snakes faster in his direction as if to say to him, "We see you!"

I ducked at the sound of a gunshot. The thug shot wildly and never managed to hit a snake. One bullet struck the car's right rear fender. Another splintered a hole in the door that led to the kitchen. I took a chance to retrieve the pencil, but it was still out of reach. I knelt and stared at the license plate until I heard pounding upstairs, the sound of Beau breaking in.

My ears were ringing. The snakes were coming at the thug from different angles. They'd trapped him by the Model T. I caught sight of a long-handled shovel near the woodpile. I might've tossed it to him, as it appeared to be solid steel and had a sharp pointed head, a weapon that, from a safe distance, could take off the head of a snake. But I didn't bother to do so. The last I saw of the thug, he was clinging to the top of Grandpa's Model T.

I ran into the house, and Beau met me at the front door, which now clung crookedly to its hinges, its knob dangling. He picked me up and carried me over his shoulder to the truck even though I could've run faster. He'd left the truck idling.

"Let's get the hell out of here," he said.

Exhausted and too worked up to speak, we headed back to the Tap. Eventually, Beau apologized for placing me in danger, which I considered unnecessary.

"Too bad we didn't get the license plate number," he said.

"It's right here." I tapped my forehead. "I memorized it."

"What the..." He stopped on the side of the road. He reached into the glove compartment and found another pencil, and said, "Write it down before you forget."

I wrote fast, challenging my memory. Of the numbers and letters, only one number caused me to delve deeper into my mind. In the fourth position of the series, I had written a "2," but decided to change it to "3." I buried the number in my pocket and was surprised to find that I still had the key to the house. Considering the door, the key didn't matter. The sun was setting and we were late for dinner with a big story to tell.

Chapter 23

Beau and I entered the Tap through the back door, knowing the front would be locked, being Sunday. Grandma sat with Henry and two of his deputies. They appeared to be having a meeting, undoubtedly about Jimmy. Their plates were empty, though a couple of sausages and red cabbage remained on a platter. When Grandma saw us, she said, "Where the heck have you two been? You'll have to share what's left."

I could hardly wait to tell them what had happened to us. Henry's deputies scowled in ways that told me we'd interrupted them. I figured it wasn't a private meeting because Grandma was there.

"Pull up chairs. Finish what's left," she said.

Henry said he didn't mind us staying to eat. They were almost done with their meeting.

Beau and I sat where we could reach the leftovers and exchange knowing glances while we waited our turn. Henry introduced us to his deputies. One of them, Bernie, stared at Beau as if he recognized him. Beau lowered his head to avoid the deputy's eyes.

"And the kid," Henry said, "is Aggie's grandson."

Each deputy made what sounded like a summary of what he'd already said.

Bernie went first. No black car with Illinois plates had been seen in the county or crossing state lines. I jiggled my feet, burning to tell our story. I reminded myself to be patient.

Oscar's report was more detailed than Bernie's. He'd visited Goose's family. Joseph was one of the last people to have seen Jimmy. Clearly Oscar was chosen to speak with the Wildgoose family on account of being half Ho-Chunk. Goose told Oscar that the two boys had met before the fireworks, which I knew, having been there. He knew nothing more.

"Okay," Henry said in conclusion. "Bright and early tomorrow. With overnight updates." The deputies stood and turned to the door.

But it was my turn now! I was kind of a deputy, too; especially after what I'd done today.

"Wait!" I said, jumping up. "We found something. You gotta listen."

"It'll blow your minds," Beau added.

Henry knew me well enough to respect my plea. He ordered his deputies to sit back down at the table.

"Okay," he said to me. "Shoot."

I looked at Beau, wanting him to begin, but he was at a loss for words. He shifted uneasily on the chair. Typically, he liked to talk, but was now too spooked to speak, I knew, on account of some mysterious history between Bernie and him.

"The car isn't black. It's dark blue!" I said, proud to have caught everyone's attention.

"What did you just say?" Henry asked. "How do you know

that?"

"Were you up to no good?" Grandma asked.

I decided on a longer version of my story since I had an audience. I reminded Henry of the day he had taken Beau and me to the lake house, a week ago now, and that I had found the key to let us in. I aimed my point at my fellow deputies to make clear Henry had been with us and that no one had broken the law. The house belonged to my family, and I had rights, I added.

Satisfied with my introduction, I explained that Beau and I were on a mission to find Jimmy, but were interrupted by a man who shouldn't have been there. A man with a gun. When I told them that Beau had pretended to be Henry, and had named me Casper, caretaker, and son, we were able to escape.

Everyone was wide-eyed in disbelief that we had concocted a plan to get the license plate number, and that I had returned to the house on my own. From the pencil to the snakes to the gunshots, I held their attention. By the time I reached the end of our escapade, Henry said, dismissively, "So, you didn't get the tag number?"

I realized that I had neglected the most important part of the story. I reached into my pocket, pulled out the paper, and handed the number to him.

"Here it is," I said.

"Mike memorized it," Beau said.

Henry studied the paper. "What's this? Is it a two or a three?"

"I'm pretty sure it's a three."

"No matter," said Henry. "We'll run it through Illinois both ways. That was damn ballsy of you," he added, "but don't do anything like that again."

"Yes sir!" I said. I took "ballsy" as a compliment, and felt proud, aware the word had to do with becoming a man.

"And what did you think you were doing?" Henry asked Beau.

"Getting the license plate number for you, sir."

Henry scoffed and turned to us deputies.

"Gentlemen," he said, and commenced barking new orders at us. Bernie would cover Highway Z where it intersected with J, and Oscar would cover Highway Z southward, to the Castle Rock causeway. He would replace Eddie with Rick, and back up Rick if need be. I had never heard of a deputy named Rick but he was apparently one of us.

On their way out, Bernie and Oscar clapped Beau and me on our backs, and Oscar whispered in my ear that Goose asked him to say hi to me if he saw me. I thanked him for the message, pleased to know Goose had thought of me.

When Henry and the other deputies were gone, Beau and I helped Grandma clean up. She told us we were lucky we weren't murdered.

Upstairs, after Beau left, I heard Joe snoring loud enough I could hear him in my room from across the hall. But it didn't matter. I'd help find Jimmy.

Chapter 24

I woke to a ruckus and Grandma shouting. I hurried downstairs in my pajamas and found her playing tug of war with the front door. She was pulling back at whoever was trying to get in. "You have your nerve!" she hollered.

Henry stood about ten feet behind her, watching, but without lifting a finger to help her. "Let him in," he said.

Her eyes, hard and angry, put him on notice. Why hadn't he taken her side?

"Come on, Aggie," came a voice. "Let me in!"

My stomach did a somersault when I realized my father was outside. I hoped he hadn't come to cause trouble or to heap pain on us for losing my brother.

"I'm not here to bother you!" Dad pleaded. "I have to talk to you!"

"If it's not about Rosie, or something you know about Jimmy, go away!" she yelled back.

"Aggie, hear him out. Bury the ax," Henry said.

"In his head?"

"Now-now," he said.

"I'll get my gun then!"

Henry took her hand from the knob and opened the door. Dad stepped inside, looking like he expected an ambush, as I would have expected if I were him, to see how Grandma was baring her teeth. Dad did a double take when he saw Henry in uniform. He recognized the sheriff from his last visit. It had been a disaster, especially for me. If I had agreed to go with my father, Jimmy would have come with me, and we both would be in Evanston now.

Dad addressed Grandma. "I'm sorry for how I acted the last time I was here." Then, directly to me, he told me he was sorry, more than I knew. He sounded sincere but after what he had put us through, and being aware of people who would lie to get what they wanted, I gave him the benefit of the doubt, which was the best alternative I had.

Henry guided my father to a chair and helped him sit down. I sat between them at their table. Grandma stayed on her feet. "What's more important than Jimmy?" she asked.

"My family's coming," Dad said. "They'll cause trouble."

"I'm sure they will," Henry said. "They're meeting me at the station bright and early tomorrow to talk about Jimmy. The person who called my dispatcher was rude. He demanded that Sylvia schedule a meeting with 'whatever clown was running the show.'" Henry chuckled. "I told her to accommodate them and see if she could find my Bozo clown nose."

Although I laughed, this all came as a disturbing surprise to me.

But Henry had another surprise, one better. A senior FBI agent, Agent Jones, had arranged to meet with him at eight a.m. tomorrow, coinciding with the time he had scheduled for the Calloways. "Since you're here, I'd like you to join us."

Fire Conditions

"Of course," Dad said.

I thought, What about me?

"And Mike," Henry said, "you come too. You're a witness."

I relaxed, knowing I could count on Henry.

"Who will be coming?" Henry asked.

"My father, for sure," Dad said. "Some uncles. Maybe a cousin. A brother. I have nothing to do with any of them. I've been disowned, but not by my mother. We talk."

"When was the last time you talked to her?"

"Yesterday. I called her right after I read the story in the *Tribune*. 'The grandson of a prominent Lake Forest family disappeared in Wisconsin.' She'd read the story already. I had to borrow her car." He stared hard at Henry. "You should have called me first. He's my son, and I had a right to know."

"I can't control the press," Henry replied in an equally firm tone. "What happened to your car?" Henry asked.

"It's in Evanston. For when Rosie is able to drive."

"Why can't Mom drive?" I asked. "Does she even know about Jimmy?"

She was in no condition to drive, Dad explained to my dissatisfaction, and that, to his knowledge, she wouldn't know what had happened to Jimmy. "It would break her heart."

He knelt on one knee and took my hands in his. I couldn't remember whether he'd ever knelt before me.

In a small voice, I asked him to tell me where she was.

"She's where she can get better."

"How sick is she?" I asked, aware she'd been sick a long time.

"I've been trying to help her, but there're things to work out."

"What do you mean, things? How do you help her? Have you finished your important paper?"

"I'm close," he said, sounding like he wanted to drop the subject.

"I'd hope so," Grandma butted in, without any idea what we were talking about.

"Let's take a walk," Henry suggested.

As we left, Grandma shouted, "Don't let him take Mike!"

The town was of little interest to my father, and Roscoe had already given me the grand tour, such as it was, that I could've shown him around myself, but when Henry offered us a tour of the jail, we bit.

Henry locked Dad in one cell and me in the other.

"What's it feel like"? Henry asked.

"Cozy," my father said to be funny, but what he said was stupid. For me, it would be scary unless I were with Jimmy. I wished whoever'd taken him would die.

Sprung from our cells, we finished the tour. Henry introduced us to Sylvia, the dispatcher, who'd borne the brunt of Grandpa's rudeness. He showed us into a conference room where, presumably, we would meet in the morning at eight o'clock sharp.

When we returned to the Tap, Grandma had hot roast beef, carrots and peas, and boiled potatoes waiting for us. This was the royal treatment, a token of peace for my father, I believed. We sat at two tables pulled together, talking. I was proud to hear Henry tell my father I was brave, and that I'd gotten the license plate number

Fire Conditions

of the prime suspect's car. Not only was I a witness but also a deputy. Within the story, Henry mentioned Beau and left the rest for me to explain who he was. I told my father how he had helped the Big Fish People build a fort and that he was with me at the lake house, where we were both brave, that he was a stuntman, and that he knew Mom.

My father ate slowly, his brow furrowed. I wondered if he was comparing himself to Beau, and what that might mean. He asked, "How does your mother know him?"

I felt strange, knowing; but not how to answer.

"Isn't he too old to hang around with kids?" he asked Henry and Grandma.

"He's on the up and up," said Henry. "He's no pervert if that's what you think."

"He's a good egg," Grandma said.

It was then that I made the mistake of asking where my father would sleep.

"Not here," she said.

"Aggie," Henry warned her by the tone of her voice.

"Why don't you stay at your hoity toity place at the lake?" Grandma continued. "With your family." Didn't she remember? He'd told her already that they'd disowned him, except for BeBe.

"Why can't he sleep in my room?" I asked. "In Jimmy's bed?"

She pouted. Henry and I stared her down. She could be reasonable if she wanted. We kept our eyes fixed on her.

"Fine," she said in a stubborn huff, and trounced into the kitchen. Henry followed her.

Dad went outside to get his belongings out of the car. When he returned, we went up to my room.

"How are you holding up?" he asked. I was changing into my pajamas. He left his boxers on, and wore no T-shirt. The room was hot and sticky. My arms were stronger than ever before from my work on the fort. He couldn't have noticed my muscles because my sleeves covered my arms. I wondered whether I was as strong as he was at my age. One thing I knew: I could outrun him, although that was unfair. Afterall, he had a bum leg from the war.

"Don't worry," he said. "We'll find your brother. Let's get some sleep."

I was happy to know he was with me and felt safe having him across the narrow gap between our beds. He fell asleep before me. I lay awake, remembering how I wrote letters to my mom and him in my mind. When he started to snore, I covered my head with a pillow, and said a prayer to keep Jimmy safe, thinking God would answer because how could He not, when I held my eyes so tight to be heard?

Chapter 25

The Calloways arrived early the next morning in a muggy heat. They parked five cars in line across from the Tap, taking the spaces on Main between East Hazel and Pine Streets, not far from where Dad's newly borrowed car, a red Thunderbird, was parked. BeBe had left her Cadillac in Evanston, as usual in Julys, or she would've lent the car to my father, I knew. She would ride to the lake house with other family members without Grandpa. He rode with the men.

Grandma spotted the Calloways first. By the look on her face, she could be witnessing little green Martians invading her world. Dad hardly ate a bite at breakfast while he poured cup after cup of Grandma's crystalized coffee and was pacing like a caged tiger. Grandma and I watched five Calloway men gather across the street on the corner. I pointed them out to Grandma and Joe: Dad's cousin Bruce, his sister's husband Phil, his brother John, father of Horace the bully, Grandpa's brother Mark, and Grandpa himself like a field marshal. He stood taller than the rest, proud, self-assured, rugged, tan, and in total command.

"Why the hell do they need five cars when one would do?" Grandma asked Dad.

"Only God knows," he said.

We watched them cross Main Street in a line parading like

geese. When they paused at the front door, Grandpa scowled as he often did in disgust.

John scratched his head. "Is this the right place?"

Mark disappeared around the side of the building and returned a short time later. He looked at Grandpa and shrugged.

"What're they doing?" Dad asked from across the room.

"Looks like they're trying to figure something out," Grandma called back. "The dummies can't tell a bar from a police station."

I saw it was 8:05. We were late. Henry and the FBI agent would be waiting for us, and the Calloways were clearly lost. I asked Grandma whether we should help them. She looked at me as if I'd lost my mind.

One of them pounded the door, rattled it hard, and after more shaking by more of them, the lock and latch ripped apart from the door. The Calloways walked in, one by one, stepping over splintered pieces of wood, their heads high, curious, yet puzzled. I wished Henry were here. If he were, he'd put a stop to this. Grandma seemed to have lost her nerve watching them roam through her tavern.

As they milled around, I felt invisible. Joe looked at them like they were zombies. Grandpa Calloway marched to Grandma Flowers, bypassing Dad who was invisible to him.

A couple of them wandered around like dogs looking for a place to do their business. I decided not to tell them that the toilet was upstairs.

"So, you're Aggie," Grandpa said, in the polite way he'd typically begin before he stabbed someone in the back. "I've heard a lot about you."

I knew she'd never crossed his mind.

Grandma looked directly at him. "And you're George II," she said. "I've heard you're full of crap. How's Rosie? I bet you don't know," she sneered. Of course, I knew, he didn't know, or care.

Grandpa squinted at her. "Haven't seen her in months," he said. "If you want to know, ask Phoebe. She'll know more than me. We're here on account of James being missing. Not to bother you."

"You just broke down my door! You're trespassing." She followed up with a pack of curses containing Jesus's name, his Father's too, along with crude bodily functions.

John, Grandpa's favorite suck-up and son, also my father's brother, came to rescue Grandpa as Grandma Flowers continued to swear. Not that Grandpa couldn't handle her by himself. But of course, John needed his daddy's attention.

Leaning close to Grandpa, John whispered louder than he should have, "You said this place burned down." This was not rescuing him, but rather a slip-up.

"That's what I heard," Grandpa growled.

Through Grandma's eyes, I saw her mind spin. I shared her suspicion, vague as it was. How would they, a rich Chicago family, know about a tavern fire in the middle of Nowhere, Wisconsin? Why would they care?

Meanwhile, Phil, my father's brother-in-law, married to his sister, and Bruce, his cousin, were eyeing the stuffed animal heads. I envisioned the Calloway men as trophies themselves, glass-eyed, moldy, and missing spots of fur.

"That one's starting to rot!" Phil proclaimed, indicating the head with the largest rack.

"This juke box is a joke," Bruce announced. "All gawd-awful crap you can't call music."

Phil scoffed. "Can you believe she's from here? But at least she's hot." He meant my mother, which made my cheeks burn.

The Hamm's bear sign sprang to life, in its beautiful neon, accompanied by the irresistible melody that had captured me the night I arrived: "From the land of sky-blue water," the lyrics repeating nonstop as the bear paddled, before he'd go over a waterfall. Mark and Phil spun around, surprised by the sound and lights, then laughed to see Joe grinning devilishly at them.

"Look at the gomer," said Mark.

"He thinks he's a hoot," Phil said.

To Joe, the joke was on them.

Grandma stood in Grandpa Calloway's face. "What you did is called breaking and entering round here."

"Send me the bill," said Grandpa, turning to his soldiers. "Seen enough, men?" They chuckled. "Let's go." They stepped around the broken door and gathered on the corner, then hesitated.

"Which way, Dad?" I heard John ask his father.

"You're supposed to know those things," said Grandpa, and peeked back into the Tap.

"Pardon me," he called to me, "but we have an appointment with your sheriff. I'm meeting him this morning. About Jimmy."

Grandma stepped in, saving me from having to answer. "Follow me," she told him. "I'll lead the way."

Fire Conditions

She led us around the block and stopped at the police station. The journey took about eight minutes, yet long enough to make me sweat. Inside, the waiting room was almost full. Two rows of three chairs faced each other. Sarah and her mother were there, which surprised me pleasantly. They looked like pioneer women, worn out and sad in a black and white photo I'd seen in a history book. I met each with a smile to cheer them up and to acknowledge the hope, if not the love, in their eyes for Jimmy and me.

Two other presumable witnesses sat across from each other. Decidedly, they weren't together. The man wore mud-caked overalls and smelled like he'd slept with farm animals last night. The thin elderly woman across from him had permed perfect hair and wore a strand of pearls. Eventually she stood, pinched her nose, and took the last seat next to the Wylers. She immediately began to make goo-goo eyes at Grandpa, who turned his back to her.

Sylvia came out from wherever she worked. Her eyes widened when she saw how many of us there were. She introduced herself to those of us who didn't know her.

"I see you finally made it," she said to the Calloways. "Can I get you chairs from the back?"

"Little lady, men can stand," said Grandpa on behalf of those standing.

She nodded okay but appeared somehow offended. When she cracked open the conference door, I heard her say, "Sheriff Tuttle. Everyone's here now."

I watched them as they whispered about how many people

were waiting to get inside. Henry adjusted his glasses and raised his head to focus, then cleared his nose with a snort in his hanky.

"Where've you been?" he asked Grandpa. "You miss your bus?"

Henry invited my father, Grandma Flowers, and me to take chairs at the conference table. I was surprised to see Grandpa Calloway on his way to sit down. He must've slipped past Henry when Henry was cleaning his glasses. In no time Grandpa began to act like he was in charge, which inspired the other Calloways to follow him in.

Grandma swore under her breath as they entered together. Grandpa had to be first in everything. He was known as a notorious cheat at golf by anyone who'd played with him. He made sure to get the first and last words of an argument, as my father knew very well.

Henry took the seat at the head of the table, an empty chair at his left, and to his right sat a man who had to be FBI Agent Jones. The standing Calloways began to compete for a chair. Grandpa apologized for being late and said, "I'm George Calloway." All of us already knew who he was. "Thank you for meeting with me," he added.

"I got your message," Henry grumbled. "You made Aggie late. You were supposed to come after she and Mike were questioned. I asked Sylvia to apologize to the other witnesses who have been waiting. Now she'll have to call them back."

"Again, I apologize, Henry. We were sidetracked. We stopped at Aggie's place. I never saw it before."

"Call me Sheriff Tuttle."

Fire Conditions

"Sorry, again. Nice to meet you, sir."

I had scooted in and taken a chair that swiveled when Uncle John walked over and told me to move somewhere else. He was doing a "Horace" on me and I told him to go suck an egg.

"George," he addressed my father, "your kid has a big mouth on him."

Dad didn't waste a breath on his brother.

I was interested in Jones, two chairs up from me. A real FBI Agent. To be more than a deputy, I saw by Jones's example, I would have to sit stone-faced, my eyes seeing while pretending they didn't.

"Well," Henry said to Grandpa, "there's too many of you. Pick one of your litter to stay." It was a foregone conclusion that he would choose John.

Calloways without another seat at the conference table buzzed like bees, asking themselves why they were there. They knew already, as I did, whom Grandpa would choose, so they walked out, bickering.

My father and Grandma took seats, as did John.

"You must be a busy man," Grandpa said to Henry. "I'm sorry for any inconvenience."

"Your grandkids are good boys," said Henry. "No kid deserves to be taken away by a stranger." He paused, then said to Grandpa, "Doesn't help to get the day off to a slow start, waiting around for you."

"I am sorry, sir."

I knew he was lying. I believed most of the people in the room knew it too.

I was proud of Henry for how he bullied Grandpa around and was honored to be one of his deputies.

The door opened and Sylvia ushered in another man. "District Attorney O'Connor," she said, and withdrew. O'Connor carried small cardboard cups of coffee for Henry and Agent Jones.

"When did they get here?" O'Connor asked as he sat down. "Hope I didn't miss anything."

"We could've taken a nap while we waited for you," said Henry.

Grandpa didn't apologize this time, as if he'd run dry of humility. Dad and I shared glances. We knew the "real" Grandpa would soon crawl out and show his true skin.

Henry cleared his throat to begin the meeting, but Grandpa cut him short. "Hey there, Army or Air Force?" he addressed Jones, friendly enough to be an old war buddy.

Jones studied Grandpa while I studied Jones. The FBI agent's rigid posture, as he sat in his steel-colored suit and blue tie, gave him an air of self-confidence. He looked too young to be an agent due to his youthful face. His hair was buzz-cut. His upper arms bulged inside the sleeves of his coat as if Superman was hiding beneath.

"Marines," Jones answered, softly and politely, his head slightly raised. "From Guadalcanal to Okinawa. How about you?"

Grandpa hesitated.

Dad knew more than I ever would know about his father, and he spoke up, stealing his father's question.

"Army here. France to the Bulge," Dad said. "Sent home before

Fire Conditions

I saw the Rhine. Our commanders got cocky. Like they thought we'd be in Berlin in a few days. Their bombs exploded above the trees. Shrapnel and sharp splinters of wood rained down on us. Most of the men in my unit, friends by then, were killed."

I had never heard him speak frankly about the war, but there was one thing he didn't mention. I said proudly, "He got a Purple Heart."

"Army here too," Grandpa said not to be outdone. "I boxed in base leagues, early thirties. Fort Jay. Bragg. Grew up near Freddie Caserio, outside Chicago. You probably never heard of him. The best army boxer in my weight class. I gave him a good fight once. Before he got his Golden Glove." He paused to give a light-hearted chuckle of pride.

Jones looked at John. "How about you?"

If Grandpa had been out-manned, John had no chance of earning respect from the FBI agent. His cheeks turned pink before he could say a word.

"They didn't take me. I have a heart murmur."

"Did you do anything during the war?"

"Worked for my father. At his company."

"I see. How's your heart now?"

"Pretty good, they say."

I'd never seen a look on my father's face like the one I saw then. Veins throbbed on the sides of his forehead above the bones of his cheeks. The rest of his face flushed. His lips trembled, and when he managed to speak, his words exploded, shaking the room.

"What in God's name does this have to do with Jimmy? So what if you were a boxer? So what if I was wounded? So what, you had a heart murmur? I don't give a damn. I want my boy back!"

The corners of Grandpa's eyes smiled to have gotten under my father's skin.

"Yes," Grandpa said, "we all want that." He then quickly directed his words toward those of us who were important to him in that moment: Agent Jones, Henry, and O'Connor. "I have something to show you." He produced a paper from his shirt pocket and handed it to O'Connor, who sat nearest to him. "This will explain a lot. I wanted to deliver it personally."

After O'Connor read the note, he passed it to Henry like a hot potato. The quickness of the district attorney's response disturbed me, while Henry's patient composure inspired hope. Jones took time to study the contents when the note came his way. He asked, "When did you get this?"

"All I know is that Phoebe gave it to me on Sunday," Grandpa replied.

"Is Phoebe an employee?"

"She's my wife."

"Did she read it?"

"I don't know. We go our own ways. As far as I know, she knows nothing about this."

"Didn't she ask you what it was? Or why didn't you tell her?"

"You don't understand. She'd get crazy if she knew."

"What do you mean, 'crazy'?"

Grandpa tossed his hands in the air. "I can't explain it."

I'd been following their banter as I'd watched my father lose patience. Jones's line of questioning was meant, I believed, to keep Grandpa on edge, which fascinated me and hardened my desire to be an FBI agent. My father's hand trembled as he took the note from Jones. After he finished reading, he asked Jones whether Grandma and I could read it.

"It's up to you," came the reply.

Grandma and I read it together. The handwriting was hard to decipher, with poor grammar and spelling, but the meaning eventually became clear. Someone wanted Grandpa to pay fifty thousand dollars in hundred-dollar bills, or no one would see Jimmy alive again. The money was supposed to be dropped in a box at Count Casimir's Saloon in South Chicago, with the name on the delivery reading "To Rocky."

"Do you believe this is on the up and up?" Jones asked Grandpa, pointing out that Casimir's had closed a year ago.

"Who says someone can't pick up money at a closed joint?"

"Have you met," Jones plowed forward, "or do you know of a person named Rocky Wisniewski?"

"Never heard of the Polack."

"We'll put up a stake-out at Casimir's, though I suspect he's still around here. When did you arrive? Last night? This morning?"

"After dark. About eleven o'clock."

"Did you find anything unusual when you arrived?"

"Yeah, the front door was broken. A house key was missing."

I smiled inside of myself to know the key was inside my pocket. I'd kept it in case I needed it.

"But not only that," Grandpa continued. "This morning, I found a bottle of my best bourbon broken on my garage floor. And there were bullet holes, too."

"So you didn't park in the garage last night."

"We have too many cars so we parked outside."

It wouldn't have made sense to me, or to Henry, O'Connor, or Jones, if we didn't already know Rocky had been staying there. I couldn't forget the snakes or the bullet-riddled Buick. Somehow, all of it oddly reminded me of my family.

"Do you and your brother get along?" Jones asked John.

"Well enough."

A big lie. Dad laughed out loud.

All the while, O'Connor had been scribbling notes. The law enforcement officers were conducting a shrewd interrogation like I would conduct in a few years. Henry asked Grandpa whether he knew Wisniewski's car was in his garage. Or did he know that Grandma had received a threat, poorly written, by an arsonist who'd burned down the wrong tavern?

Grandpa did what he often didn't; he sat quietly, listening as Henry pummeled him with facts he might not have known. His golf course tan progressed to an irritable red. He cussed and pounded his fist on the table.

"I can't believe this! I'm beginning to think you're all incompetent. Even you," he told Jones. "You read the letter. It's my money. I love my grandkids like my own sons." He shook violently. "I can't accept this! Do your job! Find Jimmy."

He stood and led John like a leashed lapdog huffing out of the room. He slammed the door on his way out. Those of us in the room exchanged glances. No one appeared particularly surprised by what had happened just now.

"I'll be treating him as a hostile witness," said O'Connor. "An accessory, if my instincts are right."

"I'll be giving him an academy award for worst actor," Henry said.

"I'll be hoping he gets bitten by a snake," I said.

Chapter 26

The next day Beau arrived around noon and paid particular attention to the Tap's broken door. Grandma fetched a lunch plate for him even though she knew he didn't like liver. I couldn't read the look on Beau's face when my father appeared from upstairs, introduced himself, and shook his hand. They spoke for a while, Beau telling him briefly about California, and Dad telling him more extensively about his research on psychological issues of trauma from war, sometimes called shell shock, other times battle fatigue.

"Maybe your father would like to see the fort we built."

I was as proud as Beau about our club's accomplishment but it felt like it would be a waste of time as long as Jimmy was missing. Not an hour went by that I didn't worry about him.

Dad agreed to see the fort. Beau suggested he should drive. He didn't consider that the truck wouldn't fit three unless someone was as small as Jimmy. Dad volunteered to drive instead. The borrowed red Thunderbird had air conditioning. Beau was left to navigate.

I had the backseat to myself. I was eager for my father to see the fort my friends and I had built with Beau's help. But as we neared the fairgrounds, Beau told Dad to pull over. Dad did as he was told but looked puzzled. Beau rolled down his window. From town, the fire siren screamed bloody murder.

Fire Conditions

"Should I go?" Dad asked.

"First, let's see which way they head," Beau said.

Dad turned to me for an explanation. Were we going to the fort or not? I shrugged. I didn't know. He wouldn't understand. This was Adams County where people liked to watch fires, and Beau still had a smidgen of home.

As we sat in the car, we watched the hook and ladder and tanker pass by. Henry followed close behind. Grandma trailed Henry but at the long-specified distance he had set for her on the way to Jasper's fire.

"Go!" Beau shouted. "Cut them off!"

Dad didn't know what Beau meant but he pushed the pedal hard to the floor. The Thunderbird took off like a plane. We caught up with Grandma at the three-way stop where J met Z. The fire trucks and Henry were long gone. Cars stopped at the intersection to take orderly turns. I imagined Grandma was frustrated, and sure enough she suddenly cut off a southbound car in the middle of the intersection, which earned her a long angry honk before she sped off.

My father, too slow in Beau's view, allowed a car to turn east on Z, then another north on J before he finally turned. Beau raised his hand in frustration to mock how my father drove. Dad didn't notice the gesture.

Soon we were on our way south. Along the highway I watched familiar buildings pass by; the dance hall, the Standard Oil gas station, a couple of old and others new. When we'd stayed here, I would accompany my mother on grocery runs to and from the

Rapids while Jimmy napped. My father would check on him when I went with Mom. She hated the lake house and all it stood for, especially the people. BeBe would give her a list and the money to purchase the food and liquor. We sang and talked like goofs and laughed a lot on our way to and from the store.

I remembered how singing "Jimmy Crack Corn" while I tickled my little brother always made him giggle.

As we neared the dead end to the lake, Dad parked at the end of a long line of empty cars. We hurried the few hundred feet to where people on the opposite side of the road were dodging traffic to see the fire. Deputies Oscar and Eddie tried to intercept them. I waved at my partners but they were too busy to notice. Those who'd crossed the highway were immediately corralled into a ditch overseen by Henry. Grandma and Beau stood with the herd.

Grandma jumped around and motioned to us when we appeared. She turned to Henry and by the sight of her she was badgering Henry for a get-out-of-jail-free card to join my father and me.

Henry raised his hand at Grandma. "Whoa there! Only family can pass."

"I'm family," she said. "Ain't I?"

"Sorry to say, you and Beau have to stay here." To the few people approaching us from the ditch, he turned and called, "One more step and you're under arrest!"

By then, Dad and I were nearly at the end of the road at the lake. The fire trucks were out of sight and had to be up the driveway at the Compound. The wisps of gray had turned into a thickening

Fire Conditions

dark smoke that was beginning to rise.

"What are you doing here?" came an angry voice.

We turned and found ourselves under the glare of Agent Jones. We were family, Dad explained, and had a right to be here.

"The boy shouldn't be here," said Jones.

I thought Jones could someday be my friend, and help me get into the FBI so I could work with him, but he wasn't friendly right now. I touched one of my father's legs to remind him I was here.

"It's okay," Dad said. But when Jones turned away, Dad stopped him short. Where were his people? Meaning the FBI team Jones had promised.

Jones admitted there were delays and that they should've been here by now. They were outside Madison, the last he'd heard. For now, Henry and his deputies would have to make do.

"So, there's nothing about Jimmy?" I asked, displeased.

"We'll find him," said Jones. "I promise."

Dad asked Jones whether he knew anything about the fire.

"Nothing yet. Maybe it's under control."

From the corner of my eye, I glimpsed something I should've seen earlier. We were being watched. People from the trailers had gathered on plastic lawn chairs, smoking cigarettes and drinking beer from bottles. I couldn't tell how many trailers hid in the thicket of trees that stretched from Captain Kidd's Marina and the Tickle My Tackle Bait Shop on the waterfront, across the road from Grandpa's property. From family talk, I knew Grandpa's purchase came dirt cheap because of the neighbors, which I hadn't understood at the time.

A grizzled old man in a sleeveless T-shirt and a sailor's cap, limping slightly, approached us from the marina like the neighborhood welcomer. Short and burly, he greeted us like we'd just moved in. Close up, his face was pale yellow. He introduced himself as "the Captain Kidd himself." He lowered his face to mine. His breath smelled like a dead fish. A handful of his teeth were missing. His bare arms revealed taut muscles like a scrawny old Charles Atlas. Inked in blue, his right arm was decked out in a wrinkled anchor. A bare-breasted woman in a sailor hat rode what looked like half a banana. An eagle, inked red and blue, wrapped his biceps. Its claws holding a skeleton extended down to his wrist. Each claw clutched a little body with a large face; one I knew from history class was Hitler, the other Tojo.

"Here for a boat? Business is slow today."

"Maybe you can help us," Jones said, flashing his credentials. "I have a few questions. About a kidnapping. You must've heard."

The old pirate put on a well-practiced look of a mischievous cat. "Might've seen him," he admitted, guardedly.

Jones showed him a picture of Jimmy. "Have you seen this boy?"

"I don't want trouble."

"Yes or no will do."

Kidd hesitated, then said, "I saw a kid looks like him. Can't say for sure it's him."

Jones asked where and when did he think he saw him.

"Saturday," Kidd said, "late in the morning."

"What was the boy wearing?"

"Some kind of cowboy outfit."

My heart thumped a couple of beats. Jimmy was alive the day after he disappeared! I felt hopeful at last.

"Was there anyone with him?" Jones continued. My father listened closely, looking distressed.

Kidd scratched his chin whiskers like an old pirate might. Whatever rolled around in his head, he eventually came clean. "There was a man with the boy. The guy couldn't keep up with the kid. The kid was fast."

Then, reaching the part that must've caused his reluctance, he told us the kid ran to the marina. The guy after him must've started his bottle too early. He knew a drunk when he saw one.

Jones asked him if he thought the boy was trying to get away.

"Can't say. The kid was as happy as a clam at high tide."

Which made no sense to me, or to Dad. Neither of us could believe Jimmy would have been happy.

"The man rented a boat and took the kid fishing," Kidd continued.

Which I knew then was why "the kid" was happy.

"What time of day was this?"

"Early afternoon," Kidd said, "the worst time to catch fish. I remembered it because Saturday was the busiest day of the week. I was running low on bait. He paid extra for a rod and red wrigglers for the kid. He bought two caps when I reminded him about how hot the sun got on the water." Kidd shook his head and grumbled, "Landlubbers. Funny, I can always spot someone that's never been in deep water."

"Do you check I.D.s? For the rental?"

"Yes," Captain Kidd said. He held on to driver's licenses of anyone who rented from him, and returned the license if the boat came back undamaged.

"Anything on the license jump out at you?"

Kidd laughed. "Just the usual. What I write down when I rent a boat. Driver's license numbers. Names, of course. Any damage I find to a boat. If they don't pony up on the spot, I keep their license. If they don't like it, tough titties, I say. It's all in my little blue book in case I get sued."

Inside the marina, Kidd handed the book to Jones who copied the last entries into his notes. Kidd looked pleased to have been helpful. Jones showed one entry to Dad and me. It read: "IL: 2659-2475-073F. Milosz Wisniewski. DOB: 2-22-10."

Jones handed the book back to Kidd and pointed to the line he'd shown us. "Do you remember this one?"

Kidd smiled, amused. "He needed a lotta help. Bait and rods. Fishing in general. Didn't know what fish he wanted to catch. When they got back, the kid showed me a bluegill he caught. Was so proud I gave him a pack of gum. The kid skipped all the way down the beach to the big house over there where the rich folk live."

This felt all wrong. Jimmy didn't smile at people he didn't know. Nobody would be happy fishing with their kidnapper. That he trusted this stranger sent shivers through me.

"Did the guy mention the kid's name?" Jones asked.

"Heard him say, 'Let's go, Jimmy.' Heard him tell the kid his dad was on the way to get him."

My father clutched his gut. He looked angry enough to kill the Milosz person and stepped outside for air. I didn't follow him. I wanted to hear how Jones finished with Kidd.

"You've been helpful. I thank you," said Jones. "Unfortunately, we'll have to impound the boat for evidence. My fingerprint people are on their way. You understand, don't you? We can't have contaminated evidence."

Obviously, Kidd understood how to take orders. "You and your boys come back someday, okay? Nice place to vacation. You'll get my best boat."

I left the marina and found my father outside. He stood at the end of the dead-end road at the edge of the lake. I tugged his arm to let him know I was there. He managed to smile. Jimmy was last seen on the beach north of us. If Dad felt anything like I did, he was frantic to run to the house and look for Jimmy.

"You've been used," I heard Jones say to my father, who lifted his face into the breeze off the lake, and said he already knew. Jones motioned for him to move away from me. They walked to where the driveway to the house began, where I couldn't hear them. Their hands unknotted important concerns as they spoke.

I shuffled, kicked stones, and sulked. When I noticed the trailer people watching me, I felt like a part of their day's entertainment. Grandma, barreling toward me as fast as she could, in her too tight daffodil dress, gasped for breath when she stopped. She pressed me between her breasts. I took a deep breath as she released me. She laughed as she told me that she'd escaped from under Henry's near-sighted eyes. It was only a matter of time, I knew. Beau was still trapped with what was left of the herd.

"Is the fire out?" she asked, disappointed. "Where's your father?"

I pointed to the driveway that led to the lake house and saw that Jones and my father had disappeared. How could they not take me with them? I thought angrily.

"Let's go up there," said Grandma. "I think I see smoke."

So she wished. I wondered what was happening, since the tanker hadn't gone up to the house. I was all aboard with Grandma.

Before we could take a step, two sleek black cars coming from the house jockeyed to pass the giant-sized water tanker on the narrow drive. The cars' horns blasted, demanding to let them pass. The tanker pulled over where the driveway ended. The Calloways' cars broke free. One lost control and came straight toward us. We jumped out of the way at the last moment.

Grandma tumbled into the trailer park's yard. I ran to help her up. On her feet she brushed off her dress, and said she was okay. "I'm a tough old bird," she added for me.

The cars passing us were the same as those parked across from the Tap yesterday morning. The windows were too dark to see who was inside. I wondered which uncle, which brother, which family, were in each of the cars.

Were they taking Jimmy away from us?

"They're not going anywhere," Grandma said with a wicked grin. "Henry's men blocked the road."

When the hook and ladder truck came back from the

Fire Conditions

Compound and reached the marina the fire chief, sitting in the front passenger seat, cranked down the window and shouted to Grandma, "Don't go up there, Aggie! The guy's off his rocker and has a gun!"

Two trailer park people approached Henry. They knew him, of course, like everyone in the county. We listened to them pepper Henry with questions. As I expected, naturally, they expressed interest in the house that drew the excitement. They clearly knew of and held attitudes toward "rich Illinois snobs" who lived there only a few weeks a year.

Would the fire mean they could hunt deer on the rich people's land now? How many cars did "they" have, by the way? And could their kids now play on their beach?

"It's not mine to say," Henry said after they finished.

"Who can say?"

Henry shrugged.

I noticed that when Henry took his eyes off Grandma, she gazed longingly at the driveway. Beau asked me how I was doing, distracting Henry for the split-second Grandma needed. Before I could answer, she took off up the driveway. I hurried after her, not wanting her to go alone. Although the gate was open, she was easy to catch. I found her clinging to one of the iron bars while taking deep breaths.

"What are you doing here?" she asked, annoyed with me. I reminded her that if she wanted to see the lake house, she would need me to show her around. She'd never seen the house. She wouldn't know her way around the grounds.

"Okay then," she said.

I saw no sign of Jones or my father or any other Calloways. I imagined Jimmy riding my father's shoulders to freedom and Jones dragging the kidnapper out of the house in handcuffs.

"That's sure one ugly statue," Grandma observed.

"It's David. It's famous."

"You don't say," she said as she ogled a certain part of its stone.

The front door suddenly flung open. I heard voices, my grandfather's, and father's. My instinct was to hide. Grandpa poked my father repeatedly in the chest and caused him to fall backward down the steps. When he tried to get up, his leg gave out and he fell again.

I didn't believe that Jones would abandon my father. He had to be somewhere nearby. When Jones appeared from inside the house, he rushed to help Dad to his feet. Grandpa raised a fist at them, cursed, and warned them not to come back.

But where was BeBe? I hoped she was safe inside the house, protecting Jimmy. Or that she'd taken him into the woods to hide.

Dad limped as Jones held his shoulders to help him walk down the driveway. Grandma and I had been standing in plain sight. "There, those bushes," I said, pointing to a long hedgerow of dogwood. The hedge was the best spot to watch Horace's comings and goings, so now I crouched down and motioned Grandma to do the same.

I watched Jones and Dad pass by us. Grandpa was watching them too. When they were gone, Grandpa didn't return to the house. He stepped casually, nonchalantly, as if to admire the statue,

Fire Conditions

not that he ever had any interest in David. Watching him gave me the creeps. He circled the flowerless garden. He would be out of my sight momentarily and then reappear. I motioned to Grandma to keep her head down.

Then the garage exploded.

Grandpa fell to the ground. The shock felt like an earthquake. My ears rang like church bells. Grandma crawled on the blacktop to me, shaking. When the sound of the impact grew into loud crackling flames I looked up and saw the garage burning. Through the smoke and flames Grandpa's antique Model T was indistinguishable from the burnt remains of BeBe's Cadillac, no longer polished and shiny. The Buick sat next to the woodpile, its tires flat on their rims. That the Buick was here meant that the thug was somewhere around here. I also wondered whether the snakes were dead.

I tried to keep one eye the fire and the other on Grandpa. When I lost sight of him, I heard him shout, "You!"

I saw him charging full bore at Grandma Flowers. She screamed and jumped out from behind the hedge and disappeared down the driveway. I retreated into the woods and hid behind a tree and waited for my heart to calm down. Maybe Jimmy would appear. After a while I returned to see what was happening. The fire trucks returned, sirens on full. I clapped my hands to my ears, but stayed to watch the men jump down and uncoil hoses, the chief shouting orders.

BeBe stood on the top step of the house, smoke seeping around the door. Two fingers touched the side of her head delicately as if she had a bad headache. She took tiny steps away from the house. She looked wounded, unsure of what to do next. The chief yelled at her. She stepped gingerly toward David. At the garden of dirt, she clenched her stomach, bent over the brick border, and threw up.

I could've cried. As she stood straight, I waved a finger to tell her to come with me. She stared at me as if I were an angel, her face lit in surprise. I took her hand. We walked like two people who didn't know each other, out of step, toddling along.

I led BeBe into the eye-popping world of rusty trailers, littered yards, and the marina/bait shop. Despite summers here, she hardly left the house, from what I knew. She looked like what people round here meant when they said a person was "caught like a deer in headlights."

"Woo-hoo!" came a catcall from the trailers. Grandma Flowers howled back like a wolf to her pack. My father nudged Grandma Flowers to remind her to be nice. No one would have noticed her if BeBe hadn't dressed fancier than anyone on their trailer-based planet. She wore what I figured were clothes she'd bought in Paris last year; a light blue and white pantsuit, with black, tight-laced boots that looked like they were strangling everything below her knees.

Grandma Flowers approached BeBe reluctantly, like an elephant skirting a mouse. "You're just like I thought you'd be," Grandma said with a sneer.

"You too," said BeBe. "Just like I pictured. A tad bigger,

perhaps."

"Be nice," said my father. Then, in a show of sympathy, he asked his mother whether she was all right.

"Does anyone know if Jimmy's here?" I asked. No one seemed to hear me. "BeBe, was Jimmy with you?"

"Jimmy? Why, no. My car." BeBe sighed. She said to my father, "Would you be a dear and get my suitcase? It's in my room. In the closet. I packed just in case."

Did she pack her suitcase wherever she went? I wondered.

"Mom, for crying out loud," he said, "the house is on fire! Can't you see I can hardly walk?"

"BeBe!" I shouted. "You're sure you didn't see Jimmy? He wasn't with you?"

"No Jimmy. He's not there. I would have seen him." She shook her head and winced. Her cheek was pink and a little puffy, maybe from all the excitement. "Forget it then," she said. "I'll go shopping."

Good luck with that, I thought. The five-and-dime's selection would come as a shock. She had only to look closely at Grandma's daffodil dress to know what she would find. Although I liked Grandma's dresses, on BeBe they would look like a joke.

"Mrs. Calloway," Henry said, "would you please come with me? I have some questions."

"Don't you see what I'm going through? I can't talk right now. I'm miserable."

"You are miserable," said Henry to mock her, though only Jones laughed, which caught BeBe's attention.

She eyed Jones. "You look like a strong young man," she said, then asked him to fetch her suitcase for her. All her jewelry was inside. Jones rolled his eyes and explained that her request was outside his duties.

"Quit dawdling. You're wasting our time," Henry told her. "If you don't hurry up, I'll put you under arrest." I knew he wouldn't arrest her, and she called his bluff, saying, "I doubt you will, doughboy." Henry brushed off the shoulders of his uniform as if to wipe her away.

Beau and I, and Dad hobbling, followed Henry and BeBe to the highway where our cars were parked. Most of the gawkers' cars were gone. Jones didn't join us. He would wait for his team to arrive.

BeBe, pointing at Grandma's Rambler, asked Henry whose little pink rat trap it was. "A wonder she fits."

"She has more class than you."

Beau and I sat in the back of Dad's cool borrowed car. He drove despite his leg. Beau asked me how I was holding up. I said, "okay," although my guilt still overwhelmed me in moments of shame. Who leaves a seven, almost eight-year-old alone in a crowd? That's what I had done. I turned away from Beau and let myself cry. Beau heard me, I knew, but my voice was too soft for my father to hear because of the sound of the road.

Chapter 27

We dropped Beau off at the farm and headed to the Tap. We arrived to find my mother sitting at the bar talking with Joe, a suitcase at her feet.

Dad stopped in his tracks. "Rosie?"

Tears poured from my eyes as I ran to her. I threw my arms around her to keep her forever.

She had color in her cheeks, her eyes were bright, and she even smiled. The fancy shoes and snazzy red dress she wore when she put Jimmy and me on the train were gone. She wore ordinary clothes, slacks and a pale green blouse, and a pair of black and white saddle shoes. A Shirley Temple sat near her elbow. After living more than a month in a tavern, I knew people who weren't regular drinkers by the syrupy, rose-colored liquid without alcohol.

"What are you doing here?" she asked my father.

"I didn't know you were coming," he said.

Grandma had gone off to the kitchen to make something for my mother to eat. When she returned, she wore a proud smile as she set a plate with a lettuce and cheese sandwich in front of her daughter. Mom asked Grandma whether she'd gotten her letter. I'd forgotten the first letter, the one she'd let me read weeks ago, and now remembered the promise of a second letter that evidently hadn't arrived.

Grandma's eyes shined spotlights on Joe. She shouted, "Did you see any letter?"

"It should've come last week," Mom wondered aloud. Under Grandma's continued glare, Joe couldn't play possum. He quickly fessed up. He fumbled a crumpled envelope out of his back pocket, and held it for Grandma to see, and announced, "You've got mail!"

"What?" Mom asked, staring at Joe.

Grandma slapped his hand and tore open the envelope. "Well, I'll be," she said as she read. Every line on her face grew angry. "It says you'll be here today," said Grandma, looking at my mother, regretfully, then at Joe, who cowered under her gaze as she gave him a tongue-lashing that lasted more than a minute.

When my mother saw me hovering around her, she turned and asked, "Where's Jimmy-Jammer," I couldn't remember her calling him that in years.

Grandma's face blanched. My stomach sank; how could she not know what had happened to him? Someone should've told her. Or was it that no one knew where she was and never bothered to look for her?

"Jimmy's gone," Joe said flatly.

Her eyes searched for my brother again. "Where is he?" In her eyes I saw a growing panic. I wanted to soften the words that would inevitably come, so I lied. I told her that Jimmy would be home soon; he was across the street playing in Lions Park. Mom stopped me right there. I wasn't as good of a liar as I'd thought I was. She turned to my father.

"Where's Jimmy?" she asked.

Fire Conditions

Dad cleared his throat. I snuggled against her.

"Where—is—Jimmy?" Her voice rose.

My father stood and did what I'd wished he'd have done sooner. He replaced my arm with his around her shoulders. When she shrugged him off, she slipped off the stool and caught herself on the rail of the bar.

"They're looking for him," Grandma said. "The FBI's gonna find him."

From the corner of my eye I watched Joe sneak upstairs where I knew he'd turn on his television to escape the real drama happening in the bar.

Mom's eyes darted in search of someone who could explain why the FBI would be looking for her son.

"Aggie!" my father said. "Please leave this to me." He led my mother several feet away. I couldn't bear to look at her, aware of what she would hear. Her hands trembled. She hugged herself and bent over as if she wanted to be in a cocoon. I was afraid she'd leave me again.

"Believe me," I heard my father say, having maneuvered myself to eavesdrop. "I love you," he continued. "I made a terrible mistake. I'm sorry." He took her arm and led her to a table away from the rest of us. I heard a chair scrape the floor, an angry sound. I turned. Dad had pulled his chair to Mom's. He held her tight to stop her from shaking. My eyes widened on the verge of tears to see him rock her in his arms, slow and easy. The sound of her sobs reminded me of when I was Jimmy's age. When my father was gone, she'd go into their bedroom and shut the door. I never understood it, but I now believed that what I'd heard then were her loud cries for baby Elizabeth, as she now cried for Jimmy.

I remembered hearing my mother tell my father that she'd leave him and take her boys with her unless he stopped seeing some woman. "Are you trying to be like your father? How can I trust you? You better not see her again, or else..."

Suddenly Henry appeared, escorting BeBe into the tavern, which stopped my father cold. She looked old and worn without makeup. After the fire, my father and I watched Henry take BeBe to jail for questioning.

"Are you okay?" Dad greeted her.

"What do you think?" BeBe snapped. "Do you think I'm all right? It's all gone. My house. My life. Now Jimmy." She dabbed at her eyes without a mention of me or that she owned another, larger house in Illinois. In her rambling I realized she hadn't mentioned Grandpa.

With Joe in hiding, Grandma told Henry to help himself to a beer.

"Ahh, that's my Aggie," he said, flirting as she tilted her head and batted her eyes back at him.

"Do you have anything for me to eat?" BeBe asked.

"I'd be glad to fix something for you," said Grandma. "I got some leftovers."

I tried to imagine what she would fix. Something with castor oil or cold liver or something worse if the first options were unavailable.

Grandma told her that there was a diner outside Big Flats if she didn't want to eat her food. "It'll close soon," said Grandma. "You'll have to hurry."

"I don't have a car! It burned in the fire. What the hell is a Big Flats? And how do I get there?"

I settled her down by volunteering to make something for her to eat. Grandma Flowers cast an evil eye at me for favoring BeBe, even though I wanted to be neutral.

"Thank you so much," BeBe said, patting my cheek.

Grandma walked away in a huff.

In the kitchen, I discovered that the day's grocery delivery had not arrived. There wasn't any cheese or lettuce left. All I had was peanut butter and jelly for a sandwich and a dill pickle. When I returned, I saw that BeBe had moved to a table far away from everyone else, including my parents. She wrinkled her nose at my attempt to please her after I set down the plate.

"What's this? It's brown. What are these red splotches? Mold?"

I thought she was probably the lone Midwesterner who'd never tasted a PB&J sandwich. Or was she only a plain old snob?

"Do you have anything with cucumber?" she asked. "Sliced thinly?"

I shook my head at her for being ungrateful.

Joe slunk down the stairs and took up his post at the bar. I knew what he wanted to do was what he did best, pour beer, but especially for Henry.

BeBe left her plate on the table after only a few nibbles and walked over to Grandma. "Who's that man behind the bar? He looks blind."

"He's not blind. He's my brother. He helps me here." Her voice was edgy at the personal offense.

BeBe took no notice.

Henry sat down with my father and mother. They began to talk. I approached them curiously. My ears were sharp, but when they caught me trying to listen to them, they moved to a more distant table, which frustrated me. Eventually I heard something about tomorrow morning and listening to a tape of Bebe at the jail.

BeBe called to my father, "Where am I sleeping? I'm not going to any old flea bag motel."

What could Dad say to his mother when she was so miserable? He asked Grandma Flowers, testing the water, whether a bed could be made available at the Tap.

"Over my dead body."

"Aggie!" said Henry.

"Do you have an empty cell?"

"Time out!" Dad said.

"I have a house," Grandma said. "Do you like dogs?"

"Why didn't you say so? I love my little FiFi."

As a deputy, I'd learned from Henry that people, even good people about whom I cared, could be as foolish and mean as kids. I suggested to BeBe that she might not want to stay at Grandma's house.

"Why not?"

"Trust me, you don't want to stay there," I said and left it at that.

The night ended with my parents dropping BeBe off at a motel

Fire Conditions

outside the Dells. Grandma waited up for them to return.

My father said BeBe thought she'd heard coyotes howling when she'd checked in. Grandma snorted.

My parents stayed elsewhere. I didn't sleep well, overthinking as I occasionally did, but not about wild animals, or girls. Only Jimmy.

In the morning my parents brought BeBe back to the Tap. Grandma made breakfast for all of us. I wondered what my parents talked about on their ride to the Dells, if they even talked. Would they talk about getting divorced, or would they stay together? By their smiles, both of them appeared to be happy, giving me hope for us as a family even though my missing brother left a void in me. We were incomplete.

As Grandma drank coffee BeBe filed her nails. When Henry went off to talk to my father, I knew they were going to listen to a recording. I'd been waiting for this since I'd overheard them. I waited a minute, then followed them at a safe distance. When they reached the corner, about twenty feet from the police station door, I called, "Hey, can I come too?"

When Henry saw me, he scowled. He told my father it was a bad idea for me to come with them. My father hesitated as if he needed time to think it through.

"I'm thirteen," I said in my defense. "I'm not afraid of what I heard."

"Why, you scamp!" said Henry. "I knew you were listening to us."

Dad appeared to have made up his mind, and he told Henry it was okay for me to come with them.

"We don't need more family secrets," Dad said. "He's old enough. What he knows won't hurt him."

Henry put a hand on my shoulder and warned me not to talk about what I would hear. I followed them into the police station, impatient to learn what Henry thought so dreadful, and what secrets Dad's side of the family were hiding.

In the conference room, a tape player sat in the middle of the table within Henry's reach.

"Mike's been helpful to me," he told my father. "He might hear something we missed. It's good he's here," Henry conceded. I felt good to know I was useful.

Before Henry turned on the tape recorder, he reminded us that the information we would hear was sensitive and had to remain confidential. Otherwise, there could be legal consequences during a trial. He trusted us, he said. His sincerity meant a lot to me. If someone (meaning me) told Grandma Flowers, or one of the Madams, what was on the tape, the whole town would know by tomorrow, and I'd be a deputy no longer.

I caught my breath in anticipation as the tape began to spool.

"Tape Recording, Monday, July 7, 1958, 7:11 p.m. Adams County Sheriff's Office. This is Senior Field Agent, Matthew Jones with Acting Adams County Sheriff Henry Tuttle."

(Jones continues.) "Please state your full name."

"Phoebe Louise Calloway." (Her voice clear but nervous.)

"Let's talk about the fire at your house. What time was the fire discovered?"

"A little after noon, I think."

"Where did it start?"

"A fireman said in the garage. They thought it was out. George told them to leave. Then there was an explosion."

"How did the fire start in the first place?"

"I don't know. I wasn't there."

"What caused the explosion?"

"I wouldn't know. The fire chief or someone else has to determine that. Ask them."

(Silence, spooling.)

"When did you receive the ransom note?"

"Saturday."

"Did you read it?"

"I didn't know it was a ransom note. I gave it to George on Sunday when he came home from golf."

"Is it true your phone line connects to his private number?"

(Silence.)

"Yes. I had it tapped."

"Any reason why?"

I wondered how that could be done.

"I had my reasons."

"About your marriage?"

(An angry sigh.)

"He cheated on me for years. I got fed up, so I had a guy fix his phone to ring mine to listen in if it wasn't my call. I have a log. Goes back two years. Evidence if he wanted a divorce. All of his floozies are listed under the names I gave them. I knew each of their voices. Piggy, Gold Digger, Pussycat, Clap Mouth, Floozies One and Two; twins, I think. I won't go on."

(Sounds of sobbing.)

The men looked around at each other uneasy. I understood they knew something I didn't and was confused. A silly thought about BeBe's nicknames replaced my confusion. They could start their own club and name it something like our club's name but with "stinky fish" in it.

"He promised every one of them that he'd leave me. Then, he'd tell me it was impossible to measure how much he loved me. Until I listened in, I thought we were happy." (Ironic chuckle.) "I didn't know how little he cared."

"I'm sorry. Now let's talk about Jimmy. Does your husband have a good relationship with Jimmy and Mike?"

What a joke.

"As good as any of our grandkids."

"Have you heard your husband on your private line, talking about Jimmy?"

(Long silence.)

"Once. A man called. George blew up at him for calling this number. George was the only one who could've given the number to him, as far as I know. The man sounded like someone you'd never want to talk to. They got angry with each other. The stranger told George he wanted fifty thousand dollars to finish 'the job.' He'd pay twenty-five apiece. I thought they were talking about work projects."

Fire Conditions

"What did he mean by apiece?"

"Mike and Jimmy. Both of them…it makes sense now."

I shuddered to think that I might've been taken, too.

"Have you ever heard the name Milosz Wisniewski?"

"Was that who he was talking to?"

"We believe so. He also goes by 'Rocky.'"

"This is the first time I'd heard his name," she said.

"Could your husband be involved in this?"

"We love the boys," she said.

The interview continued with questions about whether it was common for her husband to consort with criminals. Not that she knew of, but it wouldn't surprise her. Did he ever hit her?

(She laughs.) "He only touched me when he held my hand in public. He was hot-headed. He'd threaten me, but never hit me until today."

So that was why her face was puffy. I looked. It still was, a little, on one side. Reddish, not blue like my shiner.

"Why did he do that?"

"Angry, I guess," BeBe said. "I asked him to get my suitcase, after I called the fire department."

Nothing more was said that mattered.

"Don't leave town, we might need to talk to you again, be careful."

"Hmm."

The interview came to an end and Henry pressed the stop button.

We walked back to the Tap, quiet and somber, in the afternoon heat.

My father looked like he'd been dragged through hell, tortured by the words he'd heard from his mother. I was sad and confused, but I had plenty of hate for what my grandfather had done.

I was acutely aware of my brother's curiosity about fire but now it was way out of hand. He'd attempted—naively or not—to set a fire in the garage in Evanston, and his eyes had filled with delight as he approached Jasper's burning barn here in Friendship. He'd burned a blanket with stolen matches. Was he clever enough, or so afraid and smart, to set a fire to distract the kidnapper and escape? BeBe hadn't seen Jimmy, she said, but that didn't mean he hadn't been there. I wouldn't think about anything but that he'd escaped the kidnapper.

Once Jimmy was found, I knew I'd have to tell my parents how much he liked to play with fire. They only knew about the one time in their garage. They'd need someone smarter than me to help them before he hurt himself, or someone else.

Chapter 28

The morning of Thursday, July 10, six nights since Jimmy disappeared, I woke from a dream remembering the troubling statement BeBe had made on the recording, that Jimmy and I were worth twenty-five thousand dollars apiece. It was fortunate she was there to testify, or I would've gone on never knowing my value. Whose grandfather would do such a thing? A good grandfather would take me to a baseball game. But mine was crazy and mean.

I dressed in my jeans and cowboy shirt for BeBe to cheer her up. I'd always understood, without accepting what I knew, that I didn't know my grandmother, other than she bought gifts for us and we called her "BeBe."

Grandma Flowers, on the other hand, made large breakfasts, one now awaiting my parents for when they returned from wherever they went for the night. I ate fast. I didn't want my food to get cold. The best part of breakfast was the freshly picked blueberries the Wylers had left for us. Grandma put some in the pancake batter and saved some for herself. I saved most of the rest for my parents and a few for Joe. I wished Jimmy were here. I would've loved to have given him my share just to see his mouth turn blue.

When my parents arrived, I watched them closely, hoping to detect a spark of love, like honeymooners making up after a fight.

"Where's BeBe?" I asked.

"On her way to Lake Forest," said my father. His brother John was driving her there.

I remembered she hadn't promised not to leave town on the recording.

Mom and Dad weren't playing eye games or whispering sweet nothings, but at least they held hands. When they decided to go for a walk, I hoped they would have a good day. Maybe they'd make up and get back together.

Henry rushed into the Tap, frantic. My first thought on seeing him was that he'd found out that BeBe had left town, disobeying his order. That wasn't the case, though. He wanted to check on us, he said. The real reason, I discovered, was that he wanted Grandma to make coffee for him. When she pressed him to linger, he brushed her off, but explained. The sheriff and his deputies were needed to assist the State Police and FBI as soon as possible.

"Can I come too?" I asked.

"Sorry, not today," he said.

"I thought I was your deputy." In truth, I knew I wasn't. I was pretending, wanting to believe I'd be useful.

He came down to my level, face to face, to say it could be dangerous. He didn't want me to get hurt. I was too important to him to let that happen.

I felt better, and less resistant; he had a way with me. But I wanted a favor. I had a way too. Would he let me hitch a ride with him to Uncle Mike's farm? It was on his way to the lake. I told him I'd jump out of the car at the driveway and be gone in no time.

When he asked whether I had my father's permission to go to the fort, I lied, while telling myself Dad would've let me go if I'd asked.

"Hop in," said Henry.

As I stood on the farmhouse porch, I knocked several times without an answer. The truck was parked outside. Beau had to be around; either in the barn, the woods, or still in bed sleeping. I turned the knob, the door slid open, and I walked in. The scent of a harsh, skunky smoke caused my nostrils to twitch. In the kitchen, I found Beau drinking coffee and smoking a thin, tightly wrapped cigarette that glowed brighter each time he inhaled. When he exhaled, I coughed.

I told him that my mother had come back yesterday. This caught his attention. In a raspy voice, he asked curiously whether she was in town.

"She is."

"With your father?"

"Yes."

"Your dad's all right," he said almost sadly.

"You're all right and cool, too," I said.

He smiled. "Thanks."

"Can you take me to Castle Rock Lake?"

"We were there yesterday. All I did was stand in a ditch."

The darks of his eyes were unusually wide. I remembered the silences between my father and him and the awkwardness of each having loved my mother.

"Will you write me a letter if you leave?" I didn't want to lose track of him. Maybe he'd take me to Hollywood someday, but probably we'd go to the Dells.

"Write about what?"

"Just, you know, to keep in touch."

"Sure, Mike, I'll send you a letter."

"Can we go to the lake now?"

He mulled this over. When he said he would, I knew from his voice this could be the last favor he would do for me, after he'd done so much.

Before we left the house, I noticed he put a pouch of his weeds into the top drawer near the sink. He focused carefully on each porch step as we walked out. In the truck, he jiggled his feet. He had trouble with the gear and the clutch. His hands and feet worked against each other. The truck bucked like a wild horse. Was coming here with him a good decision? He almost veered into the ditch when he turned onto J. I gripped my seat. He yelled, "Whoops," and laughed, which I didn't find funny.

"Are you okay?" I asked.

"A-okay, here," he said with a thumbs up.

As we approached Z from J, he drove fast. I pointed to the roadblock ahead and suggested he slow down. An Adams County police car blocked the southbound traffic. I recognized Deputy Bernie, trying to redirect a long line of cars and trucks. He could've used my help. When he motioned our turn, Beau froze, and Bernie stepped to the truck, with the traffic sounding like the seventh-grade brass band warming up.

When Bernie poked his nose in for a closer look, he seemed to

Fire Conditions

recognize Beau. He sniffed and said, "hmm," and Beau squirmed.

"Have you been smoking weed? Are you high?"

Beau grinned friendly-like, but when the corners of his eyes began to twitch, I could tell he was afraid.

"Hey, remember me?" I asked to distract Bernie from Beau.

"Oh yeah, Little Deputy. Nice to see you, but you can't go that way, sorry. Turn around or go north."

Beau sat staring straight ahead. It occurred to me just what kind of weeds Beau had been growing and drying and smoking. I had heard from Rashid and Sam about drugs, but had never seen any. I felt like such a moron. But Beau seemed okay.

Car and truck horns blared. When it was our turn, Bernie motioned for Beau to turn back to Friendship or to go north on Z. He allowed no cars to go south, where the lake house had burned yesterday, about five miles away. When Bernie began to flail his arms to direct the gathering traffic, he turned his back to us, and Beau twisted the steering wheel and stepped hard on the gas.

My shoulder bumped the door. The truck swerved into a ditch. The tires must've been bald by the way they spun. As he shifted again and again, the tires finally caught traction on a slip of gravel. The truck lurched, then popped onto the highway. Pointed south, we were on our way.

Beau slowed the truck down until it rolled to a stop. I jumped out and landed flat-footed onto sunbaked sand and tall grass. After orienting myself, I noticed a small, broken-down cottage set back from the beach. I remembered the place. I'd strayed too far from

Grandpa's woods while hiding from Horace once. I'd hidden in a place that smelled like Christmas. Pine needles lay thick on the ground. I carried armloads of them to an area of large ferns and covered myself from my knees up to my neck. Horace, being dumber than his dog, passed me twice.

We stood close to where I'd come out of the woods after escaping Horace. We walked around the cottage. The wood siding was worn by the weather. Shingles were missing. The roof sagged. The door was locked. We peeked into the windows but didn't see anyone, not even a rat or a raccoon. As we walked, Beau's head must've begun to clear. He didn't stumble as much as he had in the sand.

The smell of fresh air off the lake felt like the kind of freedom I had when I was small. The herons called to each other. I imagined they were welcoming me back. Grandpa's No Trespassing sign still stood stuck in the sand by the water, pointing at the cottage where grandpa's property ended. We walked down the beach about ten yards before Beau pointed to where Grandpa's house had been. Men in uniforms and others in suits stood outside of the marina, aiming binoculars at the sky. Others with walkie-talkies stood on the beach south of us.

A plane—one like I'd seen at an Air Show with my father when I was younger—circled a particular area in the middle of the lake. Dad called it a crop duster. The plane cycled downward, appearing to dive at a boat only to zoom back into the air, and start over. I realized the plane was trying to direct the boat away from the county across the lake and back to Adams County. My heart

Fire Conditions

followed every move of the plane. From this distance the driver looked like a stick. All at once I understood. Rocky must have been in the boat, and been spotted by the FBI trying to escape. Did he still have Jimmy? I didn't see my brother, and prayed that Rocky hadn't thrown him overboard into the lake.

Euphoric, I cheered when two speedboats launched from Captain Kidd's pier. They cut through the choppy water as the plane kept the boat spinning and drifting toward land. When clouds blocked the sun, the glimmer of the lake disappeared, and it became easier to see. The speedboats skimmed the water's surface. The plane, in tandem with the speedboats, slowed as the motorboat stopped abruptly and started to bob.

"He's outta gas," Beau said gleefully. "He's screwed." I hoped he was right.

The speedboats cut their engines and bobbed alongside the motorboat. Two men, slight figures from a distance, jumped aboard. I noticed Beau wasn't watching the action across the lake but had his eye on a man down the beach who'd broke from the group. Beau froze. It had to be Henry. No one else walked like him. The heavy man stopped to clean his glasses from time to time, then afterward would stumble ahead in the sand.

"I can't stay here," Beau said. "I don't want him to see me."

But abruptly, Henry stopped halfway between the marina. He might've thought we were foraging deer. When he put his glasses on one more time, he leaned his head forward, turtle-like, and turned back toward the group he'd left.

After Bernie had asked Beau if he was high, I saw Beau in a

different light. We had one thing in common. He'd disappointed Henry, who'd looked after him when he was a troubled kid, just like I'd disappointed my father by not going back to Evanston.

The speedboats towed the runaway boat out of the returning bright sunlight. The men at the marina and lake house watched the boats drift in. No one paid attention to us. FBI agents waded into the water and hitched the runaway boat to theirs. As they neared the shore, they cut the motorboat free and let momentum take the boat to the beach. FBI agents swarmed the boat and lifted it ashore. After they pushed the man from Grandpa's garage, Rocky, face-down in the sand, they handcuffed his wrists behind his back.

A dreadful feeling sank deep in my stomach. I pictured my brother's body floating in the lake and quickly shook the thought out of my head. He was in the woods. He'd escaped before he was put on the boat. He knew the places where I'd hidden from Horace. He'd laughed when I'd told him about the pine needle trick. If he wasn't there covered in needles, he had to be hiding in the culvert that ran under County Road Z.

I motioned for Beau to follow me. I led him through the poplar trees, and when we reached the scrub pine, I told him to keep an eye out for a lump under a pile of pine needles. He laughed like Jimmy had laughed, which made me smile.

We split up to cover more ground while calling his name. I headed to the culvert, but he wasn't there. I turned back to find Beau, but he wasn't where I'd left him. I called his name. Without an answer, I wandered around to find him but soon got lost. I would've traded my watch for a compass.

Fire Conditions

The woods were quiet, without even the sound of a bird. When I heard a twig snap, I said, softly, "Jimmy, is that you?"

Nothing. Maybe it was a squirrel.

A second twig snap ruled out the squirrel.

"Jimmy?" I asked, again, dizzy with hope. But soon I heard a metallic jingling that continued in a rhythm of footsteps.

"Beau?" I asked, but Beau didn't jingle when he walked. I hid behind a tree.

Grandpa emerged, head low, a shotgun pressed tight to his side. He staggered like a mummy in a scary movie, or a regular drunk. A set of keys swung on a loop of his pants; the jingling sound I'd heard. I let him pass and followed him from a safe distance. Soon the woods thinned. Reeds of grass and sand came into view through the trees. I found myself at the cottage where Beau had parked the truck. I saw no sign of him.

Grandpa turned and walked toward the cottage, ignoring the truck. I stood watching from the fringe of the woods. As he turned the doorknob, I clenched my fists and pumped them to match the beat of my heart. The door didn't open and he gave it a kick. Then another, a harder one, when the door still didn't budge. He paused—I assumed out of frustration—and pounded the door with the butt of the gun. Finally, he blasted the door open. The sound was loud enough to be heard in Adams. I hoped Beau had heard the shot. I'd never understood the damage buckshot could do until I'd seen it close up. Splinters of wood had scattered in every direction. The doorknob dangled on what looked to be a piece of thin metal. Grandpa stepped carefully around the debris as he strode inside.

I circled around to the back of the cottage. A rear window faced the lake, and a large spider web covered the glass, making it hard to see inside. The foundation was cracked, and I pulled out a chunk of its concrete. I could hear Grandpa rummaging around inside. I knew I was alone with him, and I bolstered myself to be brave. I risked sliding the window open to take a peek.

He was running his hand across the top of a dresser like he was stroking a cat or dog. Then, abruptly, he kicked a chair across the room. He turned and rapped softly on what I assumed was a closet door. My heart leapt. Was Jimmy in there? I listened to hear a sound from him, but didn't hear anything except Grandpa's snorts and grunts.

Next, as I continued to watch him, he turned to a twin bed, the only one in the room. I lowered my head as fast as I could whenever he looked toward the window. He poked the gun at a lump under the bed sheets that proved to be a pillow, and not a boy. He walked in circles for a few seconds and looked under the bed. No boy there, either. When he tore the sheets completely off and threw them on the floor, I gasped at what I saw; yellow and brownish stains. I turned my head. My poor brother, I thought. I wanted to cry thinking about what he must've gone through.

Another gunshot rang out, destroying something in a room I couldn't see. My nerves jumped, electrified. I didn't know what to do other than to wait for my father, Henry, or Beau, or Agent Jones to come and protect me. I was on my own.

I'd set the piece of concrete on the ground in case I needed to defend myself and now I picked it up. I liked the feel of its heft, and used it to break the glass from the window. At the same time Grandpa walked into the room, pale and ill-looking, oblivious to the broken glass, unheard, possibly because of the simultaneous sound of the gunshot. He approached the closet, shotgun in hand, unclipping the keys from the loop of his belt. Unable to hold two things at once, he fumbled with the keys.

I lifted myself through the window frame onto the sill. I had to get hold of those keys.

I wanted to crack his skull.

Pivoting on my butt on the windowsill, I lost my balance and my left hand came down on a sharp piece of glass. I winced but managed not to scream. Still on the edge of the sill, the chunk of concrete at my feet, I began to wiggle the glass out of my hand, all the while keeping an eye on Grandpa.

With the glass out, I licked my blood like a wounded animal, which I found soothing, then jumped into the room, landing feet-first.

Grandpa greeted me by aiming the gun at my chest. He followed up with a hard punch to my head. I found myself on the floor with stars in my eyes. When I looked up, I saw him standing over me, the keys now in his hand. My concrete weapon lay outside on the ground. He lowered the gun to test the keys in the lock of the closet door. He tried four or five without success.

My head had begun to clear. The first thing I saw was an ugly yellow spider angling downward on a thin silky fiber toward the bare part of Grandpa's neck. Its legs were light brown and long for a spider, longer than any spider other than a tarantula, but without the hair.

"Ow!" Grandpa shouted, slapping his neck. I grabbed his keys from his hand and ran to the door, hoping the bite was poisonous.

"Get back here, you bastard!" Grandpa pointed the gun at me again, and he snarled, "Sit down."

I dropped the keys. Then I sat on the bed and wrapped my bloody hand in a pillowcase. So far I'd been quiet, but decided to try to distract him. And maybe find out if Jimmy really was here. "Do you know why everyone hates you?" I asked.

He glared at me. "Everyone loves me."

Only because of his money, I knew. "I don't love you. I hate you." Talking to him gave me the weirdest feeling, knowing that he wanted me dead.

"I'm scared!" Jimmy's voice.

I jumped up, exhilarated and terrified for him, hoping Grandpa wouldn't hurt him. "I'm right here!" I called out.

Grandpa aimed the gun at me again. Since the gun had two barrels, and two shells had been spent, by my account, the gun was empty.

I lowered my right shoulder, felt my adrenaline rising, and hurtled my body into his privates. He doubled over and I grabbed the keys back and began to test them in the closet door.

He grabbed my foot. I wriggled out of my shoe and freed my foot, the whole time checking the keys.

The first didn't work. Nor did the second.

"I'll shoot," Grandpa said.

"You're out of shells," I said.

Fire Conditions

"No, I'm not. I reloaded."

I hoped he was bluffing.

The third key clicked. I opened the door and Jimmy rushed into my arms, leaving Grandpa with either an empty or a loaded gun. Fifty-fifty, we'd live. We rushed out of the room.

I helped Jimmy go through the broken window and told him to watch out for glass. If Grandpa wasn't prowling around with his gun, Jimmy and I might've been able to run out the front door.

I yelled, "Run!"

"You too!"

"I'll catch up."

And he was gone.

I stayed back for a moment, behind the corner, and watched Grandpa stagger out of the door. Then I ran too.

I met Jimmy behind the cottage, waiting for me. I tousled his hair as I gave him a one-armed hug to avoid getting blood on him. Feeling him next to me, full of life, I gushed tears of joy.

Then I heard Beau calling, "Over here!" He stood about twenty feet down from us on the beach.

I ran toward him, with Jimmy, gripping his hand the whole way.

Beau, Henry, and Agent Jones raced from the lake house toward us on the beach. All of us took turns lifting Jimmy to give him a hug. I had smeared blood on his shirt. I told Jones and Henry what had happened. Henry asked whether Grandpa was still in the cottage. I'd seen him leave, I told him. Jones asked whether I saw where he went.

"Into the woods," I replied, "and he still has his gun."

Immediately, Jones radioed his men. "Suspect is armed. I repeat, armed. Proceed with caution."

A few minutes later, we heard a gunshot. I knew where Grandpa probably was, based on the location of the sound. When we arrived, we found his body on the path he'd taken through the woods away the cottage. His gun lay near his feet.

"Don't look," Jones said.

But of course, I had to look, and when I did, I didn't recognize him. Aside from some scalp and face tissue, the rest of his head was gone. Within an hour, the coroner arrived with his team and pronounced my grandfather dead.

I couldn't have cared less.

Chapter 29

That night, people drifted in and out of the Tap to celebrate Jimmy's rescue. He should've been exhausted but he had the perpetual energy of Wile E. Coyote. Beer was on the house. Joe poured, of course. The mood was cheerful and grew increasingly loud and boisterous. The crowd was about the size of a packed Friday night. Grandma, who said she wouldn't mind going bankrupt for the occasion, was too busy entertaining to spare a moment for Henry, which he didn't seem to mind. He walked around the tavern to thank folks who'd been in the search group, but especially those who'd brought bloodhounds the day after Jimmy disappeared.

Rocky sat in jail after his interview.

District Attorney O'Connor, Mayor Larsen, and Edgar, the editor of the *Friendship Reporter*, each paid a visit. The editor brought a photographer to take pictures for the paper. Jimmy hammed it up, posing with a goofy smile whenever the camera turned on him. Soon, he had both the photographer and editor in stitches, laughing and calling him "buddy" and "pal."

Unlike large parties with strangers in Evanston, no one here required introductions to understand family and friend relationships. My father was in the kitchen breaking the news to Grandma Flowers about his phone call to BeBe to inform her of her husband's suicide. I felt sorry for her but on the other hand, if I were her, I'd be jumping for joy.

Dad came out a short time later. I took it upon myself to keep an eye on Jimmy, who was at the bar, holding court, basking in his unexpected fame. I turned my attention to my parents, hoping to detect a sign of affection. I spied them across the tavern. They were in the midst of a conversation with a woman their age. I worked my way through the crowd to listen in. From what I heard, the woman was an old high school friend of Mom, based on talk of a Homecoming and teachers. The friend sounded drunk.

"You caught yourself a fine man, Rosie," the old friend said with a sloppy nod at my father. "I wouldn't mind taking him home myself." She winked at my mother.

Mom tightened her grip on my father's arm. I came up behind her and touched her wrist with my good hand. She looked at me and immediately positioned me in front of my father to shield him from the old friend. Proudly, Mom said, "This is our oldest son, Mike."

"What happened to him?" the old friend asked, eyeing my bandaged hand and black and blue shiner. "You should take better care of him."

As we walked away, Mom said, "No Christmas card for her this year."

When I looked back at Jimmy, he was surrounded by the Madams. One of them said, "And what happened then?" They were the last people he should be talking to. I assumed they were trying to dig up dirt to spin stories and rumors for the web of gossips across the county.

"Excuse me," I cut in, and pulled Jimmy off his chair. To the Madams I said, "Our friends are here. They want to see Jimmy." I led him away quickly before they tried to delay us.

The first friend I saw was Roscoe, who'd arrived with his mother. She was clearly here to keep an eye on her son and appeared shy to be in a crowd. Jimmy was as happy as I was to see Roscoe. While we talked about how we met, and how he had invited me without hesitation to join his club, my mother approached Roscoe's mother to learn how their boys had become friends. As they talked, I teased him about his "rigorous" meeting agendas. The big lug blushed. I said, "But we did it. We built a fort!"

"We did!"

Jimmy asked Roscoe's mother, "Why isn't Gertie here?"

"It's her bedtime," she said.

"Oh," said Jimmy. "Who's watching her? So she doesn't get kidnapped."

The question stopped her a moment. "Her father."

Sarah and Esther Wyler arrived soon after Roscoe and his mother left. We spoke about Will until we felt comfortable with each other again.

"How's he doing?" I asked.

"Doing well and praying for Jimmy. For all of you," Sarah said.

"The prayers worked," I said.

Grandma approached Mrs. Wyler and they began to speak. She'd never been inside a tavern, she said to Grandma.

"Well, this night's good for a first."

"It is, I guess. I'd love to have you come to our church."

"I did go to Jasper's funeral. Does that count?"

Mrs. Wyler tipped her head and gave Grandma an indulgent smile.

"Remember when you went with Will to his appointment," Sarah said to me, when her mother moved off to speak to other people she knew. Our words flowed once we got started. Our reminiscence ran through Wisconsin Dells to the hospital in Madison, where we waited for Will to finish his appointment, to the ice cream store where we butted in on Hansel and Gretel on their bench, and then home again late at night when she suggested we go to the fireworks together. Neither of us mentioned our kiss behind the grandstand; not because it wasn't memorable, it was for me, at least, but also because we carried the burden of knowing we shared fault for what had happened to Jimmy.

Goose poked his head into the tavern after the Wylers were gone. He motioned for me to meet him in the doorway. As surprised as I was to see him, I was glad he was here. Joseph, Goose's kid brother, hid shyly behind him. By then, Jimmy had caught sight of us. His curiosity drove him to whatever was going on, and soon the four of us were outside on the street corner.

"We brought you something," said Goose, then glanced back at a battered old car parked across the street. "My mother," he said, "she brought us. We know not to go to town at night. She promised my father she wouldn't get out of the car."

As Goose led us across the street, the car window rolled down. His mother removed a cigarette from between her lips, exhaled a

Fire Conditions

stream of smoke, and handed Goose a paper sack through the open window.

"Joshua," she said, "give this to them."

Inside the sack was a mix of nuts and dried berries like she had given Beau, Jimmy, and me when we first visited their trailer; and also the snack Goose had swapped with me for half of my sandwich the day we finished the fort.

"Pinagigi," I said, which I recalled as the word Beau used to thank her.

She acknowledged my gratitude with a nod, then gathered her boys into her gaze. "Joshua, Joseph, let's go. Your father's waiting."

Goose and I looked at each other. I wanted him to stay; he didn't want to leave. We both knew it. If I were him, I would have at least tried to finagle a way to get what I wanted, but my way wasn't his. He said, "Will you leave soon?"

I couldn't lie to him. "Probably," was all I could say. In the meantime, Jimmy and Joseph had promised to ride bikes together tomorrow, without any idea of how to make that happen.

The streetlights crackled to life as they drove away.

I expected Beau would have shown up by now. Despite his bad day—his weed problem and the trouble with Bernie—he deserved to celebrate. Without the both of us, Jimmy might not have been found. If that wasn't enough, he was my friend, an adult who paid attention to me, and gave me the strength to build a fort with the others.

"Why so glum?" Agent Jones asked. I hadn't noticed him come in. He pulled out a chair and motioned for Henry to join us. "In the morning," he said, "your parents will listen to your brother's interview and Rocky's interrogation. They say you can join them if you want."

"Yes!"

"But you can't tell anyone what you hear."

"I understand."

Jimmy and I stayed up and enjoyed being the center of attention. As I continued to watch for Beau, my patience felt more like anger the longer I waited.

Finally, upstairs, Jimmy dragged himself to bed, exhausted. I tucked him in. As soon as I thought he'd sleep for hours, he rolled on his side and said, "I love you, Mikey."

I choked up, but managed to say, "I love you too, silly goose. Now sleep before I give you a noogie."

Chapter 30

In the morning, Henry, Agent Jones, and the District Attorney were waiting for us in the conference room. This time, my mother joined my father and me. We were still worn out from celebrating last night. The tape recorder sat on the table between us. First, we would hear Jimmy's interview after his rescue yesterday, and then Rocky after he was captured and arrested. We'd also hear the voices of a special FBI agent and a psychologist we hadn't met. Henry explained that they had invited our family to listen to the interviews to spare them from attending the trial, which would be held in Adams County. Madison, Wisconsin's capital in Dane County, had no federal court; only a county courthouse, so the location made sense.

"Ready?" Jones asked.

We nodded to brace ourselves.

Henry pushed the button and sent the tape spooling.

"Recording, Thursday, July 10, 1958, Adams County Sheriff's Office, three p.m. You'll hear Senior Field Agent Daniel Collins and Doctor Julie Tucker, a special consultant on crimes against children. She has been on call from the university since the weekend and has stayed in the area to assist with the victim and his family. Now let's begin."

(Collins calling.) "Bring Jimmy in. Please state your full name."

"Jimmy Calloway."

"How old are you, Jimmy?"

"Eight."

He lied. I laughed to myself. He wouldn't turn eight until November.

(Dr. Tucker's voice.) "Before we continue, we want you to know that you are not to blame for what happened. Some boys your age blame themselves, and that isn't good to do. The only person to blame is the man who took you. Do you understand? Let the record state that Jimmy nodded his head yes."

(Collins speaks.) "Can you tell us, Jimmy, what happened to you the night of July fourth?"

"You mean when Mike went with Sarah?"

"Yes."

"A man came with popcorn. Said if I went with him, I'd see my dad."

"Why did you think he knew your father?"

"He said he did. I missed him. He wanted to see Mike, too, but Mike didn't come back."

"Did he ask you where Mike was?"

"I already told you! He was with Sarah."

My father grew angry and angrier. My mother cried.

"Now I'm going to show you some pictures. I want you to tell me if one of them is the man you went with."

Silence except for the tape whirring. I guessed Jimmy was looking at the pictures.

"This one."

"Are you sure?"

Fire Conditions

"Yeah."

"Let the record state that Jimmy Calloway has identified Milosz, aka Rocky, Wisniewski, as the man who kidnapped him."

(Jimmy laughs.)

(Tucker's voice.) "Is his name funny?"

"He's Booger Man. He picks it a lot."

"Well, you're a brave boy, Jimmy. Like your brother. We're glad you're safe."

"Can I see my mom and dad now? Mikey, too?"

"You'll see them soon."

"Are you mad at me?"

My stomach churned as an extra reminder of my guilt.

(Dr. Tucker says soothingly.) "No, no one's mad at you. Let's take a minute." (Recording stops then resumes.) "Jimmy, are you okay to continue?"

"I'm okay."

"My questions might be uncomfortable. If you can't, or don't want to answer, tell me. Did the man touch you in places that felt weird or made you afraid?"

(Tape is paused.)

"Booger Man held my hand."

"Is that the only time he touched you?"

"Yeah."

"Not in your bed? Or asleep?"

(Jimmy laughs.) "He'd be too fat."

(Tucker continues.) "I hear he took you fishing. How did that go?"

"It was fun. I got one! My dad never took me."

My father lowered his head and covered his eyes with his hands.

"So, you'd say the man was good to you?"

"Yeah. Pretty much."

"Were you ever afraid of him?"

"No, Dad was coming."

"Did you ever see or hear your grandfather?"

"I heard shouting. I think it was him."

"What do you know about the fire?"

(A long silence.)

"I was bad. I used matches and I'm not supposed to."

"Remember, you are not to blame for what happened."

"I am. I burned down the house."

(Dr. Tucker talking.) "Why did you burn in it down? Let the record state that Jimmy shrugged. Again, why did you do it?"

"I wanted to."

"Is it because you were afraid? Let the record state that Jimmy nodded. Do you know how to set a fire?"

"I learned about gasoline. I put it on the ground, then used a match."

"What happened then?"

(A long whirring silence.)

"I got scared. It got really big."

"What did you do then?"

"Booger Man took me back to the little house and put me in a bad boy closet. Then Mike came and got me!"

Fire Conditions

(Another sound of long whirring.)

We all took a breather for a bathroom break and to get some water. Then we gathered back in the conference room. Agent Jones asked again if we were sure we wanted to hear the kidnapper's interview.

Of course, Mom, Dad, and I wanted to hear what the criminal had to say. Before playing the tape, he warned us Rocky Wisniewski had a long criminal record beginning with shoplifting before he graduated from high school to car theft, robbery, assault, and eventually an attempted murder. We listened.

"Tape Recording, Thursday, July 10, 1958, Adams County Sheriff's Office, five p.m. This is Senior Field Agent Matthew Jones speaking. Please state your full name."

"Up your ass."

"Milosz Wisniewski?"

"Rocky."

"Current address?"

"Up your ass."

"Did you kidnap Jimmy Calloway on the Fourth of July, 1958, from the Adams County Fairgrounds?"

"Why would I?"

"Answer the question."

"I'm not guilty."

"You're not on trial here, but your cooperation will bear on any charges. You've been arrested for a serious federal crime."

"It's not federal. It's state. Parents have rights."

"You're not his parent. Explain what you mean."

"I picked the boy up for his father."

Dad cursed, then added, "That's a lie! That's what he was told to say."

Jones stopped the recording and asked my father not to interrupt him. He then waited while Dad nodded. Jones pressed play.

"Wasn't it to pick up the boys for their grandfather?"

"Yeah."

I knew that was what Dad had wanted to say.

(Jones continues.) "When a state formally requests the FBI investigates a crime, jurisdiction is turned over to the federal government. You're right, Wisconsin doesn't have the death penalty. But since the Lindbergh baby, kidnappers go to the chair everywhere else, and you'll fry when you get to Statesville, and that's in Illinois."

"I didn't hurt the kid."

"Did you write this? Note: suspect is reading the ransom note related to Jimmy Calloway. Now this. Note: reading the threat to burn down Mrs. Flowers's house. See similarities? Letter sizes are consistent between them. Some stick-like. Others have the same flourish. Not to mention, your grammar is lousy."

"Let's get this straight. He never paid me a cent. He stiffed me. He promised me twenty-five grand for the little guy but never squared up. I'd get the same for the older one. Since he'd stiffed me on the little guy, I figured he'd stiff me on the older kid if I caught him. A slippery S.O.B."

I felt proud to have played a part in saving my brother as Rocky

Fire Conditions

rambled on.

"I could've got extra but I burned down the wrong joint. I could've taken the Florida job. My second mistake. Up here's just bullshit."

"Shit'll fly outta your ears when they flip that switch." (Jones speaking.) "Do you want to confess?"

"To what?"

"Your sins."

(Wisniewski laughs.)

We spent another hour listening to Rocky's interrogation. He had burned down the Crapper, but when he learned he'd burned the wrong tavern, he wrote the note threatening to burn down Grandma's house.

"Did you ever think you could've killed the boys?" Jones asked. "They slept at the Tap, not at the house. Didn't you think about how much ransom you'd lose?"

(A long silence.)

"I've done a lotta bad stuff in my life, but I don't hurt kids."

"How much were you paid to take the boys? It was both of them. Not just Jimmy. Calloway's wife heard her husband talking to you over the phone. Twenty-five grand per kid, you agreed. What would he pay you to burn the tavern?"

"Ten grand." (Starting to ramble.) "I liked the kid. Took him fishing. I'd like to have a kid like him."

"Do you know why their grandfather wanted you to bring them to him?"

"So, when they grew up, they wouldn't be hillbillies."

Jones paused the tape as if to let the dead man's insult sink in. My father took my mother's hand in a tight grip. Dad's face turned red. My mother shook her head slowly, not appearing angry, but looking more like she pitied her father-in-law.

"Do you know you could've caught Mike if you were smarter?"

"I looked around for him for weeks. Never saw him."

"He was 'Casper' to you."

After a long pause, he said, "Well, I'll be damned."

I grinned. I had been Beau's son Casper, and he'd been Henry, the caretaker, when we were confronted in the lake house. How clever were we without knowing it! I could hardly wait to tell Beau.

I never got the chance.

Chapter 31

My mother, Jimmy, and I remained in Adams Friendship until mid-August. Dad stayed two days to help BeBe arrange transportation of my grandfather's body to be interred in Rosehill Cemetery at the family mausoleum. He also had to prepare to defend his dissertation after Labor Day.

Dad told Mom and me about the funeral. My uncles who'd broken the door of the Tap had served as coffin bearers. A handful of grandpa's business colleagues made brief, awkward appearances before hurrying off, presumably to their limos and lunch. Another group looked like mobsters. They wore pin stripe suitcoats, matching ties, and fedoras, and failed to conceal the shape of guns beneath their coats. Two of them roughed up a *Tribune* photographer. My favorite part of the story, and I think it was Mom's, too, that two floozies in heavy makeup, wearing inappropriately revealing dresses, hovered like vultures should any money like carrion come their way. Apparently, BeBe remained dry eyed, nor did Dad shed a tear.

A major partner of the law firm that Grandpa used for personal business welcomed BeBe and conveyed his condolences on her loss. My father and John, Dad's brother, were asked to stay for the reading of Grandpa's last Will and Testament. The other members of the immediate family were led to a room down the hall, grumbling for being excluded. When the will was read, my father was pleased that his mother had inherited all of the money and shared personal property. John, Grandpa's favorite, would manage the family's insurance business, founded nearly a century ago.

"Did he leave anything to you?" Mom asked Dad, indifferently.

Dad laughed. "That's his way of slapping my face from the tomb."

Before my family returned to Evanston, the Big Fish People promised to keep in touch with me. I gave them my address. They gave me only their names, which of course I knew, but not their streets or rural route numbers. Roscoe informed me that if I added "Adams," they'd get the letters, regardless. The mail carriers knew where everyone lived.

I corresponded with Roscoe soon after we went back to school. His first letter arrived in early October. I smiled as I read.

> Hi, Mike,
>
> This is from all of us. Can you come back next summer? Gertie says to say hi to Jimmy. Will misses playing chess with you. I still don't know how to play. Sarah got in trouble with her father. I don't know what that was about. Good news! Gary's alive. He ran away from home and is living on a farm in Iowa. How are you? Have you heard from Beau?
>
> Your friend,
> Roscoe

I wrote in return.

Hi, Roscoe and all of you,

I'm fine. I miss you. You guys are the best. Let Will know I'll send him a letter too. I haven't heard from Beau. Don't know if I will. He'll always be cool. Jimmy's in therapy. He still likes to draw. He's good at horses.

I'll write again soon. You write too.

Mike

A few weeks after we'd left for home, Grandma told us that Henry had proposed to marry her and that she'd told him, "Why should we get married when we're already friends?" After a month, Grandma and Henry invited us to celebrate their marriage in September on Rattlesnake Mountain. Lena would serve as the Wedding Officiant, just as she'd married my parents years ago. I liked the thought of Henry being my grandfather.

That Thanksgiving, Dad, Mom, Jimmy, and I celebrated the holiday on the farm outside Friendship. Grandma, Henry, who was back to being a retired sheriff, and to some extent, Joe, helped prepare the dinner. The group was smaller this year, Grandma told us; Jasper, who occasionally joined them, was dead. Grandpa Frank, who'd died long ago, was still missed, even by Henry, and now, according to Grandma, Uncle Mike was dying at St. Michael's Hospital in Stevens Point.

Grandma asked me to help her by doing the usual chores I'd done at the Tap. My first task was to find a potato masher for her. She had been searching and was now giving up. I searched cupboards and drawers in the kitchen without success. But when I opened the drawer where Beau kept his weed, there was an envelope with my name. I hurried outside to the porch and read.

    Mike,

    I don't know where I'm headed. Or where to stay. But I'll be okay. Don't worry. Okay? I'm sorry to say bye like this. You might not find this. I hope you do. I'm happy for Rosie. Your dad, too. He's nice. Tell Jimmy hi. Sorry I'm not a good person all the time. Someday I want to have a son like you.

    Beau

I wiped my eyes when I heard Grandma call, "Where's my masher?"

I turned to stuff the envelop in my pocket and went back inside to close the drawer when I spied the masher. It had been under Beau's letter.

"It's coming! I found it."

Epilogue

In December, while sitting in the kitchen, doing my homework, the phone rang. When I answered, Grandma BeBe greeted me. She told me how nice it was to hear my voice, but could she talk to my mother?

I found Mom reading Dad's dissertation, long after he'd graduated and gotten his new job. When I told her BeBe was on the line, she said, "Tell her I'm busy."

"Why don't you just say hi?"

"What does she want?"

"I don't know. Ask her!"

Mom set aside the paper and stood, muttering, "For crying out loud."

About a minute later I hid in the hall listening to Mom's voice crack. "Hello." After the greeting, she fell quiet. I peeked at her and saw a puzzled look on her face. "Okay. I see," she said at last. "What time? –You'll pick me up? –Let's. It's about time."

I thought so too.

Jimmy's child psychiatrist explained to my parents there were two general forms of child fire-setting disorders. Jimmy's was categorized as impulse-control. My father, now a Clinical Psychologist, was able to relate to what he heard from his colleague in the Department of Psychiatry, even though he dealt with war veterans with post-traumatic stress syndrome.

She explained Jimmy's issues weren't straightforward, or typical, if the trauma of being kidnapped was factored in. Otherwise, she didn't peg him to be a true pyromaniac; his fire-setting was a cry for help, which occurred when he burned the lake house. It wasn't surprising, she said. Medication was useless other than to control his behavior, which often failed. She recommended we keep a close eye on him; and didn't I already know that! For now, he'd have follow-up appointments every two weeks.

Either Mom or Dad searched his pockets for matches each morning before he left for school. They searched our room when he was gone. Having his own bedroom was off limits. Since I already knew the tricks of his trade, I was responsible for keeping an eye on him.

According to my parents, after their first parent-teacher conference, they had learned other parents had complained about Jimmy. He bragged about being kidnapped more times than his classmates could bear. Generally, no one liked him. He was a loner, with one or two sort-of-friends. His bragging sounded like another "cry for help." His teachers weren't aware of his therapy; it wasn't a physical diagnosis like epilepsy where they had to intervene if he had a seizure.

With continued therapy, by winter his grades were near the top of his class. Lacking were his social skills, marked as "needs improvement" on his December report card along with his straight A's. On weekends, when I wasn't playing my cello, practicing with the symphony for a performance, I played Chinese checkers, Pick-up-Stix and new board games to be a good brother.

What he enjoyed was the time to be alone and to draw pictures. He'd used up the supplies from the James Nagy Learn to Draw Kit that BeBe had sent in June. He no longer needed a kit. My parents kept him well supplied. Before each bedtime he would show me his day's work. I took interest in watching his artistic skills develop. Whether he had real talent or not, he became more accomplished. His face drawings began to surface from solid figures into ones with signs of emotion. Without obvious flattery I praised his work to inspire his interest, as he was truly quite good. I imagined that within a few years the drawings of his favorite superheroes would rival the ones in comic books. If he drew horses as well, I figured he might find a girlfriend someday, based on National Velvet's ongoing popularity with girls his age.

A year later, two weeks after the anniversary of Elizabeth's death in January, my parents announced that Mom was pregnant, and due in April. She would need a lot of rest to carry the pregnancy through. That spring my mother started to see her doctor quite often. BeBe went with her once, as far as I knew. They were cordial now. Mom confided in me that she'd had two miscarriages after Jimmy was born. She explained what a miscarriage was and why Elizabeth died.

Joy was born April 5, 1960, a week after my fifteenth birthday and eight months before Jimmy would turn ten. She was healthy and loved enormously. Jimmy drew pictures for her, one of which my parents framed. Grandma Flowers couldn't wait for us to bring Joy to meet her. We drove to Adams Friendship in early June. When

Joy cried, Grandma cried heartily out of happiness.

Little did any of us Big Fish People know how the sixties would turn out when we gathered the summer of 1959. The fort had held up well over a long hard winter. We shared a belief, or perhaps a hope, that we would gather each summer for years untold. Our numbers dwindled, of course. Squirrel didn't show up in 1960. None of us was surprised, knowing how erratic he could be.

But as the sixties progressed, I slowly lost touch with my Big Fish friends; and Beau long before that. I made a vow to myself to learn where they were and how they were doing. They remained dear to me. My wife and best friend, Michele, said I was sentimental and she was right. And nothing was wrong with that.

As good as my life is, memories of the summer of '58 (except for the kidnapping) stir sentimental longings in me; years of when big decisions weren't made by big bankers, lawyers, and businessmen, but by the likes of Roscoe on where to build a fort with Beau, and like Henry and Grandma and others in the town called Friendship, its first name being Adams, where we Big Fish People played and worked and cared deeply about each other.

Acknowledgements

For their kindness and generosity I acknowledge those who were instrumental in guiding me through the process of writing my first novel, *Fire Conditions*: Kim Suhr, Director of Red Oak Writers; Lisa Lickel, Manager of the Wisconsin Writers Association Press; and Luella Schmidt, President of WWA; and the many writers, readers, and friends who took the time to critique parts or the entire book: Rick Whaley, Ellen Smith, Elise Riepenhoff, Janis Falk, my loving spouse, and Jane Hamilton for the personal workshop experience at Write-On Door County.

Finally, I offer my gratitude posthumously to my two grandmothers for being as loving and eccentric as they were in real life.

About the Author

Tom Malin spent the first five years of his life in Adams County, and his family returned frequently to visit the quirky and loving relatives there. *Fire Conditions* honors a fictional Adams County that might have been.

A former administrator at the Medical College of Wisconsin and USC Children's Hospital in Los Angeles, California, Tom was also a visiting professor in the US and Ulaanbaatar, Mongolia.

His short stories have been published in the *Kansas Quarterly*, *Rosebud*, and others. He's a Jade Ring and Hal Prize winner. He's a member of Wisconsin Writers Association and attends workshops at Red Oak Writing Studio.

Tom is married to his childhood sweetheart, Shelly, and has three adult children and six grandchildren.

Wisconsin Writers Association
www.wiwrite.org

Founded in 1948, the Wisconsin Writers Association, Inc. is a creative community dedicated to the support of writers and authors. WWA sponsors and hosts year-round workshops and events throughout Wisconsin, offering discounts and exclusive resources. WWA aims to share experiences and knowledge while encouraging members in their pursuit of this most noble art.

Develop your craft.
Discover resources.
Expand your network.
Build your audience.

WWA Membership

Membership in WWA is open to anyone with an active interest in developing their writing craft. WWA welcomes aspiring and also published writers, librarians, educators, artists, students, dramatists, musicians, filmmakers, translators and others.

A passion for the written word is the #1 WWA criterion.

Join now at wiwrite.org/about-wwa-2/join
Facebook www.facebook.com/WIWrite/
Linked In www.linkedin.com/company/wiswritersassoc/
E-mail: hello@wiwrite.org

Wisconsin Writers Association Press

We are looking for manuscripts that feature Wisconsin in setting, culture and theme, whether historical, contemporary, or futuristic.

Submission guidelines, contact information, and pertinent FAQs can be found on the WWA website page:
www.wiwrite.org/WWA-Press

Wisconsin Writers Association is a 501(c)3 not-for-profit organization.

Milton Keynes UK
Ingram Content Group UK Ltd.
UKHW020706191024
449793UK00011B/103/J